THE E[...]

Brian Moore w[...]
1921, emigrated [...], and now
lives in the Unit[...]tes. His first novel, *The
Lonely Passion of Judith Hearne,* was published
in 1955 and immediately acclaimed. This was
followed by *The Feast of Lupercal* (1956);
The Luck of Ginger Coffey (1960), which has
been filmed; *An Answer from Limbo* (1962); *I
Am Mary Dunne* (1968); *Fergus* (1970); *The
Revolution Script* (1972); *Catholics* (1972),
winner of the W. H. Smith Literary Award in
1973; *The Great Victorian Collection* (1975);
and *The Doctor's Wife* (1976). Among the
honours Brian Moore has received are a Gug-
genheim Fellowship, an award from the U.S.
National Institute of Arts and Letters, a Canada
Council Fellowship, the Author's Club of Great
Britain First Novel Award, and the Governor
General of Canada's Award for Fiction.

The Emperor
of Ice-Cream

BRIAN MOORE

PENGUIN BOOKS

Penguin Books Ltd, Harmondsworth,
Middlesex, England
Penguin Books, 625 Madison Avenue,
New York, New York 10022, U.S.A.
Penguin Books Australia Ltd, Ringwood,
Victoria, Australia
Penguin Books Canada Ltd, 2801 John Street,
Markham, Ontario, Canada L3R 1B4
Penguin Books (N.Z.) Ltd, 182–190 Wairau Road,
Auckland 10, New Zealand

First published in the United States of America
by The Viking Press 1965
Published in Penguin Books 1977

LIBRARY OF CONGRESS CATALOGING IN PUBLICATION DATA
Moore, Brian.
The emperor of ice-cream.
I. Title.
[PZ4.M819Em5] [PR9199.3.M617] 813'.5'4 77-23322
ISBN 0 14 00.449 3

Printed in United States of America by
Offset Paperback Mfrs., Inc., Dallas, Pennsylvania
Set in Linotype Times Roman.

ACKNOWLEDGMENTS
Grateful thanks to the following for permission to quote from their copyrighted works:
Brandt & Brandt for lines (p. 53) from *Till the Day I Die* by Clifford Odets. Copyright 1935, 1963 by Clifford Odets. Alfred A. Knopf, Inc., for lines (pp. 5, 22, and 186) from "The Emperor of Ice-Cream" from *Harmonium* by Wallace Stevens. Copyright 1923, 1951 by Wallace Stevens. The Macmillan Company, New York, Macmillan & Co. Ltd., London, and Michael Butler Yeats for lines (p. 4) from "The Second Coming" and (p. 109) from "Easter 1916" from *Collected Poems* by W. B. Yeats. Copyright 1924 by The Macmillan Company, Renewed 1952 by Bertha Georgie Yeats. Oxford University Press, Inc., and Faber & Faber Ltd. for lines (pp. 4, 59, 76, and 80) from "An Eclogue for Christmas" from *Eighty-Five Poems* by Louis MacNeice. Copyright © 1959 by Louis MacNeice. Random House, Inc., and Faber & Faber Ltd. for lines (p. 4) from "Consider This and In Our Time" from *The Collected Poetry of W. H. Auden*. Copyright 1934, Renewed 1961 by W. H. Auden. Shapiro, Bernstein & Co., Inc., for lines (p. 37) from "South of the Border" by Jimmy Kennedy and Michael Carr. Copyright 1939 by The Peter Maurice Music Co. Ltd., London, England. Sole Selling Agents—Shapiro, Bernstein & Co., Inc., New York, N.Y.

TO JEAN

one

The Divine Infant of Prague was only eleven inches tall yet heavy enough to break someone's toes if he fell off the dresser. Although he wore the coronation robes of a monarch, he was, in reality, a desperate little preacher whose aim in life was to catch Gavin Burke's eye. He managed it now as Gavin, shivering in his undershorts, picked up the new battle-dress trousers. Mind your own business, Gavin told him. You are my business, said the Infant. Your mother put me in this room to watch over you and Owen. I knew it would come to this. This uniform. This job. What else could be expected from a boy who gives in to every weakness that enters his head? Sloth, self-indulgence. Smoking, stunting your growth. That's one reason you look silly in those togs. And lust. Lying in that bed over there, defiling innocent girls in your mind when you should have been studying for your Schools Leaving Certificate. No wonder you failed. Oh, yes, it's all part of a pattern.

I know what's working you, Infant, Gavin said. To put it coarsely, which I will, you're getting your water up because I'm escaping from you and the likes of you. No more school. I'll have wages in my pocket. I'll be able to go out and buy myself great scarlet whores if I feel like it. What whores? asked the Infant. If you met a whore you'd be stiff with fright. Maybe so, Gavin said. In that case, I might have to get drunk first. I'll be able to afford that too. Just try and stop me. Work a miracle, Infant. Miracles are supposed to be your racket, aren't they?

But as he said this, it occurred to him that he might be tempting fate. He touched wood at once. Fat lot of good that will do you, the Infant warned. Do you realize that you've invoked a pagan superstition to avert the wrath of God? It just shows how confused you are about the whole question of religion.

"Hey, let's see your uniform," said his older brother, Owen, coming in and thumping down his law books on the bed. He picked up the black steel helmet and read the white lettering on it. "F.A.P. What's that supposed to mean?"

"First Aid Party."

"Fap-fap-fap." Owen put the helmet on his head and fired an imaginary machine gun. He ran to the bedroom window, shouting: "Here's the A.R.P., missus, pull your blinds down, missus. Put your clothes on, missus. There's a war on, you know."

"Easy. Mother might hear you."

"Is this the jacket? O.K. if I try it on?"

"Help yourself."

"Hup, two, three, four. Will they drill you?"

"Don't know yet. I don't start work until tomorrow."

"Work, he calls it. What work? Do you think the Germans have any intention of bombing dear old Ulster? Are you daft, lad?"

"And why wouldn't they? There's plenty of military targets here."

"Go on. Hitler never heard of this place. Look, he's got France to beat first. And after that there's the whole of England, Scotland, and Wales. It'll be years before he gets around to this benighted outpost. I'll tell you something. The war's been on how long, two months? Know how many fellows in my year at Queen's have joined up? Four. Which just proves there's no difference between Loyal Prods and bomb-throwing papists when it comes to laying down our lives for Stuttering George. And, anyway, why should the Germans worry about a place where half the population will take to the hills at the first rumor of a conscription bill?"

Pleased with his peroration, Owen removed the steel helmet and handed it back to Gavin with a flourish. "Here," he said. "Stop trying to pretend you're a bloody hero. I know you, sonny. Air Raid Precautions, my foot. First Aid! You just joined up in this thing to dodge going back to school for another year. You're a mug, sonny."

"Stop calling me 'sonny.' "

"All right, then." Owen sat down on his bed and stared at his bitten fingernails. "Look," he said. "I don't subscribe to Daddy's bunk about education making you a better man. I just know it gets you a better job. The only reason I'm doing law is because I need a degree to get into the firm. And once I have it, I'll never starve. Dammit, do you want to wind up on some street corner, standing around with a lot of layabouts?"

"At least I'll be better off than the others. I'll have the benefit of free legal advice."

"Stop codding. I'm serious. Drop this A.R.P. job and go back to school. It's not too late."

"It is too late. School's started and this job's all arranged. Besides, I'll have bags of free time to study for the London Matric. The math is supposed to be much easier in the London. You said so yourself."

"Well, bloody well study then. Promise me."

"I promise. End of sermon?"

"No, dammit," Owen said. "For some idiotic reason, which I won't go into now, I happen to be fond of you. I like you, you stupid ape. I think the old man's both callous and careless to let you drift into this thing. It could wreck your whole life."

"It won't. This time, I'll pass my London Matric and get three pounds ten a week while I'm doing it. Afterward, I'll go to Queen's and procure myself some monetarily useful degree. All right?"

"I hope so," Owen said. "I bloody well hope so." He stood up and turned on the lamp by his desk. A moment later, setting an example, he bent over his books, studying with an unwavering concentration which Gavin had never managed to emulate. The room was cold. Gavin put on the battle-dress trousers. The man at the A.R.P. stores had said they would fit. That man was a liar. The pants were an inch too long, the jacket was too big, by far. He looked at Owen's bent back. How could you explain to Owen the feeling you had before every examination, a feeling that the authorities had somehow predetermined your failure? Owen did not vomit up his breakfast on examination mornings, Owen had never sat trembling before an unused answer book, listening to the minatory creak of the monitor's boots. How could you explain to Owen that you suspected there were things wrong with you, that, for one thing, you were a sex maniac whose every moment was plagued by thoughts of girls, that you sensed you would become a drunkard the first chance you got, that you no longer believed in God or His One, Holy, Catholic and Apostolic Church, yet remained unreasonably in dread of God's vengeance for the fact of this unbelief? How could you tell the likes of Owen that, tinker, tailor, soldier, lawyer, doctor, minister, thief, it was all the same to you, that your only thoughts of the future were elaborate daydreams, the one about becoming a famous foreign correspondent, or the youngest actor to dominate the English-speaking stage? How could you tell Owen that the real future of your generation had been foreseen by a group of modern poets whom Owen had never read, would never read? The poets knew the jig was up; they knew the rich and famous would crumble with the rest:

> You cannot be away, then, no
> Not though you pack to leave within an hour,
> Escaping, humming down arterial roads . . .

Or MacNeice, an Ulsterman:

> We shall go down like palaeolithic man
> Before some new Ice Age or Genghiz Khan.

Yeats said it too:

> Things fall apart; the centre cannot hold;
> Mere anarchy is loosed upon the world . . .

It was all prophetically clear. Hitler was Yeats' "Second Coming." He was the rough beast, its hour come round at last, slouching toward Bethlehem to be born. Yeats knew what nonsense it was, in this day and age, to talk of futures and jobs. But how could you explain that to Owen, who had read nothing for pleasure since his *Boys' Own Weekly* days? How could you tell him that, for you, the war was an event which had produced in you a shameful secret excitement, a vision of the grownups' world in ruins? It would not matter in that ruined world if Gavin Burke had failed his Schools Leaving Certificate. The records would be buried in rubble. War was freedom, freedom from futures. There was nothing in the world so imposing that a big bomb couldn't blow it up.

So put on this policeman-blue shirt, this tie, and these cheap black shoes and don't look back, but give thanks for this job which will grant you independence from your father and your father's do's and don't's.

> Let be be finale of seem.
> The only emperor is the emperor of ice-cream.

He liked that line. He was not quite sure what it meant, but it seemed to sum things up. He went to the window and looked down at a clothesline on which a girl's knickers flew. Beyond the narrow garden was a back entry and beyond that were the backs of the houses in the adjoining avenue. From habit, he looked at the window where the typist sometimes stood, her dress off, brushing her long chestnut hair. But her blackout blinds were drawn. He reached for his own blind. Would German raiders ever fly through those rain clouds up there, hurling down bombs on the city? He saw himself, wearing his steel helmet, dashing into the house across the way to carry the typist downstairs, she half-naked and hysterical in her relief. Or was this, as Owen said, a cod? Would life go on unchanged, would he, by refusing to go back to school, really mess up his future?

The battle-dress pants were tripping him. Maybe his mother could turn them up. She had not yet seen him in this uniform. He went downstairs to the empty sitting room, where a fire burned in the grate. The painted French clock on the mantelpiece gathered its coils and struck five times as he stared into the round looking glass behind it, seeing his familiar self, unfamiliar now in the ill-fitting A.R.P. uniform. Had smoking really stunted his growth? He was certainly an inch or two smaller than most other fellows of seventeen. Had masturbation made him pale, or was that just a stupid yarn? God, not self-abuse, had given him his face, all beaked nose thrusting out blindly like a day-old bird's, his thin lips which seemed to bite each other, his hated girlish hands. If he were a girl, would he go with him? He had to answer: no. And in this uniform, in this steel helmet, his wrongness was compounded. He turned the helmet back to front, hiding the F.A.P. letters, and tried to imagine himself a Siegfried Sassoon commando, crawling through no man's land with a dirk in his teeth. But this wasn't no man's land; it was, indisputably, his parents' sitting room.

He looked into the looking glass. In that world, encircled by the looking glass frame, he had acted and reacted, had left his mark, and had, in turn, been marked. His bare knees had helped wear down the old Turkey carpet, battleground of a thousand childhood games of Snap. A Hornby locomotive, thrown by him twelve years ago, had made the big dent in the brass fender in the fireplace, and the broken lock of the rosewood gramophone cabinet was the work of himself and of his brother, Owen. From that gramophone he had heard his first record, a scratchy rendition of "Yes, We Have No Bananas," a favorite of his father's youth. Over his mother's writing desk, a fierce stag peered from a dark forest glade. His mother had told him that the artist meant the stag to seem afraid. Yet the stag was not afraid: it made him afraid. It had been his first lesson in the duality of art. Night after night during the family rosary, he had knelt at those chairs and sofas, until now, eyes shut, he could see the shape and color of each faded rose on their slipcovers. This room was part of him: he had grown up in it. Would he ever again know any room so well?

Not bloody likely, whispered his Black Guardian Angel. That sort of stability is a thing of the past. Sell your birthright for three pounds ten a week, would you? That London Matric talk is all hogwash and you know it. I think you took this job just to feed your cigarette addiction. Wasn't that the first thing you thought of? Oh, boy, now I can buy all the packets of twenty I want. You're still a kid, you know. Three pounds ten a week may seem a lot now, but how will it sound when you're a middle-aged man of thirty?

His older sister, Kathy, came into the room, stopped, and shrieked: "God help us! Charlie Chaplin."

"Not funny."

"But it's true. Charlie Chaplin." She fell onto the sofa, giggling.

"Where's Mother? I need these pants fixed."

"She's downstairs. Aunt Liz is here. They'll be up in a minute. Oh, Gav, you look so *funny.*"

Pay no attention to her, whispered his White Guardian Angel. Put on the helmet and look in the mirror again. Not bad at all.

He had two guardian angels. The White Angel sat on

his right shoulder and advised the decent thing. The Black Angel sat on his left shoulder and pleaded the devil's cause. The White Angel was the official angel: everybody had one. It had all been explained to him in catechism class when he was a little boy. In catechism class the Black Angel was barely mentioned. Yet, the trouble was, the Black Angel seemed more intelligent; more his sort. If, as now, looking into the looking glass above the mantelpiece, he noticed that nineteen-year-old Kathy had her legs up on the sofa's armrest, exposing white thighs and peach-colored knickers, his angels at once went to work. *Black Angel:* "Nice legs. Hot stuff." *White Angel:* "Stop that at once, she's your sister." *Black Angel:* "Remember last week, going past the bathroom? You looked." *White Angel:* "Mortal sin!" *Black Angel:* "Is it incest you're talking about?" *White Angel:* "Don't even mention that word!" *Black Angel:* "I know, but is it really so unnatural? It doesn't seem unnatural to me. It might be rather a good idea to marry one's sister, you'd have a shared family background, know the same jokes, never be shy with each other. The Pharaohs did it all the time." *White Angel:* "That's a sin you can't get absolution for!" *Black Angel:* "Are you sure? Common enough, I'm told. Lord Byron and *his* sister." *White Angel:* "You're diseased, that's what you are. I mean *you*, Gavin. Degenerate, that's what they call the likes of that." *Black Angel:* "Oh, stop being so serious. I just said they're nice legs."

Into the sitting room came his mother, followed by Aunt Liz, a heavily mustached widow who wore unchanging black in memory of Gavin's uncle, killed twenty years before in the Irish Troubles.

"Gracious God," Aunt Liz said. "Did I ever think I'd live to see the day when my own nephew would stand in this room dressed up like a Black and Tan."

"Now Liz, that's not fair. He *is* funny-looking, though."

"Funny? Is that, or is it not, a British uniform that child of yours is wearing?"

"Oh, Gavin," his mother said. "Do you really have to?"

"Have to what?"

"Do you have to come home in it? Couldn't you leave it at the First Aid post and come and go in your own clothes?"

"There's a war on," he said, his face growing hot. "I

have to report in uniform tomorrow night. In the meantime, I need these pants shortened."

"If you were my son," Aunt Liz said, "I'd shorten them all right. I'd burn them."

"But I'm not your son."

"Now Gavin, don't be rude. Go on upstairs. I'll do the trousers later."

"It wasn't me was rude, it was Aunt Liz."

"I admit it," Aunt Liz said. "Truth sometimes hurts. Deirdre, surely you realize that these A.R.P. places will be filled with the scum of the Orange Lodges. Are those the sort of companions you want for a boy of his age?"

"Now Liz, dear, that's enough," his mother said. "Gavin, go up and change."

The house was small, the corner house in a row of red-brick workingmen's dwellings in a street sown with children who played chalk games on the pavements, wound ropes around street lamps to make Maypoles, and scrawled NO POPE HERE and UP THE PRODS in its narrow back entries. It was a street to which cloth-capped, collarless men returned heavy with porter when the pubs shut, a street in which husbands slapped pinafored wives, wives slapped small children, and grandmothers screamed imprecations at grandfathers who urinated too near the weekly wash in the back yard.

But this house, the corner house, had been transformed into Crummick Street First Aid Post 106. It had been chosen because it was only three blocks away from a large Catholic hospital. In the event of an air raid, the post members would serve as stretcher-bearers and ambulance attendants, collecting casualties and bringing the more seriously injured to the hospital for treatment.

Gavin knew Crummick Street. He had often walked down it on his way to the Nurses' Home near the hospital where his girl, Sally Shannon, was in her junior year of nursing training. But he never really looked at the street until that first night, when, reporting for duty at half-past six, he knocked on the front door of the little house and was opened to by a peroxide blonde in a blue A.R.P. smock. She had a good figure but was oldish—thirty, he guessed.

"Yes?"

"I want to see the officer in charge."

"He's in he's office."

She indicated a tiny front parlor just off the front hall. She told him to knock.

"Yes?"

The front room contained a filing cabinet, a kitchen table and chair, a telephone, a map of the city, and a man. The man's pale skin glistened like a newly peeled potato. His hair was combed from the back, where there was some, toward the front, where there was none. On the right-hand pocket of his blue battle dress he wore three enameled first-aid badges. When Gavin stated his business, the man did not speak but reached out a hand for Gavin's letter of appointment, slit open the envelope with a black-rimmed fingernail, read the letter, his lips moving silently, then put the letter down on the table. He opened a drawer, took out a rubber date stamp, and stamped it on the top of the letter. Still silent, he unscrewed the top from a shilling fountain pen and, with the tip of his tongue between his lips, wrote something across the top of the letter. His hand was large and Gavin was able to read it: A. CRAIG. POST OFFICER, POST 106. REC'D WITH THANKS.

Carefully, the man blotted this statement, then stood and went to the filing cabinet. He found a clean cardboard folder, put it on top of the cabinet, and again wrote laboriously. This time he wrote Gavin's name on the folder. He filed Gavin's letter of appointment in the folder, filed the folder in the filing cabinet, shut the cabinet drawer, and returned to sit at the kitchen table with the air of a man who has performed an immensely complicated task. He looked up at Gavin. He screamed.

"Stand up straight. How old are you?"

"Seventeen."

"Childer, they're sending me. And cheeky childer. Say 'sir.' "

"Yes, sir."

"Anybody is cheeky around here, I'll learn them different. Just you mind that. I won four medals lifting weights."

He glared at Gavin.

"My name is Post Officer Craig. I have *rules*. Nobody

goes off these premises without my permission. No sleeping on night duty. No man alone with any of the ladies in any room after midnight. Do you follow me?"

"Yes, sir."

"The shift is on duty twelve hours, not one minute less. We'll be one month on nights and the next month on days. You see this book?"

"Yes."

"I told you, say 'sir.' "

"Sorry, sir."

"I draw a line in this book. At seven. If you come in after seven, you sign under that line. Mister Harkness of City Hall, he checks this book. If you are late twice in the one month, you get your cards. Do you follow?"

"Yes, sir."

"All right. Sign in."

As Gavin signed his name in the book, the telephone rang. The post officer seized it. "Crummick Street First Aid 106, Post Officer Craig speaking. . . . What? Missed the bus? That's *your* worry, mister. You'd better clock in here before seven, that's all." He slammed the receiver down. "Hear that? A new man like yourself, and he has the blooming cheek to ring up he's first night and say he's missed he's bus." Craig opened the drawer again and produced a thick red pencil. "See this? That's the old red line. I draw that line on the stroke of seven. O.K. Go on in the kitchen. I'll be in directly."

In the narrow hall Gavin passed an old woman and a girl. Both wore blue A.R.P. smocks. The girl was tall and had a nice figure but wore spectacles. The old woman wiped a wavering tear from the end of her nose as she directed Gavin to the kitchen. In the kitchen six men sat around a coal fire, wearing the blue A.R.P. battle-dress uniform, quiet as pensioners in a park shelter. One man, a heavy soldierly figure, with crow-black hair and a lined face, stood and came forward in the manner of a hall porter. "Good evening, lad," he said.

"Good evening."

The soldierly one looked keenly at him. "Tell me, boy. Does your cock stand in the morning?"

He heard the men's laughter breaking about him, saw himself as they must see him, too young, with girlish hands, his nose beaking forward like a day-old chick's, his face flushing, his lips tight. He stared at the old joker, who put out his hand, asking amnesty. "My name's MacBride. They give me 'Soldier.' Soldier MacBride. What's your name, lad?"

"Gavin Burke."

"Well, and so, I'll introduce you to your mates. This is Wee Tommy Bates."

Wee, he was. Almost a dwarf, Gavin decided. He sat hunched over the fire, all prognathous jaw, monkey forehead, and protruding teeth. "And the big man here is Frank Price," Soldier said. Frank Price nodded gently. He was sad and stout and ludicrous in battle dress.

"And this here's Jimmy Lynan." Who was bald and who hawked, spat in the fire, and offered his hand.

"And Hughie Shaw." A clerkly little man, who was filling his pipe from a flat tin box filled with cigarette butts.

"And this is Mick Gallagher." Who said in a harsh voice, "There's three new men due the night. Yourself is the first. I wonder is all of them going to be young uns."

"There's all ages in this job," Hughie Shaw decided. "I was over at Stannup Street Depot the other day, there was all kinds there."

The others nodded at this profundity. Soldier MacBride began to cut slivers from a plug of pipe tobacco. All looked into the fire, and the Black Angel nudged Gavin, saying, have a look at that bloody dwarf, will you? If that idiot can read and write, let alone pass a first-aid certificate, then I'll be a monkey's uncle. Which *he* is. For once, the White Angel agreed. Maybe your Aunt Liz is right about these jobs going to the Orange Lodge faithful, said he. How else could some of these freaks have got here?

The kitchen door opened and an officer entered. The men stood, instinctively. Yet, on examination, the newcomer's battle dress differed in no way from theirs. It was the officer face, the straw-colored mustache, the receding chin, the cigarette in the trembling, yellowed fingers, a cigarette which was only half-smoked when he impulsively cast it on the coals of the fire. That gesture at once set him apart from the other men. It was the gesture of a man who had not known the dole, had not smoked each cigarette to its last wet dottle.

"Good evening, all," the newcomer said. "My name's Lambert."

The men nodded dutifully, as though they had received an order to memorize it. Lambert offered a packet of Gold Flakes. Wee Bates and Lynan each took one, with an air of grateful humility which made Gavin's resentment rise. Who was this officer type, what was he doing here?

"Am I the only new boy?" he asked. He looked around and then, aware that he had not been understood, rephrased his question. "Anyone else's first night?"

"It's mine," Gavin said.

"Oh, good. Sorry, didn't catch your name?"

"Burke. Gavin Burke."

"Oh, good."

At that moment Gavin saw Soldier make a meaningful face at Jimmy Lynan. The tension was lifted. By now, they all had noticed Lambert's trembling fingers, his fixed smile, the purplish veins over the bridge of his nose. There was a reason why this gent was among them. It was the drink that brought him here. Drink, the great leveler.

The kitchen door opened again and a man came in, a tall man in a tweed jacket, well-cut flannels, and highly polished brogues. His thick-lensed, tortoise-shell-rimmed glasses did not seem to belong on his handsome face. He went straight to the fire, turned his back on it, and, lifting the skirts of his tweed jacket, warmed his thighs at the flames. "That's a right sod of a fascist you have there," he suddenly told the company.

No one spoke.

"I was late, you see," he continued. "I rang up to explain that I'd missed the bus. I was in Antrim at the time. And then, of course, I wasn't wearing the bloody uniform. I think that's what sent the rocket up. Bloody uniform doesn't bloody fit, so, naturally, I had to have it altered. God, you'd think I'd committed treason."

"Aye, your man is a right bastard, all right," said Mick Gallagher, he of the red face.

"Hsst," murmured Soldier, nodding toward the kitchen door. Footsteps sounded in the front hall and Post Officer Craig entered the kitchen. "O.K., ladies, in here," he said. Five women filed in behind him, including the tall girl and the peroxide blonde whom Gavin had seen earlier. "Everybody sit down," Craig said. "I want to have a few words."

He waited. When everyone was seated, he went and stood with his back to the fire. "Some of youse have heard this before. Some of youse have not. We have three new men and two new ladies here the night. We are now at full strength. Under me. I have *rules*. If anyone breaks them rules, I will shop that man or woman to the inspector the minute he walks in the front door. I am not saying this to cause nastiness. I do not like nastiness. But there's a war on. I said, there's a *war* on.

"So I am putting youse all on notice. I am tough. I am tough because it's my job to be tough. At H.Q., at City Hall, they have inspectors. I repeat, inspectors. It is the inspector's job to catch us out. The inspector will come in here without any warning at any hour of the night. The inspector will want to know if we are all present and correct. The inspector will look to see if anyone is asleep on the job. If anyone is asleep on the job, that will reflect on me. I said, on *me*. Now I warn each and every man and woman here that I do not intend to let it reflect on me. Not if I can help it. And I can help it. I can.

"The post officer on the day shift is Mister Bob Greenwood. Like yours truly, Mister Bob Greenwood holds the advanced training certificate from both the Red Cross Society and from the Saint John's Ambulance Brigade. Mister Greenwood is keen. Very keen. I am keen too. The inspector—I said, the inspector—will want to see which shift is better trained. Yes, the inspector will want to know that. Now you know what I want. I want this shift to be the best. And what I want I will get. Is that clear now? I said, is that clear?"

He waited. Heads nodded in agreement. The women, in particular, seemed anxious to please him. Yes, yes, yes, their heads went. Don't annoy him. Yes, yes, yes.

"Good. Now, tonight we will start with splints. Splints is very important. There's many different kinds of splints. There's many different kinds of splints because there's many different kinds of fractures. Now . . ."

"Ah, you're very right," said Soldier MacBride.

"What do you mean, I'm right?"

"I mean, sir, begging your pardon, sir, don't you be worrying your head now, Mister Craig, we'll all of us train up and be a credit to you. Won't we, lads?"

There was a confused grumble of agreement.

"And the ladies too," said Soldier. "I know we can count on the ladies, sir."

"Oh, yes, Mr. Craig," said the peroxide blonde.

Gavin looked over at the tall man, the one who wore civvies. He sat hunched against the wall, smoking a cigarette. He winked at Gavin.

"Right then," Craig said, in a pleased voice. "Back to splints. As I was saying, there's many different kinds of splints bècause there's many different kinds of fractures. . . ."

Yes, there's many different kinds of splints, mimicked the Black Angel. Strange, how quickly one's life can change. No need to sail seas or cross frontiers to lose your bearings, you can do it here in this room, less than a mile from your parents' house. Is this your grown-up future, sitting among these frightened men, listening to this bullying ignoramus talk about splints? Look at your colleagues, will you. The one opposite you, the big, sad, stout one with the face of an informer. Price is his name. He was introduced to you. Are you going to become, like him, a creature to be bullied?

Frank Price watched the post officer in the same way he had, years ago, watched his schoolmaster. It did not matter if you listened, as long as you kept your eyes fixed on the speaker's face. Frank was a big man, but timid: he had a bad heart. His sisters had not wanted him to take this job: they said it would kill him. His sister Minnie had cried for a week. Lifting stretchers, said she, what are you thinking of, in your condition. It's suicide, plain and simple. But Frank was not old. Forty-five wasn't old. He looked older, he knew, but then he had always looked older. Bald at twenty-five, and he had lost most of his upper teeth in the days when he used to go on the batter and be carried home from the pub by strangers. He didn't drink nowadays; had not had a drop pass his lips in five years, thanks be. And the old ticker had been steady for a long time. Couple of years since he'd even felt it flutter. Until tonight. And that you could understand, it was nervousness, plain and simple. This was his first job since he'd got the sack from Knights the Chemists, six years ago next month.

Frank was a pharmacist by trade. He had his certification. He had always lived at home, first with his mother, and after, when she died, he and his two unmarried sisters had gone on living in the old house. A sheltered life, you might say. And lonely too, in these last years. Desperate lonely. Getting up in the morning after sleeping as long as you could manage, then having to go out, rain or shine, because Maggie and Minnie didn't want you hanging about the house all day: it wasn't right for a man to hang around the house. He usually went to the Carnegie Public Library in Royal Avenue. There was a periodicals room there: he read the newspapers. Sometimes he had to wait a long time for the paper he wanted, because, in those Depression years, a lot of men hung around the library to keep warm. A funny thing. He made no friends in those years. Not since he went off the booze. Pubs were where you met fellows. A funny thing. He never could have a real chat with another person unless he had a few jars in him. So, now that he was teetotal . . .

Still, he had great hopes for this job. He meant, in the way of meeting people. It had been a godsend, landing it, no two ways about that. Just so long as he avoided lifting anything too heavy and kept his eyes open for that gaffer Craig. Craig was the sort would take advantage, all right. If he knew you were afraid of him, he would jump on your back and ride you home. The thing to do was do your work and not let on you were afraid of anything. Minnie would get over her crying. She and Maggie had no idea how much it meant to him to be able to bring home his share.

"You there," Craig said. "You're a big fellow. Lie down on that stretcher and we'll get a couple of these lads to carry you upstairs. I want to see if youse lads can handle a stretcher."

Well, it was better than having to carry the stretcher. Frank did not envy the fellows who had to carry him. He weighed sixteen stone. He lay down on the stretcher and noticed, with alarm, that Craig had picked Wee Tommy Bates to take the head of the stretcher. What would happen if Wee Bates tipped him downstairs?

Freddy Hargreaves was one of the two men picked to carry the stretcher. He was not surprised. From the moment he had set eyes on that fascist bastard Craig, he'd known he had an enemy. "Come on, you," Craig snapped. "Get a move on."

"What's the hurry? Can't I take my jacket off first?"

"If you'd showed up in your uniform the way you were told, you'd have no call to be taking no jacket off."

Freddy ignored this. He folded his jacket carefully and asked the kid, Burke, to hold it for him. He had no bloody intention of wearing their fascist livery until it fitted him properly. He was vain about his appearance: his clothes were his armor. How many times when he hadn't a shilling in his pocket had he landed a job, got off with a good-looking girl, or managed a few pints on tick, simply because his clothes were good.

"All right, Bates," he said.

Bates was crouched down like a little dog waiting to fetch a stick. Freddy stepped between the stretcher poles and lifted. *Christ.* He played scrum half for Glentoran Wanderers and, beer or no beer, he was in fair condition. But this sod, Price, weighed a ton. Of course, Wee Bates collapsed at his end of the stretcher, almost spilling Price onto the floor.

"Youse are not lifting right," Craig said. "Youse have to lift together."

"Balls."

"What did you say, Hargreaves?"

"You heard me."

"Shut your dirty beak. There's ladies present."

Freddy, ignoring this, turned to Wee Bates. "Price is too heavy for you, lad. You'll get a hernia trying to lift him."

"Bates," Craig screamed. "You listen to me. You got this job because you're supposed to be able to carry a stretcher. If you can't do the job, just say so."

"It's all right, Mr. Craig," Wee Bates mumbled. "I can lift it."

Sod it, Freddy thought, what's the use in talking. Spineless Irish proletariat, they'll let you down every time. Touching their forelocks to every bosses' hireling, sabotaging every effort to protect their rights or improve their working conditions. "All right," Freddy said to Craig. "If we drop this man on his head, it's your responsibility."

"Come on, get the lead out, you. Sorry, ladies."

The ladies smiled forgivingly at the post officer. Freddy hoisted his end of the stretcher, stooping his body so as not to toss all the weight onto the poor bloody dwarf up front. Bates staggered toward the stairs and, as he began to go up, the entire weight of the stretcher was thrown back onto Freddy. Fair enough. Freddy could stick it. He ignored Craig, who followed him upstairs, shouting useless instructions. He thought of Comrade Billy MacLarnon's jeer about the Home Defence services being a paradise for parasites. Comrade Billy Mac should try this on for size.

Freddy considered himself an independent Marxist. He had never been a C.P. member or a Trotskyite, although members of both groups had accused him of belonging to the other one. He had once been arrested for selling the Trotskyite newspaper, *Socialist Appeal*, at the corner of Bank Street, and at present he was associated with a C.P. group in putting on social-realist plays. Freddy couldn't see the Old Man as a latter-day Jesus Christ, but then neither could he agree with Uncle Joe and Harry Pollitt on what made the world go around. He was aware that some local C.P. theoreticians had put out a rumor that he, Freddy, hung around party groups simply to seduce girls. That was utter balls. If Freddy wanted girls, he went to the Plaza or the Floral Hall and picked them up on the dance floor. His tango was damn nearly championship class. He didn't need any party to organize his sex life, thank you very much.

"All right now, put him down in the corner," Craig ordered.

Wee Bates, relieved of his burden, sat weakly on a wooden bench by the wall. Frank Price started up off the stretcher, but Craig pushed him down again. "Stay there a minute. Now, which of youse ladies is going to put a tourniquet on this man's leg?"

The ladies, uneasy, jostled each other. Finally, the peroxide blonde, she of the tight brassiere, allowed herself to be pushed forward. "What was your name again, dear?" Craig asked, eyeing her as though he would eat her.

"Mrs. Renee Clapper."

"Right. Come over here, dear. Now, we'll suppose that this man has a large wound in he's calf. He's bleeding freely and profusely. What would you do?"

"I'd put a tourniquet on he's leg, Mr. Craig."

"Aye, but whereabouts on he's leg, dear?"

"On the thigh, Mr. Craig."

"Show us where, dear."

Mrs. Clapper knelt and put her hand on Frank Price's thigh, just about the knee.

"Right," Craig said. "That'll do nicely. Now, he's bleeding like a pig. I'd say he has an artery cut. Time is of the essence. Hurry now, dear."

Mrs. Clapper took the bandages and stick which Craig handed her. "Excuse me," she said, genteelly, to Frank Price. "But would you mind lifting your leg?"

"No, no, no," Craig screamed. "*He* can't lift he's leg. You lift it."

Mrs. Clapper raised the leg.

"Now roll he's trouser leg up. Higher. Won't go any farther, will it?"

"No, sir."

"Then you would have to tear it. How far would you tear it?"

"Up to here?"

"No dear. You'd tear it all the way up to he's *crotch*. All right. Put on the tourniquet."

The woman was bent over Frank Price, her breasts within an inch of his face. Frank could smell her scent. O Lord, something was happening. His man was beginning to stand. Did anyone notice it? He shut his eyes and using an old trick to divert his mind, began to recite the confiteor. Shame and concentration drove out the embarrassing sensation, and when Craig knelt down to inspect the tourniquet, Frank was all right again. But that mean gaffer suddenly gave the stick two twists and Frank was hard put to keep from crying out. His leg would go dead if this was left on. Far too tight, it was.

"Now, gather around, the rest of youse. That's pressure, that is. That would stop the bleeding and save he's life."

Save my life, Frank thought. My leg is numb already. Circulation's stopped. Oh, that's a bit thick, isn't it. That hurts.

"MacBride. Get some bandages and put a splint on he's other femur."

"Very good, sir. His femur, sir."

"My leg is numb," Frank Price said, looking up at Craig.

"It's supposed to be. Is that the phone, did any of youse hear the phone? Wait a sec."

Craig ran out to the head of the stairs and called down to the bespectacled young girl whom he had left to mind the phone. She called back that the phone had not rung. By this time Frank Price was in pain.

Craig came back into the room. "Now, let's see that femur splint," he said. "MacBride, how are you getting on?"

"Just trying to recall, sir. It was the femur, you said?"

"Aye. Not on he's arm. On he's *leg*."

"Ah, right sir, very right, sir."

Well, dammit, Frank thought, damn my femur, what about this tourniquet? If I speak up, this mean gaffer will have it in for me. Bear with it would be best. Jobs are hard to find. But the circulation has stopped.

"Excuse me, Mr. Craig, but this tourniquet is stopping my circulation. That can be dangerous."

"Who has the advanced training certificate, me or you?"

"You, Mr. Craig. But I'm a chemist by trade, Mr. Craig. I know a wee bit about these things."

"A chemist, are you? Is that a fact. Well now, Mr. Chemist, we'll just leave that tourniquet on a wee while longer. Just till MacBride gets his splint arranged."

"No," Frank said. He was surprised at himself. "I want it off now."

The tall chap who had helped carry him upstairs on the stretcher, Freddy something, suddenly knelt down and pulled the stick out of the tourniquet.

"What did you do that for? Who told you to touch he's leg?"

Freddy ignored Craig. "Can you stand?" he asked Frank, helping him sit up. Frank felt funny, but he did get onto his feet. It was as if his left foot wasn't there at all. He fell over, but this chap caught and held him.

Craig clapped his hands, walked around the two men, continuing to applaud. "Oh, that's good, very good. Oh, you're a good actor, Price. That was a first-class performance."

"Leave the man alone," Freddy said.

"You call me SIR, do you hear? I can put you in the charge book for cheeking me."

"You're the one may go in the charge book," Freddy said. "If Price here will make a complaint, I'll be glad to back him up."

"Is that a fact. Price, are you making a charge against me?"

"No, sir."

"I should think not. Making a charge over a training exercise."

"Do the rest of you think it's just training, trying to cripple a man?" Freddy asked. He looked at Lambert, the fellow with the drunken officer face. Lambert wouldn't be intimidated by a tick like Craig. "What about you?" Freddy said to Lambert.

"Me? Well, one must be careful, of course."

"We're *being* careful," Craig snapped. "But there's a war on. I said, there's a war on. Now, let's have a look at this splint of the femur. What's wrong with it?"

"There's the phone, sir," Soldier said, suddenly.

"The phone?"

"I think so, sir."

"Right." Craig left the room at a run. Soldier smiled at the others. "One of you, fix this splint, will you?" he whispered. Fat Mrs. Cullen came forward and expertly went to work on Frank Price's leg. Soldier grinned at her and, in a whisper, but loud enough for a couple of the lads to hear him, asked: "Tell us. How are you girls going to like it, cooped up every night in this wee house with a gang of strange men?"

"There," said Mrs. Cullen giggling. "That's it." She stood back and surveyed her handiwork. Soldier nudged her plump middle. "I'm not joking," said he. "This is going to be hard on us fellows. It's an unnatural class of a situation being cooped up twelve hours a night in close proximity to a lovely bit of a woman like yourself. Ah, I don't know if I can stand it."

"Go on with you."

"Tell us," he whispered. "Does your man mind you being on nightwork?"

"M'husband's not here. He's in the Navy."

"Is he now? Well, I'll tell you one thing. There's no lovely girls like yourself aboard His Majesty's ships. And, speaking of girls, tell us. Craig, the boss man, do you know if he's married?"

She said she did not know. Which was a pity, because Soldier was more interested in Craig than in any piece of skirt. He was having her on for his reasons. It made him seem younger, all that woman talk. That was important to Soldier. But his curiosity about Craig was another thing entirely. They were all new here, even Craig, and it took an old soldier to see that Craig would need a deputy on his nights off. That deputy might as well be Soldier, and if getting the job meant kissing Craig's Royal Irish arse, then Soldier could do it, on his soul he could. "Oh, my dark Rosaleen," he sang, winking at Mrs. Cullen as Craig returned to look at the splint. He must get beside her at supper. He put his will to work on that.

It worked grand. At suppertime, Craig elected to eat alone in the front office, so there was a good bit of jollity at the table in the kitchen. Soldier, well placed, drank his tea and ate his slice, and then, still laughing and joking, put his hand up Mrs. Cullen's skirt. He took good care a couple of the lads saw him do it. It never hurt to let them see there was life in the old dog yet.

Freddy Hargreaves got up from the kitchen table and, waiting his turn to wash his dishes in the sink, noticed that young Burke was sitting apart from the others, eating his sandwich alone by the fire. Freddy guessed the kid was shy. He went over and sat down beside him. He lit a cigarette, blew a smoke ring, and asked: "Play Rugger?"

"No, I'm afraid not."

"I play a bit," Freddy said. "Not much good at it, but I like the game. Do you dance at all?"

"A bit."

"There are some hot tarts hanging around the Plaza ballroom these nights."

"Oh?"

"We might look in on a night off," Freddy said.

The kid nodded. Freddy watched Soldier groping under that fat woman's skirt. "Wonder why he dyes his hair," Freddy said, softly.

The remark drove out the kid's shyness. "Who dyes his hair?"

"Soldier."

"Honestly?"

"Of course. Come here a minute."

Freddy led the kid over to the scullery door. From there they could look down at Soldier's black head positioned right under the light bulb. "Well," Freddy said, "what do you think?"

"It looks funny, all right."

"I wonder how old he really is. Look at the lines on his neck."

Behind them the scullery door opened and Captain Lambert, wearing his overcoat, entered from the darkness of the yard. He seemed alarmed to find them there. He went unsteadily across the kitchen and hung his overcoat up in the back hall.

"There's another quare one," Freddy said. "It's a wonder the powers that be didn't put *him* in charge of us."

"Might be an improvement on Craig," Gavin said.

"That sod," Freddy said. "One of the low on whom assurance sits, as a silk hat on a Bradford millionaire."

"That's from T. S. Eliot, isn't it? Do you like him?"

"He's good," Freddy said. "He's an anti-Semite and a high church fascist, but he's a first-rate poet."

"You know Eliot," Gavin said, excitedly. "You read modern poetry. Who's your favorite?"

"Auden, I suppose."

"Do you know Wallace Stevens' stuff?"

"Isn't there something by him in the Faber book?"

"My favorite is in that book," Gavin said, " 'The Emperor of Ice-Cream.' Do you know it?

> "Call the roller of big cigars,
> The muscular one, and bid him whip
> In kitchen cups concupiscent curds.
> Let the wenches dawdle in such dress
> As they are used to wear, and let the boys
> Bring flowers in last month's newspapers.
> Let be be finale of seem.
> The only emperor is the emperor of ice-cream."

"I remember," Freddy said. "There's another verse about a corpse, isn't there?"

"There is, indeed." Gavin stared at him. It was an absolute miracle finding someone who read poetry, who knew Wallace Stevens' work. It was an omen, a thing that filled him with joy.

"Listen," Freddy said. "Is that a car outside?"

"Sounds like it. An inspector?"

"Or the emperor of ice-cream," Freddy said. "Anyway, it's moving off."

"There's a war on," Gavin shouted, suddenly trying an imitation of Craig. "I said, there's a *war* on."

They both began to laugh. They had become friends.

two

He tried to tell Kathy, but she didn't understand. "Oh, go on. You always make out that things are special even when they're perfectly ordinary. You're a reverse snob, Gav. Just because these people are peculiar, doesn't make them romantic. If there's one thing I wouldn't want, it would be to spend night after night cooped up in that little house with all those men just off the dole and all those old Missus Dears from the Shankill Road."

"But they're not all just off the dole. This fellow Hargreaves is very interesting. And there's Captain Lambert, the boozer."

"What's so great about boozers? I see them every day, hanging about the labor exchange opposite our office. Oh, the A.R.P. is a perfect place for them. Honestly, Gav, haven't you any idea what other people think about you and your precious colleagues?"

"Not romantic enough for you, eh? I suppose you'd have preferred me to join up in the British Army?"

"Don't be silly, you're not old enough. Besides, our sainted father would have a fit."

"Never mind him. Even if I *could* join up, with my luck I'd spend the whole war scrubbing out army latrines."

"Here we go again. With *your* luck. You make your own luck in this world. You just took this job because you found it easier to pass some simple first-aid certificate than go back and pass your Schools Leaving Cert. Your motives had nothing to do with the war and you know it."

"What war?" asked Mr. Burke, who had just come in to breakfast. "Haven't you heard the news? The Poles have surrendered at Lublin. Hitler's won. Of course, he'll ask for a few more perks, but the British and the French are in no position to refuse. They're quaking in their boots."

"Daddy," Kathy said. "It's occurred to me that you could be arrested, the way you talk."

"Let them arrest me," Mr. Burke said, grandly. "I've said it before and I'll say it again: when it comes to grinding down minorities, the German jackboot isn't half as hard as the heel of John Bull. All this guff about Hitler being a menace to civilization is sheer English hypocrisy. The things we've seen *them* do."

"Oh, Daddy, let's not have the Troubles for breakfast. You're beginning to sound like Aunt Liz."

"You can laugh at your Aunt Liz," Mr. Burke said, unfolding his *Irish News*. "You just don't know anything, either of you." He shook the paper out and began to read, his full lips pouting at the news. Gavin, watching him, decided that his father read the newspaper as other men play cards, shuffling through a page of stories until he found one which would confirm him in his prejudice. A Jewish name discovered in an account of a financial transaction, a Franco victory over the godless Reds, a hint of British perfidy in international affairs, an Irish triumph in the sports field, an evidence of Protestant bigotry, a discovery of Ulster governmental corruption: these were his reading goals.

These days he's well satisfied, Gavin thought, as his father read Hitler's Reichstag speech, his left hand absentmindedly smoothing back the gray ruff of his chair, his head nodding agreement with Hitler's new demands. His father, a solicitor, believed that his legal training had made him impartial, logical, and reasonable in judging issues. Actually, Gavin thought, he's one of the most prejudiced, emotional, and unreasonable people I've ever met. It was more than a year since he had decided there was no longer any point in arguing with his father. Silence and silent rebellion were the only defense against his father's pious prate about Catholicism, his father's fascist leanings in politics, his father's literary pronunciamentos. His father's opinions were laughable. Or, perhaps, enough to make one weep.

"By the way," Kathy said, lowering her voice, "a friend of yours rang up last night."

"Who?"

"You know who. She wants you to ring her. She thinks

you're avoiding her. You're right next door to the hospital now, why don't you go and see her?"

"Student nurses aren't allowed visitors. And we're not allowed to leave our post."

"Well, you'd better phone her. She sounded hurt."

He nodded, pretending unconcern. The truth was, he was terrified each time he went into the hospital that he'd bump into her, she in her student nurse's uniform, all white starched apron and black stockings, a getup which played the devil with his guardian angels. And he in his hated A.R.P. battle dress. But, now that she'd phoned him, he couldn't put it off any longer. He would have to phone her back. Later. Yes, later.

Kathy and his father went off to their respective offices. He went to bed. At eleven a.m. his mother woke him. "Your lady love is on the phone." He went downstairs in a shambling run, his mind not yet awake.

"Gavin, it's me. Listen, Sister's letting me off for two hours this aft to buy shoes. Can we meet?"

"Campbells'," he said.

"Good. Say I meet you in Campbells' at five, after I get the shoes? Then we can be together until six-thirty."

"Perfect."

But, of course, it was not perfect, it was hopeless. No sooner had he put down the receiver than he remembered that meeting her downtown at that hour would entail his showing up in the A.R.P. rig. He went on duty at seven, no time to go home and change after seeing her. Panic. Phone the hospital.

"May I speak to Nurse Shannon, please?"

"Nurse Shannon! Is this a private call? Probationer nurses are not allowed private calls excepting it's an emergency."

"This is an emergency."

"One moment, please."

A new voice. An old voice. "Hello? Can you tell me what the emergency is? This is Sister Mary Immaculata speaking."

"The Pope's dead," he said and hung up. From hairy old nuns, deliver us, O Lord. Face it, if Sally's feelings for you depend on what clothes you wear, then she's not worth your while. Stop acting like your mother with her snobbish little joke about you coming in the back door so as not to disgrace her with the neighbors. Wear that uniform to Campbells'.

It was an Indian summer's day, warm, wet, and close, and the university students, as they passed through Campbells' ground-floor bakery shop and started up the stairs toward the coffee room, began stripping off their raincoats and long woolen university scarves. In the coffee room, the only male still wearing his raincoat was Gavin, sticky and ill-at-ease in a window seat, his steel helmet and gas mask hidden under his chair. Unless one noticed his boots and battle-dress trousers, one might suppose him to be just another student. Uniforms, however, were in vogue. Across the room, lording it over two admiring girls, was an R.N.R. lieutenant, the gold braid on his cuffs so new as to make him seem an imposter. An O.T.C. cadet with white shoulder flashes on his battle dress was getting coffee for a girl in ballerina stockings, and a very studious-seeming private in the Royal Ulster Rifles was reading the coffee shop's copy of the *New Statesman & Nation*.

Well, Burke, said the White Guardian Angel. Are you a man or a mouse? Take off your raincoat. Yes, and put your tin hat on while you're at it, mocked the Black Angel. Salute that naval lieutenant, he's your superior. Nonsense, the White Angel said. You're a civilian, he has no authority over you. How can you be sure, the Black Angel whispered. It's wartime and he outranks you. He holds a King's commission.

Sometimes the Black Angel was too cheeky for his own good. When he put that particular bee into Gavin's bonnet, Gavin was obliged to take the dare. No bloody little West British naval person was going to frighten him. He removed the raincoat and, as he walked toward the self-service counter, he deliberately stared at the lieutenant, daring him to God knows what. The lieutenant cast a cold eye. He was probably the sort of fellow who wore a hanky up his sleeve, the cold Protestant sort who considered Catholics somehow vulgar and Southern Irishmen untrustworthy peasants. Gavin felt his anger jump as he passed him. The lieutenant had done absolutely nothing to him, yet in Gavin's mind he had already dragged the lieutenant to his feet and knocked him flat.

"Is it you?"

She said it almost shyly. He could see the white collar of her nursing uniform at the opening of her overcoat and those black silky stockings, sweet to his Black Angel. "Coffee?" he asked, in a whisper. He always whispered in public places. He hated strangers to know his business. He took a tray from a rack, put two cups of coffee on it, and led Sally toward the window seat. As he sat down, her foot touched the steel helmet under his chair.

"Is this yours?"

"Yes."

"What does F.A.P. stand for?"

"First Aid Party."

"Oh."

"What do you mean, oh?"

"Nothing. I was just curious."

"You meant something. Spit it out."

"No, honestly. I was just wondering what it looks like on you."

He bent down, disentangled the chin strap on his helmet from the gas mask satchel, and put the helmet on his head. Deliberately, he wore it, dead center, at its least dashing angle. "Well?"

"Mnn."

"Go on, say it. I don't cut a fine military figure, like that hanky-up-the-sleeve naval hero over there."

"I didn't say a word."

"Ah, but you meant it."

"What are you talking about, Gav? What's the matter?"

"I embarrass you, that's what's the matter. I look like Charlie Chaplin. Well, let me tell you, the people I work with look even funnier. Our post officer is an illiterate ex-weight lifter. He's a scream. And we have an old soldier, a dwarf, some old charladies, and a blonde semi-whore. Most of my fellow workers haven't had a job since the Depression started and I can see why. We're the unemployables, we're a joke and everybody thinks we're a pack of loafers. We are. I don't blame you one bit for laughing."

"I wasn't laughing at you, Gavin. What's got into you today?"

"Nothing's got into me. You don't know what I went

through on your account, having to come into this place in my uniform."

"But it was you who suggested Campbells'."

"Oh, never mind."

"But I do mind. If you hate this job, why don't you resign?"

"And go back to school. I thought you said you wouldn't go out with a schoolboy any more?"

"I never said any such thing. Of course I'd go out with you."

"Yes, better a schoolboy than some awful A.R.P. joker."

"Stop it, Gavin. Did I ever say that?"

"You didn't have to say it."

There was a silence. She picked up her coffee cup and sipped for a moment. She put the coffee cup down. "Face facts," she said. "You're the one who said those things about the people you work with, not me."

"How could *you* say anything about them? You don't even know them."

"Exactly." She reached across the table for her handbag. "I might as well go now."

"Go ahead. I won't embarrass you by coming with you. You won't have to be seen walking down Donegall Street with an A.R.P. layabout."

"Gavin, do you know what? You're a snob."

"*Me?* It's you's the snob."

"Oh, shut up and listen!" she said. "If you think this job's beneath you, why don't you resign? If you were so dead set against going back to school, why didn't you join the air force or something? You could go in as a cadet."

"Since when did you become such a loyal little West Briton, Miss Shannon? My uncle was shot by the English. What do you think my parents would say about my joining up?"

"I don't know. Do you care about your parents?"

"Of course I care."

"If you did, you'd have gone back to school and got your Leaving Cert."

"What do you know about it? I'm getting my London Matric, it's the same thing. What are you, my mother?"

"Come to think of it," she said. "I'm not." She stood up, slipped on her raincoat, and went across the room in a great hurry. Go after her and apologize. Hurry!

He would run downstairs, out into the street, see her in a crowd. Run after her, catch up, and begin to walk alongside her. Abase himself. Tell the truth, at last.

—Sally, you were right, I *am* ashamed of this job, and you're right, I should have gone back to school—

No answer. Still angry.

—Sally, please slow down, don't walk so fast. I want to tell you something. I'm in love with you—

Her eyes, looking at him.

—I said all those things today because I was mad with worry, I'm afraid you'll get tired of me, stop going out with me—

—But Gavin, that's silly—

—Sally, wait. I can't tell you this, here in the street. Come into this teashop, it's half empty. We'll take a table in the corner. Let me take your coat. Now, listen to me, I want to tell you the truth about me. I haven't been able to tell it to anyone, and that's what's been driving me mad. I'm serious. I sometimes think I *am* mad. Well, there's something wrong with me. I'm peculiar. No, that's not the whole truth. I want to tell you the real truth—

Her eyes, those large, lovely eyes. Watching him. Warm eyes. He could tell her. If he couldn't tell Sally he couldn't tell anyone. And if he couldn't tell anyone, it was all up with him. He knew that.

—Darling— Yes, call her darling, have the nerve to say it. —Darling, you were right, I *am* ashamed of this job and I'm ashamed of being ashamed, if you know what I mean. I'm just as snobbish and small as my parents, when I get right down to it. I want to be friends with people like Freddy and Captain Lambert because they seem "nice." I like to think I'm a socialist, but when I sit down with some of the men on our post . . . I mean, they're the sort of men who never wear collars and ties, the sort my father says wear their shirts "drawn simply to the neck, by a brass stud." They're men who were years on the dole, the men you see hanging around street corners on the Falls and Shankill Roads, the men who wear those cardboard suits, you know the jingle?

> When I was a lad, I went with my dad,
> And we always were clad at Sackman's.
> Now I'm a dad, I go with my lads,

> And we always are clad
> At Sackman's.

—And always will be clad, Sally, *sicut erat in principio et nunc et* bloody *semper*. They and their condition are what I fear; they are my failing future. I'm no different from my father. Like my father, I don't want to be them, not them. All other talk of futures is false, Sally. You're not a snob, Sally, you wouldn't understand me—

—But I do understand— She will understand. But she'll say I'm being silly, I'm not like them.

—I am like them, Sally, that's the thing that scares me. Don't you see, I'm a part of this A.R.P. farce, I fit in, perfectly. I'm the kid who failed his school exams, the boy going to the dogs—

—Nonsense, Gavin—

—Not nonsense! I'm part of the farce, that's the truth of it. Sally, what's happening to me, what's going to happen to me?—

Her eyes, I love her eyes.

—What do you mean, Gav, what *is* happening?—

And I must tell her everything. Everything, it's my only hope. I'll tell her that I haven't been to confession in fourteen months, that I never pray any more. She'll be shocked, she's holy. Well, in a way. All girls are holy, in a way. And I'll tell her that I'm not holy, that I never was, even when I was a kid. I'll tell her the real trouble, which is that I have sex on the brain, that I think about it every waking minute, day and night. —But not when I'm with you, Sally, because I love you and that's different—

Lie, lie, lie, there's no hope for you if you tell even one lie. A confession must be total.

—Even about you, Sally, I have dirty thoughts about you—

Not that I believe they *are* dirty, those thoughts, they're perfectly natural, that's the trouble. No, I'd better not go into that. I'll go on and tell her about the other signs. The fact that I'm only seventeen but I drink. —Yes, and have been drunk twice, once with the A.R.P. crowd. At twenty I'll be a drunkard, probably with V.D.—

—V.D.?—she'll say.

Go on, tell her. Because my friend Freddy Hargreaves,

he's a lot older than us, he's nearly thirty. Anyway, he wants me to go out with him on my next night off and we're going to pick up a couple of hot tarts in the Plaza Dance Hall. And I don't know how to get out of it, I don't even know whether I *want* to get out of it. Unless I go out with you, instead, Sally. Sally, please, don't leave me. If you walk out on me now, I'm done for. If you love me, it means there's some hope for me. Forget all the awful things I said today, will you?

But there was no sense asking that question. By now, Sally must be halfway back to the hospital. He sat in Campbells', staring at the naval officer's cap which sat on a chair nearby, arrogant and elegant, symbol of an authority he would never command. As usual, he had said all the right things—but to himself. As usual, he had done nothing to save himself.

three

In the lounge bar of a pub called The Hole In The Wall Freddy Hargreaves ordered two pints of porter and two half uns of whisky. He put one of each in front of Gavin. "The trick is to drink both in two minutes. Ninety seconds for the pint, then down with the chaser. Then straight out of here and over to the Plaza. Fit to dance but just a little lit. Ready?"

Gavin picked up the pint, which seemed as big as a vat of Guinness. He sighted down the bar at the red-headed girl he had noticed the moment he came into this place. She was stunning, not much older than he was, yet completely at home in this world of pubs and pints. A strand of her red hair fell over her brow and she was laughing delightedly at something a fat, blond pig of a man was telling her. Maybe she was a little tight? Or just happy. She should be happy, she was a girl, she didn't have to drink pints of porter against the clock.

"On our marks," Freddy said, glancing down the bar to see what interested Gavin. "Wait a minute. See that fat character, the one with the girl."

"I see the girl, all right."

"Well, the fellow she's with is Bobby Luddin, his people are Luddin's Southern Cream, the whisky barons. He's the one was in the papers a while back, you must have read about him. He got turfed out of the English Army."

"Why?"

"He got a peacetime commission about a year ago, got fed up with it, I suspect, and then went around England writing his name in the visitors' books at national monuments. Only he wrote it as Adolf Hitler. They caught up with him at Salisbury Cathedral. The *Daily Sketch* wrote it up."

"And who's the girl?"

"Don't know. Girls are his hobby. I'll bring him over. He's a gas man sometimes. And he always pays the drinks."

Bobby Luddin's face was pimpled, his fair hair so thin it showed his pink and gleaming skull. His clothes were expensively cut. The girl looked rich, too, in her silk dress and fur coat. She was Sally's age, a little too tall, though. What could a stunning girl like her see in a pig like Bobby? *You* know, said the Black Angel. £.s.d. Money.

"Oh, you read about it, did you, Freddy? Yes, they cashiered me. Said I'd gone bonkers. Bonkers not to stay on and get slaughtered for King and bloody country, what do you think?" Flutteringly, Bobby closed an eye. His smile was wet. He had bad teeth.

"This is Gavin Burke. Bobby Luddin."

"Burke. How do you do. My wife, Sheila."

"When did you get married?" Freddy was surprised.

"Six months ago—is it six, Sheila? Tell you something else too, she was unmarked merchandise when I acquired her. I've got a medical certificate to prove it. We have it framed over the bed. 'This is to certify that Miss Sheila Collins was examined by me and was found to be *virgo intacta*.' Signed by the quack."

"You're joking."

"Not at all. Perfectly reasonable precaution, don't you agree, Burke?"

Say something, the Black Angel warned. Don't stand there looking shocked. Nod your head, at least. That's better.

"You see, Burke agrees. After all, I've stuffed something like four hundred females in my life. Fact. I keep scores and I don't joke about holy things. Well, after that, one suspects that very few women remain virgins after puberty. So I decided that, with my money, I could afford a genuine, untouched hymen. I bloody well insisted on that. I wanted to be able to say that I was the first that ever burst into that silent sea. Poetry. Are you still fond of poetry, Freddy?"

"You always were a prick," Freddy said.

"But, a big prick," Bobby agreed delightedly. "Eh, Sheila?"

The girl stared at him with the wide unfocused stare of

someone who is drunk. Then turned away. And no wonder, Gavin thought. Poor kid.

"Surely, that's not a pint you chaps are swilling down? No, no. Pints aren't a fit drink for anyone but a carter. Mick? Change these pints for double whiskies, there's a good fellow."

"Don't be deceived by Bobby," Freddy said to Gavin. "He's really a revolutionary. Simply by being his odious self, Bobby makes a thousand converts to Marxism-Leninism every year. Even to getting cashiered. That was a master stroke, Bobby. 'Degenerate Capitalist Dodges Fight.' "

"Thank you," Bobby said, raising his glass in toast. "Have you heard about my court case with the Royal Lane Cinema?"

"The French letters you stuffed in the éclairs?"

"Oh, you know about that." Bobby seemed disconsolate. "Ah, but you didn't hear about my little game last month in Portstewart. Tell him, Sheila."

"You tell him," Sheila said. She drank her drink.

"I got heaved out of a Methodist church. We were passing by, Sheila and I, and we heard these sweet young voices singing hymns. So we went in, went up to the church loft, and there were all these children. And a lovely little soprano, about fourteen, I think. When she started her solo, I slipped in beside her and put my hand up her skirt. She ended on a very high note indeed. What was the hymn, Sheila?"

Sheila shook her head. She sighed.

"But didn't they call the police?" Gavin found himself asking, despite the Black Angel's sneer that this was gauche.

"They did," Sheila said, grimly.

"Yes, I had to make a very large donation to the church fund," Bobby said. "Worth it, though. Have another whisky, chaps."

"Just one, then," Freddy said. "We have to dance tonight."

"Where?"

"Plaza."

"Oh, that's more like it. Let's all go. I feel like skirt tonight."

"But, what about your wife?" Freddy said. "It won't be much fun for her."

"Young Burke here, can dance with her. She's a good dancer, Burke. And she has a sweet little arse on her, don't you think?"

Gavin looked at her and then could not look. He was aware that his face was red. Bobby, ignoring his embarrassment, pulled out an expensive leather notecase and slipped a five-pound note from it. He held the fiver up like a handkerchief, fluttering it in an effeminate manner. "Mick?" he called. The barman came. Bobby paid. Freddy winked at Gavin.

If I were you, the White Angel said, I'd think about this, really I would. I know you feel I'm silly when I talk about bad companions, but if ever you were out with a bad companion in your whole life it's this fat, rich pimple with his fivers and his foul mouth. Oh, come off it, the Black Angel said. Imagine when you tell fellows like Rory Hare and Tony Clooney about this. Imagine a man offering you his wife, even in a joke. And what a wife!

"Come on, Gav," Freddy said. "This way, we'll ride up there in style. Bobby has a car."

A car he had. It stood at the back door of the pub and, even in the blackout, revealed itself as a gleaming, high, old Bentley tourer, all huge, silvery headlamps and rakish mudguards. Bobby, in belted raincoat and cloth hat, bowed as he held the back door open. "You and Sheila in the back," he told Gavin. "You'll notice that seat. I had it made specially. It reclines. Freddy, you hop up front with me."

As the Bentley went up the back street with an arrogant elderly roar, Mrs. Luddin put her head close to Gavin's. "Can you dance?"

"Yes. A bit."

"I love dancing. Before I got married, I went to dances all the time."

"Did you?" Was that a tremor in his voice: there was certainly a tremor in his legs. The Bentley rounded a corner and slowed down, purring along the pavement's edge. "Trouble with this blackout," Bobby said. "You can't see what you're hunting. I'll risk the sidelamps."

Light flashed on the pavement. A girl gave a mock scream. "What about those two, Freddy, will we pick them up?"

"Your wife," Freddy said. "They'll spot her."

"Hey, young Burke, are you there? Lie down in the back seat with Sheila, there's a good chap. Hello, girls. Want a spin?"

Crouched beside Mrs. Luddin, her hair in his face, her arm around his shoulders, Gavin heard the girls' footsteps come close. "Come on in," Bobby's voice said. "Lots of room in front."

"Away on home," cried a broad Belfast accent. The engine roared and the Bentley accelerated. "Christ," Bobby's voice said. "I stepped on the gas, just in time. One of them was a pig and the other was her sister."

The redheaded Mrs. Luddin sat up, suddenly, releasing Gavin. "You and your games," she said to no one in particular.

The doorman on patrol outside the Plaza Dance Hall was the sort who is hired, not to open doors, but to throw people out of them. He shoved his brutish ex-serviceman's mug in the side window as the Bentley stopped at the front entrance. "Shift it," he said. "Youse can't park here."

Bobby did not appear to hear. He got out of the car, produced a ten-shilling note from his notecase and tucked it between the first and second button of the doorman's tunic. "The key's in the car."

"Yes, sir, very good, sir. I'll just slip it round the corner for you. I'll keep an eye on it, sir, don't you worry."

Mrs. Luddin allowed Gavin to help her out of the back seat. She leaned heavily on his arm and turned her face up to his. She smelled of whisky and expensive scent. "You're younger than I am, aren't you?" she asked. "Are you a Queen's student?"

"Yes." He let one answer cover two awkward questions, all the while aware that Bobby was buying four admissions at the ticket booth, aware too, that Freddy had made no effort to pay for their tickets. What sort of fellow was Freddy, really? What sort of fellow would consider Bobby a pal?

"I want to dance," Mrs. Luddin murmured. "Let's go in."

On the dance floor she was all clinging thighs, pressing breasts, and face in his neck, so much so that Gavin could not help an uneasy glance at their table each time they passed. But Bobby sat blissful, surrounded by mugs of tea, each of which contained illicit whisky. Freddy, on the dance floor, stalked the ballroom with panther glides, a masher, a champion, at home and admired. See, said the Black Angel. Nobody gives a damn. You could take her out in the dark and kiss her and feel her up and nobody would notice.

The music stopped, leaving them close to Bobby and the table. It would have been rude not to go back. "Enjoy the dance, Burke? Here, have a little tea. What do you think of that tart over there, the one with the odd shoes?"

If you drink that neat whisky on top of what you've had already, the White Angel said, there'll be no going home tonight. Your parents will catch you out. It's late, after ten, and you'll have to be sober again by midnight. If I were you, I'd slip away, get my coat and walk for an hour in the fresh air before risking it home. If he listened to you, the Black Angel said, he'd still be sitting in Classroom A in St. Michan's. Exactly, said the White Angel. Where he belongs. Gavin, these people are degenerate, disgusting, and silly. Oh, shut up, the Black Angel said. She's absolutely stunning, she hates that fatty, he probably bought her from her parents or something, she likes you, you're her generation and certainly more her type than that fat porker ever was. You know what I'm thinking, don't you? Young Mrs. Luddin might break your jinx. She might be the one to start you off. Can you think of anyone better? Have a drink and dance with her again.

They danced under a shifting ceiling of colored lights, danced slowly and very close and, suddenly, he was happy and drunk, the war, the A.R.P., the exam, all were forgotten, and someone on the bandstand was singing "South of the Border," a song he had first heard last year in Bangor on a camping holiday with Rory Hare. What would old Rory say if he saw him, Gavin, dancing with this stunning girl, his nose in her titian hair, listening to her sing:

> "That's where I fell in love, when stars above
>   Came out to play.
>   The mission bells told me
>   That I mustn't stay
>   South of the border
>   Down Mexico way."

He meant to kiss her on the cheek, but missed and kissed her eyelids. She did not seem to mind. He kissed her again, this time on the neck, and the music stopped and she led him, hand-in-hand, back to the table, where there was no sign of Freddy but where Bobby was offering a teacup full of whisky to an ugly, tarty-looking girl in a green frock and red high-heeled satin shoes. "Don't you love her shoes?" Bobby said, staring down at them. "This is Sheila, my daughter," he told the girl. "And this is young Burke, her boy friend. This is Imelda MacConaghy, you two. Shall we dance, Imelda?"

"Not if *she's* your daughter," Imelda said in a flat, angry voice. "*I'm* only twenty."

"Oh, but I was just joking, my dear. Sheila's no relation to me. Now come on, dear. Let's have a dance."

He stood, guiding the ugly girl toward the dance floor. As he passed Gavin, he leaned over and reached for Gavin's hand. Something metal was in his damp palm. "The car key," he said. He giggled, his pink skull suffusing with blood. "Don't be too long."

He went out onto the floor. They watched him dance with the girl called Imelda, rubbing his gross body against hers, as though he were a heifer with itch. Freddy glided by, a girl in his arms, executing masterful reverse slow foxtrot turns. Gavin and Bobby's wife sat in silence, the car key on the table among the whisky cups, a key symbolic of flight, of sin.

"Can you drive?" she asked.

"A bit."

"Do you want to go for a drive?"

"Whatever *you* like."

"I don't like anything. I don't like it here. I don't like it at home. I mean, where we live."

"Where you do live?"

"In the country. Before that, we lived in England for a while. Pass me one of those teacups."

"Why did you get married?"

She put her head down and laughed. Her red hair tumbled all over her face, hiding her from him. Through the mask of hair, her voice asked, quietly, drunkenly, "How old are you? Don't lie to me. Tell me."

"Seventeen and a half. I know I look older."

She went on laughing.

"Tell me the joke?"

"Oh," she said. "I was like you. I wanted to be grown-up. I wanted to leave Portstewart and smoke and drink cocktails and neck and never, never, never have anyone say again that I mustn't do this or mustn't say that. I got married, I suppose, because I wanted to be grown-up. Does that answer your question?"

"Maybe."

"Gavin . . . Is that your name, Gavin? Tell you something. Don't grow up. It's bloody awful being grown-up. Come on, we'll dance."

"I'd better take this key. Somebody might steal it."

On the dance floor she took him in her arms and put her cheek against his. They began to dance. "I know," she whispered. "I know what you're thinking. I know why you put that key in your pocket. You're all hot and bothered. You're like me, three years ago. I like you, Gavin. And you're going down, down, down, aren't you Gavin?"

"You're beautiful," he whispered. He felt sexy, but also sick.

"And rotten," she said. "Oh, yes, you think I'm rotten. Come on, stop pressing into me. Dance a little."

They danced, they danced past Bobby, who stood, barely moving, pressing against Imelda, his eyes shut, his wet lips open in a smile. "Kiss me," said Sheila Luddin. He kissed her. The whisky whirled in his head and he missed a dance step, he stumbled and she caught him. Dizzy, colored lights blurring in front of his eyes, he saw her face, a face which blurred into pinwheels of color. Then it came, hot, sudden and full, and he turned quickly from her, vomit rushing from his mouth. She took his hand, led him to the table and sat him down. "I told you," she said. "Better not grow up. Come on, I'll drive you home."

"I can't. Too soon. My father."

She laughed. "I remember that problem. All right, we'll go for a walk. You need air. Come on."

"No." He loved her, it was stupid to say so, but she was stunning, she was Bobby's captive and he loved her, you see, but there was vomit on his suit, he was sure he stank to high heaven of it and there was no point in her being with him now, he'd be ashamed to touch her, he was drunk and must be sober and this lovely other rotten, lost, damned soul, the only person in the whole world who understood him, must stay here and not see him reeling in the street outside. "I love you," he said. "Even though you're married. What's your phone number? May I ring you up?"

She bent over the table top, her red hair falling down to touch the teacups. She laughed and laughed and laughed. It was horrible. She looked up, still laughing, and said: "Just don't grow up. Don't grow up."

If only he could think of some crushing reply, if only he could pay her back for laughing at him, pay her back for mocking something very, very serious. But as he sat there, stiff with rage and shame, his stomach heaved. He bolted for the gents'. There, kneeling amid carbolic smells, he began his night's penance.

four

"Nurse Shannon," said Sister Mary Paul. "Take this slide down to Dr. Hanson in the V.D. clinic. And don't hang about. I need you back here for ward rounds."

Sally Shannon took the slide. It had to happen sometime. You just couldn't go on forever avoiding that part of the hospital. Sister Kane had told her that the A.R.P. people practiced their drills and classes four times a week in the V.D. clinic and most of the other probationer nurses had seen them coming and going through the hospital. But Sally had not. It was not that she had consciously avoided them: she had just been lucky. What was the point in seeing him again? It was over. If he had telephoned or made any effort to see her after that awful afternoon in Campbells', she would have been quite willing to make up. But not after seven *weeks*. That was too much.

The trouble was, she had been more than keen on Gavin Burke, even though he was a year younger than she and an awful baby in some ways. He wasn't like other boys and, certainly, he wasn't like the medical students in this hospital, always trying to maul you on the back stairs. Or like Tony Clooney, her present beau. His father was a rich publican, he had pots of pocket money and had taken her to a dozen dances and plays, yet had hardly exchanged more than a dozen words with her on each occasion. Gavin liked to talk: he was a boy you could talk to. He *listened* when you talked about male-female equality, women's rights, and stuff like that. He didn't consider you daft because you had a mind and were interested in other things besides dances and dates. Yes, she had been more than keen on him until that stupid business of the A.R.P. and the uniform. Which had ended it.

Still, as she went through the hall of the extern department and up a flight of steps toward the V.D. clinic, she began to feel nervous. If he were there and cut her dead, it could be worse. Still, there was no excuse for his not having called for seven weeks. No excuse, whatsoever.

She went in. Dr. Hanson's office was in session and there were a couple of old V.D. regulars waiting for their injections. In the big outer room, sure enough, the A.R.P. people were going through all that nonsense of stretchers and splints. A terrible-looking case in a white helmet was shouting out orders and there, sitting on a bench, was Gavin. He had not seen her. He looked so shabby and pale and miserable in his unform, was it any wonder he was ashamed of it? She had to remind herself that nobody had forced him to join this A.R.P. thing. Would she pretend she hadn't seen him? But, as she wondered about this, he turned around on his bench.

Hup-la! the Black Angel whispered. Wouldn't you just meet *her,* today of all days.

He stood up. Would she see how sick he was, would she guess that he had spent half the night tossing up? It's up to you to speak, the White Angel warned him. Remember the good resolutions you made this morning. Thou shalt not go to the Plaza, thou shalt not drink, thou shall phone Sally Shannon. Well, here she is, in the flesh.

"Hello, Sally."

"Hello."

"I'm sorry about not phoning you. I've been on night duty all the time."

"That's not true, Gavin, but never mind. It's not of the slightest interest to me whether you phone or not."

"That's blunt enough. Sorry, Nurse. We A.R.P. rats will now crawl back into our stinking caves."

"Gavin, it has nothing to do with the A.R.P. It has to do with you not phoning me for *seven weeks.*"

"I know. I'm sorry. But I want to explain something to you. I've been thinking about you all the time, Sally. Look, can we go to a flick on your next night off?"

"I'm sorry. I have a date."

"Can't you break it?"

"I have no intention of breaking it. Someone I know is taking me to see *Hamlet* at the Opera House and afterward we're going out to supper.

"Who is this millionaire?"

"I don't think that concerns you. Excuse me, I have to deliver this slide."

But he was waiting for her when she came out of Dr. Hanson's office. "Sally, please. I wish we could talk."

"Well, really. If you'd been so anxious to talk to me, you could have phoned me any time. You wouldn't have had to wait until I walked in here to be reminded of my existence."

"Do you know what you are, Nurse? You're a little Catholic bourgeois prig whose main interest in life seems to be the rules of courting etiquette. You should take a good look at yourself some time."

"So should you."

"What's that supposed to mean?"

"Oh, *nothing*," she said and ran out of the room. She could kill him, so she could, talk about stuck-up, look who was calling other people stuck-up. Oh, he was the end.

"Hey, you, Burke," Craig called. "Who gave you leave to talk to the nurses?"

"I know her."

"Doctor MacLanahan told me none of us was to annoy the hospital staff. He told me that, the doctor did. Now, you leave them nurses alone, Mister Romeo, or I'll learn you a thing or two. Get on to your drill."

Tomorrow night they would go back on the night shift. That meant he could see her only one night out of seven. His night off rarely coincided with her night off. Fat chance of making up with her under *those* conditions.

On the night shift he sat, glum, in the kitchen pretending to read a book so as not to have to talk to anyone. Gallagher, nicknamed "Your Man," passed him coming out of the scullery, going upstairs. Gallagher was thus nicknamed because he never referred to anyone by his given name. Man or woman, he spoke of his colleagues as "Your Man." Out of boredom and to try and raise a smile, Freddy Hargreaves now called after Gallagher: "Is Craig out in the yard?"

"No, your man's in he's office with the door locked."

"Where's his girl friend, is she with him?"

"Aye, your man is in there with him."

Gallagher went upstairs. Although he never referred to anyone by name, he always knew where everyone could be found at any hour of the shift. He was, Gavin and Freddy had decided, a rum one, but decent.

Your Man Gallagher had no idea what the likes of Gavin or Freddy thought. Nor did he care. He always volunteered for the bandage-folding job because he liked to be alone in the attic storeroom. He preferred being alone to mingling with Orange gets. Your Man was thirty-four and fat, with a red face which made him look like a boozer. In fact, he was a life member of the Pioneer Total Abstinence Society. He lived with his tubercular wife and four children in the Falls Road, a fiercely Catholic, fiercely nationalist, working-class district. What most of his Falls Road neighbors felt about this war could be summed up in the fact that they considered it a point of honor to leave a light shining in their upstairs windows at night in case any German bombers might come over the city. Your Man, a former member of the I.R.A., agreed with the slogan that England's adversity is Ireland's opportunity, but he no longer had great hopes of the I.R.A. as a force to overthrow the British. He put his money on Hitler. When Hitler won the war, Ireland would be whole again, thirty-two counties, free and clear. In the meantime, a man must earn a living. So he joined the A.R.P. He had taken first-aid training in his I.R.A. days. He kept to himself. He also kept a powerful flashlamp in his overcoat pocket. He knew what he'd be doing when, and if, any bombs dropped.

As he went up the narrow flight of stairs to the attic, his footsteps sounded in the upper front room below him. "Who's that?" Mrs. Clapper whispered. The other ladies listened. " 'Tis only Your Man," said old Mrs. MacCartney, who had sharp ears.

The ladies relaxed a little. Miss Albee, who had summoned them together for a private chat, tried to get the talk back on the subject. Miss Albee considered herself more refined than the other ladies; she could not, on her life, see herself making a friend of the likes of old Mrs. MacCartney, who took snuff, kept her teeth in her smock pocket, except when she was eating, and ate bread and dripping with her tea. Nor with fat Mrs. Cullen, and was it any wonder she was fat with all the bottles of stout she put away on the sly. It might have seemed possible to be friends with Mrs. Renee Clapper, but really, when you came right down to it, Mrs. Clapper was the last person in the world a lady should make a friend of. She was, to be blunt about it, too free in her ways.

But still, Miss Albee needed each and every one of them tonight. If something was to be done, it must be done through a group complaint. Who would heed her if she complained alone?

"He's taking advantage," old Mrs. MacCartney said. "He's using his position to take advantage of that wee girl."

"And him a good twenty years older than her," Mrs. Cullen said. "Somebody should tell her mother, so they should."

They were discussing Maggie Kerr, the tall bespectacled girl whom Craig had designated as post telephonist.

"There *is* no mother," Miss Albee announced. "I took it upon myself to make inquiries. It seems she shares a flat with another unfortunate girl like herself."

"Something should be done," Mrs. Clapper decided.

"Exactly. We should lodge a formal protest," Miss Albee said.

"But, who'd believe it?" Mrs. Clapper said. "Sure, none of the other men ever gave that girl a second look."

You did your best to make sure of that, Miss Albee thought, eyeing Mrs. Clapper's short skirt and tight bra; but said: "It's not a matter of other men, it's not even a matter of proving any irregularity between her and Mr. Craig. It's simply that the telephonist's duties should be rotated among us. In case of an air raid, all duties should be interchangeable."

Mrs. Cullen giggled. "There's some duties *I* could do without."

"That's not the point," Miss Albee said. You vulgar lump, she thought. God help me, that I've fallen in with such people. "The point is that girl does no other work. The rest of us have to shoulder her burden, cleaning up and so on. We must sign a formal complaint and hand it in to the City Hall inspector."

"But who'll write it?"

"I will," said Miss Albee.

In the scullery, Frank Price was keeping dick for a few of the lads who were having a hand of twenty-one. Cards were forbidden, you see, and while Frank would have liked to take a hand himself, he was not one for doing anything that would endanger his job. It had worked out very nicely these last months. His sisters had stopped complaining: he bought them little presents from his pay and, of course, put his share in the kitty. When you no longer drank, you see, there was not much to spend your money on. He wanted to buy a few racing pigeons and keep them on the roof, but Maggie and Minnie said they were dirty beasts. Besides, with a war on, it might be thought that keeping racing pigeons was fishy. Spies kept pigeons. No, no, Frank thought. Just sail a straight course and hold your tongue.

He looked in at Soldier MacBride, who was running the game. *There* was a man with a mouth on him.

"Hit me," Soldier said, beckoning for a card. "That'll do. Yes, there's no question but that the higher-ups stand to each other. Once an officer, always an officer. I'd like to see what would happen to us if we came in night after night, half-seas over like our friend, the Captain."

That's one blessing, Frank thought. Thanks be to God. I'm no longer a slave to drink. He felt sorry for the Captain, a nicely spoken man, a sad case.

"Give us a card," said Hughie Shaw. "Aye, the Captain's one of the higher-ups, all right. Even ould Harkness, the inspector, pretends not to notice when the Captain's away with the band. Soldier is right. The Captain must have connections."

"Pay twenties," said Soldier, who was dealer.

"Pay me," said Jimmy Lynan.

"Aye," said Soldier, turning up the cards, "we should all stand in with the Captain, mark my words. Boozer he may be, but he's one of them."

"That's you all over, Soldier," Hughie Shaw said contemptuously. "Stand in and suck up to every mortal man. Wasn't that how you got made Craig's deputy?"

"And why not," Soldier said. "Isn't it well for the rest of you that it's me's in charge on Craig's night off? You owe me fourpence, Hughie."

Hughie Shaw pushed fourpence to Soldier.

In the ping-pong room upstairs, the White Angel nagged Gavin as Gavin played his seventh straight game. Work, did I hear, said the angel, study, did you say? The curfew tolls the knell of passing months as you ping-pong your way into failing your London Matric. Have you opened your books once in the past three weeks? I know you won't like this, but that old one about the road to hell being paved with good intentions seems pretty apt in your case. Look around you. How do you think people get ahead in life? By playing ping-pong? Do you want to wind up like the Captain over there? He must have had all the advantages, a good school and so forth. Did he fail in school, too? Ask him, go on, ask him.

"Nineteen-eleven," Freddy said, taking over the service.

The Captain, sitting on a bench, was listening through earphones to his crystal wireless set. From time to time, his hand sawed the air as if he were conducting a concert. His eyes were shut, his straw-colored mustache seemed in danger of catching fire from the cigarette which burned, forgotten, between his lips.

"Twenty-eleven," Freddy said. He served again, an ace service. "Game," Freddy said. "Want another?"

"No. Need a rest." Gavin put his bat down on the table and went over to the Captain. "Concert?"

"Bach," the Captain said. "The D major harpsichord concerto, you know."

Gavin did not know. It was terrible to be a musical moron. Removing his earphones, the Captain offered his vague, timid smile. "It's a rearrangement," he said, "of the E major violin."

"Did you take up music at school?"

"Well, yes."

"Where did you go to school?"

"Ampleforth," the Captain said. "English school. You're Catholic, aren't you?"

"Yes." The idea of the Captain's attending a Catholic school had never crossed his mind. And Ampleforth. Gavin was impressed.

"I didn't much like it, going to school over there," the Captain said. "It estranged me from the other boys at home."

"But you're English?"

"No, I'm a Kerryman."

It was as though a Kenya planter had announced that he was black.

"Oh, come on," Freddy said. "You're Anglo-Irish."

"No. My father had a small mill in Kerry."

"But, you were in the British Army, Captain, and all that?"

"I wish people wouldn't call me Captain," the Captain said. "Actually, I held a temporary commission during the last war, wasn't even a soldier, had to do with a fleet of ambulances. I never fought, dammit, wouldn't have. I've always been a pacifist."

"You're joking," Freddy said.

"No. Serious. Hated the army, got out the first chance I had. I . . . " He stopped speaking. He had begun to tremble. "Back in a moment," he said. He got up and walked out of the room.

"Admit," Gavin said to Freddy. "We were dead wrong about him. A pacifist, a Catholic, and a Kerryman. Jesus."

Freddy was not convinced. "Don't believe all you hear. Haven't you noticed how he tries to suck up to everybody? Tell them what he thinks they want to hear and then tries to spring them for ten bob until payday."

Pacifist or fascist, said the White Angel, the Captain should be a lesson to you. Finishing up here in Crummick Street, his hands shaking so much he has to nip out and have a drink to steady them. That's what booze does. That's what comes of being lazy and lacking any real ambition. Think about that.

"Want another game?" Freddy asked.

"No, I'd better study a bit."

The new man, Old Crutt, who had at once become Craig's stoolie, watched the Captain come downstairs. He followed the Captain through the kitchen and scullery and out into the back yard. He saw the Captain go into the coal shed and shut the door. Old Crutt turned and went back into the house. Soldier and the others looked up from their game of twenty-one. They did not speak to him. Old Crutt went down the hall and knocked gently on the door of Craig's office.

"What's up?" Behind the partly opened door, Craig's

face glistened with sweat. His battle-dress blouse was unbuttoned.

"He's just gone down the yard again," Old Crutt said.

"Is he all right?"

"Aye. He was listening to the wireless."

"O.K."

"Right then, Mr. Craig."

Craig shut the door and slid the bolt. He liked heat.
He kept the two electric stoves in his office going all night.
The inspector had made his nightly visit. The coast was
clear. Craig turned to the tall slender girl who sat by the
telephone. She had taken her glasses off, and now she
looked up at him with the narrow stare of the near blind.
She held the front of her smock bunched together in her
clenched fist.

"It's all right," he said.

She removed her hand from her smock. The buttons
of the smock were undone. He went to her and eased the
smock back on her shoulders so that her breasts came out.
She wore no brassiere. He had forbidden it.

"I love your nellies," he whispered. "Nice soft nellies."

"Oh, love."

He stared at her naked breasts. They were large and
well formed. He knew that she was a bit afraid of him.
He reached forward and caressed her nipples. He knelt
beside her and kissed her breasts. Then he noticed the
clock. "I have to go for a wee while. I have to stir them
up, eh, Maggie?"

"All right, dear."

He took off his boots and went out in stockinged feet.
He went quietly toward the kitchen. He saw Frank Price's
face retreat hurriedly into the scullery. At the kitchen table,
Captain Lambert sat, a mug in his hand. Craig went to
the shelf, took down a clean mug, and went up to the
Captain. "Give us a drop of your tea, will you?"

"Out of this cup?"

"Just a wee sip."

The Captain poured half of his tea into Craig's cup.
Craig drank. It *was* tea. He got up and went out into the
scullery, where Soldier MacBride sat with four other men.
Soldier, as usual, was talking his head off. "So I says to
him, what post are you from? Darby Street First Aid,

says he. A very decent class of a man he was too. And do you know what he told me? He told me that in Darby Street every man jack on the night shift gets into his blankets the minute the inspector's past."

Why did I ever make that bloody Fenian my deputy? Craig wondered. That was my first mistake. "This isn't Darby Street," Craig shouted into the scullery. "There'll be no sleeping here. Where's Gallagher?"

"Up in the attic, sir."

He went out quickly. If only he could catch Gallagher in a nap. He went up the stairs in his stockinged feet, up and up until he reached the attic door. There was no light on inside. He opened the door, careful not to make a noise. The blackout blind was up and he could see the moon. He peered around in the moonlit shadows, looking for a sleeping figure.

"Do you want the light on, sir?" a voice asked.

"What's the blind doing up?" Craig said, rattled.

A hand came out of the darkness and pulled the blind down. Gallagher's boots sounded on the bare boards. The light clicked on.

'You were sleeping, weren't you?"

"No, sir, I was looking at the moon. The rising of the moon."

"Sitting here in the dark, looking at the moon? I never heard tell of that."

"There's no harm in it, though," Your Man said, defensively.

"Well, cut it out, keep that blind down, there's a war on. I said, there's a war on. Is all the bandages put away?"

"Yes, sir."

Craig shut the storeroom door and went down the attic steps toward the room he called the henroost. Pack of bitches, clucking away in there. He knocked. Miss Albee had complained of his habit of throwing open the door on them.

"Good evening, ladies. How're we getting on?"

"Rightly, sir," said old Mrs. MacCartney.

"I just want to remind youse all that first aid class is at three sharp. And remember, next week is divisional exercise with casualties from the Boy Scouts."

"Yes, Mr. Craig."

"Right then. Three o'clock."

He went on downstairs. There was no noise from the ping-pong room. He went in for a look. They were reading books, Hargreaves and the kid. Always reading books, they were. He went over, picked up the ping-pong bats, and said: "These bats is to be put away when not in play. I said, these bats is to be put away."

Hargreaves looked up. "Sorry," he said, and went back to his book. Rage filled Craig. In his mind he picked that big drink of water up by the neck, threw him to the floor, and kicked his nuts in.

But he did nothing. He looked at the book Hargreaves was reading. He knew Hargreaves did not like people looking over his shoulder. "The Waste Land," he spelled out. "What's that supposed to mean?"

"It's a poem."

"A pome, a pome—what do you want to read pomes for? Only girls read pomes."

Hargreaves played deaf. Craig looked at young Burke. "What are you doing?" he asked.

"Studying."

"Studying what?"

"History. For an exam."

"That's against A.R.P. regulations, sonny boy."

"What is, sir?"

"Doing another job on the premises."

"What job—sir?"

"Studying for an exam, that's a whole-time job."

"Is it—sir?"

"I say it is. I say studying for an examination is a whole-time job, that's what I say. I'll have to report this to Mister Harkness. And I know what Mister Harkness will say. He'll say you'll have to cut that out."

"Will he, now?" Hargreaves said.

"I'm not speaking to you. Shut your beak."

"Look, Craig. If Gavin wants to study for his exam during a recreation period, he's perfectly entitled to do so. What do you do on your rest period, Craig?"

"*Mister* Craig to you. And what I do is my business."

He turned and left the room. What did Hargreaves mean by asking him that, what did Hargreaves know?

Old Crutt was waiting for him downstairs. "Soldier and Bates and Shaw and Lynan was at twenty-one in the scullery a while back."

"O.K., Tom. Thanks."

"Right, Mister Craig."

He went back to his office. He had a free hour before he gave them their first aid class. He thought for a moment of Captain Lambert and, as usual, felt uneasy. He had shopped the Captain as a drunk, the first month on the job. But H.Q. had ignored his report, and when he rang up about it, some snotty bastard in H.Q. told him the matter was pending. He had complained to Mr. Harkness about it, but Harkness had done nothing. Since then, Craig had often wondered if it had been a mistake to shop the Captain. Maybe the Captain knew some higher-ups at H.Q. Maybe the Captain was, at this very moment, making trouble for him. It worried Craig: he had Old Crutt keep an eye on the Captain. Some night, if he was lucky, he would catch the Captain so drunk it could not be ignored.

But he had not been lucky tonight. He had caught nobody out, had no sport at all. It made him angry. He thought of Maggie Kerr. He knocked on his office door, using a signal. She opened the bolt and let him in. He saw that her blouse was still undone. He slid the bolt shut.

five

Ernst Tausig, a German Communist leader who had been tortured and compromised by the Nazis, looked across the room at his brother and his mistress. He weighed a revolver in his hand. "Tilly, Carl," he said, "our agony is real. But we live in the joy of a great coming people! The animal kingdom is past. Day must follow the night."

At the back of the Grafton Players' Hall, the four art-student girls who had painted the scenery leaned forward in their seats. The one nearest Gavin was sobbing.

"Now we are ready," said Ernst. "We have been steeled in a terrible fire, but soon all the desolate places of the world must flourish with human genius. Brothers will live in the soviets of the world! Yes, a world of security and freedom is waiting for all mankind!"

Ernst looked meaningfully at Tilly and Carl. He walked to the wings. "Do your work, comrades," he said. He went offstage.

Tilly stood still for a moment, then started after him. Carl held her back.

"Carl, stop him, stop him."

"Let him die. . . ." said Carl.

"Carl. . . ."

In the wings, Archie Henderson fired the stage pistol.

"Let him live. . . ." Carl said.

Meg Hunt, who was assistant producer, led the applause, a long ash from the cigarette between her lips spilling unnoticed on her skirt. The girl students clapped until their hands hurt. Harry Boyle had trouble getting the curtain down and was forced to appear on stage, dragging the curtain behind him. It stayed closed for a moment, then jerked open to reveal the entire cast, assembled in their dress rehearsal costumes. Ernst Tausig came forward, bowed to the audience, then straightened up, put on his glasses, and, in his normal voice, the voice of Freddy Hargreaves, asked for a cigarette.

Billy MacLarnon, the producer, appeared on stage and told everyone to be on time tomorrow night. The dress rehearsal was over, and Gavin went to the dressing room to see Freddy. Two girls were there ahead of him.

"Freddy, you were the whole show," said fair hair and freckles, her eyes round with admiration.

"I cried," murmured small and serious.

"Is it true that you're really a professional? Meg said you acted with the Gate in Dublin."

Freddy smeared cold cream on his chin. "That's right."

"You were just perfect," said small and serious. "Especially in that last scene. And the play is so *true*. Just to hear someone say the truth. I cried and, normally, I'm not the sort who cries."

Gavin, standing at the dressing room door, noticed the look on her face. She would do anything Freddy asked of her, that small and serious girl. *Anything,* said the Black Angel. Imagine if it were you she looked at like that. You should investigate this. Remember your dream of becoming an actor?

"The *what* players?" asked Mr. Burke, ten days later.

"The Grafton Players. They have a hall in the Ormeau Road."

"Protestants?"

"Some of them, yes. They're not really affiliated with any group."

"The Grafton Players, I remember them," Owen said. "They did something at Queen's last year. Some left-wing thing."

"Gracious God," Mrs. Burke said. "Is that true, Gavin?"

"Of course not."

"Well, what's the play?" Mr. Burke wanted to know.

"It's an American play by a man called Clifford Odets."

"Never heard of him," said Mr. Burke, in a voice which clearly indicated that if he had not heard of Odets, Odets would not be heard from.

"What's the play about?" Owen said.

"It's about Germany."

Is it, now, the Black Angel whispered. Is that an honest answer? Tell them what it's really about. Stand up for yourself, you're not a kid any more. You're nearly eighteen.

"Well," said Mrs. Burke, "we must go and see you in it."

"It's only a small part. Maybe next time, I mean if I get a part in their next play."

"There won't be another play," Mr. Burke said loudly. "There's the little matter of your London Matric."

"Yes, Daddy."

"You'd better make up your mind to pass, this time. And, after that, you're going to Queen's and you're going to get a degree like anybody else."

"Yes, Daddy."

"This time," said Mr. Burke, "the play is *not* the thing."

If only he knew, the Black Angel whispered. The luck you had, with the fellow who played Carl taking sick. Oh, yes, you're a natural-born actor, Meg Hunt said so. And the naked admiration of those girls who paint the scenery. So, the play's not the thing, eh? It's *your* thing. You scored a triumph.

What triumph? the White Angel wanted to know. What good is it to be acting in a play you're afraid to let anyone come and see? What would your mother say if she heard you deliver that line in the play about there being "no deeper mother than the working class." Isn't it a fact that you're dying to ring up Sally Shannon and ask her to come, but you're afraid to do it because she might tell Owen or Kathy what sort of play it is?

Never mind him, said the Black Angel. And never mind Sally Shannon. I hear she's going around these days with some big lump of a medical student who's probably feeling her up in the back seats of cinemas.

O God, no. Black stockings, her kisses. I still love her, no matter what.

Come off it, the Black Angel said. You want her lily-white body, that's what. And if that's what you want, those girls who hang around the Grafton Players' Hall are hotter than Sally will ever be. They're not Catholics, not even Prods, they're probably Communists. Free love and all that. Why don't you ask Freddy tomorrow?

"Freddy? Not that it makes any difference to me, of course, but I was wondering if the Grafton Players are a Communist group?"

"Not officially. Billy MacLarnon's C.P. And so are some of the others."

"Are you?"

"Christ, no. I'm independent."

"And what about the audiences?"

"Well, a lot of them are Party faithfuls. The trouble is, we're preaching to the converted. Anyway, there isn't much of an audience. Did you notice how few people were in the hall last night?"

"No. I was too busy admiring my own performance."

Half in joke and whole in earnest, the White Angel sneered. You, an actor. What's so marvelous about being an actor, anyway. Look at Freddy. He acted with the Gate, didn't he?

"Freddy, why didn't you stay with the Gate?"

"Never was there. That's just something I tell the girls."

"You mean you never were a professional?"

"No, I started too late. You have to get into it when you're twenty."

Do you hear that? It's an omen, everything about this play has been an omen. I'm only seventeen and already I've played an important role. David Garrick, Beerbohm Tree, Edmund Kean, Gavin Burke. Maybe they'll name a theater after me. The Burke.

A whistle blew. Craig's voice screamed. "Downstairs on the double. Inspection. Inspection."

Freddy put aside his copy of *Letters from Iceland*. "Sod it, this day shift's three times worse than night shift." He and Gavin went down to the front hall to line up with the rest of the personnel. Mr. Harkness, the A.R.P. inspector, had arrived for roll call.

Mr. Harkness wore a civilian suit, never a uniform. He was a permanent Local Authority employee and, before the war, had been an inspector of City Work gangs. "Now, it's no-work gangs," he would say, puffing irritably on his cigarette. "Biggest waste of public funds that ever was invented. Take this war. The whole of the British Empire quaking in its boots over a few Huns that never in a million years could beat us. It's the newspapers' fault. Take these Russians, ignorant bloody moujiks, that's what they are, and let me tell you I'm not one bit surprised they couldn't even beat Finland, a wee country the size of a postage stamp. If the Finns can hammer them, then what are *we* worrying about? It's these bloody newspapers with their scare stories. These air raids, that's all scare stuff too. What damage have they done over in England? None, am I right? Just like the Zeppelins in the First War, scare stuff, nothing more, nothing less. And when you have my job, checking up on these loafers of A.R.P. people, day in, day out, I tell you it would make an honest man sick to his stomach."

It made him so sick he no longer bothered to read out the roll call himself. He simply took the lists and counted heads as though the personnel were sheep. As for the training schedules he was supposed to check on, he initialed them as soon as the post officer handed them to him. "Training for what?" he said to his wife. "Who's going to bomb Ulster? I wish the Gerries would. I do. I wish they'd drop one big bomb, just on these A.R.P. loafers."

And did those loafers complain! Always some complaint or other. This morning, as he initialed the inspection sheet roll at Crummick Street Post, the post officer, Craig, took him into his little office and shut the door. Always some daft question.

"Tell us, Mister Harkness, it's a point of order I want to clear with you. Is the people on this post allowed to indulge in other activities for profit?"

"What do you mean?" Mr. Harkness said, moving downwind of the fellow's bad breath.

"Well, there's two men on this post has spent the last week rehearsing a play on the premises."

"Did they attend drills and classes?"

"Oh, yes, I seen to that. But the question is, sir, is a man entitled to do the like of that? One of them, the young lad, spends his time studying for an examination. I mean that is *work*. He's doing other work on A.R.P. time."

"Exactly," Mr. Harkness said. "That *is* work. Good for him. I'm glad to hear somebody's doing something useful in these posts."

"Well, I just wanted to know if it was O.K."

"Where's my coat?"

"Here, sir. I'll see you to the door, sir."

Harkness knew why Craig wanted to see him to the door, it was because there were probably four other loafers waiting in the hall with some complaint about *him*. It was always the same in these posts: there was one woman here complaining last week about the telephonist's duties. Typical. They had nothing to do but think up ways to make trouble for one another.

"Has your man left?" Gallagher asked Freddy and Gavin.

"Just gone. Is the ping-pong table free?"

"Aye."

But no sooner had they got a game going than the whistle blew again. "Men only," the voice screamed. "Men only. Decontamination drill in the hospital. Everybody into he's suit."

The antigas decontamination suits were heavy, yellow oilskins, high rubber boots, and oilskin mitts. They were nonporous and caused the men to sweat. Grumbling and fumbling, eight men got dressed and were paraded out into the rainy street. "By the right, quick march."

The hospital was four streets away, four streets mined with public humiliation. As the eight men marched raggedly along the pavement, doors opened and women appeared, smiling and shaking their heads. Small children grew to a noisy swarm, dancing around the A.R.P. men like outriders, attracting more spectators by their yells.

"Here's the yellow men."

"Hey, mister. Is it goin' to rain?"

Heads down, sweating in their stiff, yellow oilskins, the A.R.P. men ignored these taunts.

"Hey, mister, are you goin' fishin'?"

"Thon's a gas suit he has on."

"What does them men do, Ma?"

"Hey, mister, when's ould Hitler comin'?"

Public humiliation ceased at the hospital gates, but there was no sanctuary within. As the eight men marched past the door of the outpatients' surgery, Sister Keogh, the senior extern nurse, raised her eyes to heaven.

"Listen to that noise, would you. Tramping across my floors in their big bloothers of boots. And not one mortal one of them, man or woman, that you could trust to stick a bit of Elastoplast on a child's cut finger."

"They're a desperate looking bunch, all right," said Dr. Donlon, a new intern. "What's that rig they're wearing?"

"Something to do with gas. They use the V.D. clinic. It suits them, I'd say."

The Venereal Diseases clinic, a suite of three rooms, had been rented by the Local Defence Authority from the hospital and partly converted as a contamination center. Craig's practice drill consisted in a run-through of the decontamination procedure. First, he would pick two men, usually men who were shy about undressing. Two other men, wearing the cumbersome gas suits, would undress the victims, placing their "contaminated" clothing in large zinc bins. In the second room, two men gave the naked men a shower, washed their eyes and covered them with bleach paste. In the third room, the victims were to be given a hospital nightshirt. However, in the practice drills, there were no nightshirts. The victims must re-shower and dress themselves.

This morning, piqued by the inspector's refusal to take action against Gavin and Freddy, Craig designated them as gas victims and ordered Old Crutt and Jimmy Lynan to strip them naked. In the shower room, he turned on the cold water first, then, apologizing, turned the water on very hot. In the application of bleach paste to victims, he took charge himself, scrubbing it on with a large, hard brush. He was silent during this operation.

Just look at you, the White Angel said. Standing here naked with a lunatic sadist smearing paste on your bum. Seven months you've been in this farce of a job, seven wasted months. Just suppose that everyone is right and that there'll be no air raids here. Suppose Hitler doesn't win. The war will be over one day and Sally will marry a medical student, Owen will be in the firm, and all the boys you went to school with last year will have finished their university and have good jobs. But where will you be?

A boozer, an ex-A.R.P. stretcher-bearer, a sometime amateur actor, an ex-Catholic, a masturbator, a marginal loafer, still waiting for some revolution, for the day when:

. . . the sniggering machine-guns in the hands of the young men
Are trained on every flat and club and beauty parlour and
    Father's den?

There'll no no explosion and you know it: your father's world will not be blown up. This war is a phony war

The Emperor of Ice-Cream • 59

and one day it will be over, with the only Irish casualties you and your buddies who will then be out of work. Take a look at yourself. You're what you feared. A flop.

"Sod this," Freddy said, scrubbing off paste in the shower. "If there's much more of this guinea pig stuff, I'm going to transfer to the Fire Service. Listen, let's nip out for a pint after lunch."

"Hey, Billy, here's the yellow men again."

Childish voices, singing a mocking folk song, pursued the A.R.P. men down the street.

"Will you treat your Mary Ann,
To some dulse and yellow man
At the Ould Lammas Fair at Ballycastle-O!"

Captain Lambert, ignoring the singing, turned to Gavin, who marched alongside him. "I say, Gav, I don't suppose you could spare five bob until Thursday?"

"Sorry." The Captain had borrowed or tried to borrow from every man and woman on the post.

"I get an allowance," the Captain said, "from my family. Paid each quarter. Should have it by Thursday."

Well, five bob wasn't such a lot. "All right," Gavin said. "That'll be fifteen bob you owe me. With the other lot."

"Right. Yes, I have a note of it."

"Give it to you when we change."

"Thank you."

He was waiting, a cigarette trembling between his nicotined fingers, as Gavin changed back into his battle-dress. As usual, when loaned money, the Captain offered to buy his creditor a pint. "Perhaps we can nip out after lunch?"

"Freddy and I are going to the Crown."

"I'll join you then, if I may."

"O.K. See Soldier."

Soldier was the man to see, because Soldier generaled all illicit movements. Pub time on the day shift was between one and three in the afternoon, a period when Craig was closeted in his office in the company of Maggie Kerr, the post telephonist. If Craig left his office during those hours, or if an inspector arrived for roll call, Soldier's scout, posted in the hall, would make a surreptitious dash down the back entry to the pub and the warned men would flee back to ground, going hard over the back wall and into the yard.

So, they saw Soldier. He allotted them the first forty minutes of the grace period. Frank Price, who was to stand guard, was promised a packet of cigarettes for his trouble, for Soldier, a good general, liked to see his troops kept happy.

"Thanks very much indeed," said the Captain to Gavin as they moved, single-file, down the back yard.

"What's that in aid of?" Freddy whispered to Gavin.

"Loan of five bob."

"More fool you. Come on, let's ditch him."

They entered the Crown at a half-run, leaving the Captain half a block behind them. But when he came in, shaking rain-drops from his hat, peeling off his old chamois gloves, smiling his glassy smile at the barman, he spotted Gavin at once and went up to him, ordering a Guinness all around, an order that took two shillings and threepence from the five shillings Gavin had lent him. "Your health, gentlemen," he said, lifting a shaky glass.

They drank. The Captain gave a prefatory cough. "I say. Would either of you know of some cheap digs?"

"For you?" Freddy asked.

"Yes. People I'm staying with now, they need my room. I have to leave at once. Tonight, as a matter of fact."

"And have you somewhere to go for tonight?"

"Afraid not."

"But, good God!" Freddy might not have much time for the Captain, but a man without a bed was a man in conflict with the system. "What are you going to do?"

"Well, I might pop back to the post and ask the night-shift people to put me up on a stretcher."

"Wait a minute," Freddy said. "If you do that, old Greenwood will make sure it gets back to H.Q. No, no, we'll have to think of something else. Where's your stuff?"

"At my digs. Have to move it."

"Gav and I will give you a hand, eh, Gav?"

"Of course."

"And I can get you a bed for a night or two. A friend of mine runs a sort of club. He'll put you up until pay-day. I'll ring up now and ask him."

"Very kind of you." The Captain had already finished

his pint and now signaled the barman for a refill. Which was three shillings gone out of the five Gavin had loaned him. Well, said the White Angel, that's how it goes with drunkards.

Freddy came back from the pay phone. "It's O.K. My friend will give you a camp bed at his place until Friday. After that, you'll have to make other arrangements."

"Thank you very much, indeed. May I buy you a pint?"

Did Freddy blush? It seemed like it. "No, no," he said, crossly. "You've already bought a round."

"Never mind. Thursday, I get fifty quid. To pay off some debts."

"Mind you get your five bob," Freddy whispered to Gavin, provoking one of their spontaneous outbursts of laughter. The Captain looked puzzled. "What? Something, some joke?"

"No, no," Freddy gasped, still laughing.

"By the way," the Captain said. "About moving. I have quite a few records and my gramophone is rather large. Still, we might get it in a taxi."

"I can borrow a car," Freddy said.

"Oh, splendid. Sure you chaps won't have another pint?"

"Yes. But it's my round," Gavin said.

The Captain smiled. He already seemed woozy. "Thanks very much. I'll have the same thing."

six

Freddy offered to pick Gavin up at Gavin's house and drive him across town to the Captain's digs. On his way home from the post Gavin worried about this. His parents had never met Freddy. He did not want them to meet Freddy, or Freddy them. Was it, he wondered, because he was ashamed of Freddy, or was it because he was ashamed of his parents? One thing: they would not get on together. He could just imagine his father telling Freddy about the progress of the war. Two days ago the Germans had invaded Belgium, Holland, and Luxembourg, and this, on top of the British retreat from Norway, had made Mr. Burke a very happy man. Since then, he had been tuning in gleefully to the wireless, waiting for the downfall of the Chamberlain government.

Gavin was thinking about these things when he entered the house. Thinking made him absent-minded, and so he did not examine the overcoats on the downstairs hallstand. Usually, if there were strangers in the house, he went upstairs to change out of his uniform. Tonight, he went straight into the drawing room.

Tony Clooney rose up from the armchair nearest the door, very grown-up in a blue pinstripe suit, with a striped, tab-collared shirt. "Lights out," Tony said. "Here comes the warden."

He let the crack pass, for there *she* was, sitting opposite Kathy at the fire. He looked at her: she looked at him. "Hello, Gavin," she said.

What's *she* doing here, the Black Angel wanted to know. She answered him as though the angel had spoken aloud.

"Tony and I were at the pictures and met Kathy there. We all came back together."

His mother had provided tea. Now, he was asked if he wanted a cup. His wrinkled battle dress versus Tony's pinstripe. "No, I have to go up and change. I'm going out, right after supper."

And fled, going upstairs two at a time, mentally punching Tony Clooney's mug half a dozen times on the way to the bedroom. What was she doing with a clot like Clooney, the smutty-minded son of a rich publican, a former classmate of Gavin's remembered mainly for his boasts in the jakes about things he had done to girls he'd gone out with. What about all her fine talk of wanting to go out with boys she could talk to, boys who would treat her as an equal. Clooney had never really talked to a girl in his life, only cuddled them. Clooney treat her an an equal, well that would be the day! Gavin slammed the bedroom door.

"What's eating *you?*" Owen asked, looking up from his desk.

"Nothing. I have to change."

And downstairs again on the double, praying they hadn't gone, for he had sounded rude running out like that, she would think he was still dodging her, whereas he was in love with her. After all these months, it made no difference, the moment he had walked into the drawing room tonight he saw her and only her. Oh, Sally. To hell with moving the Captain, he would ask her out to the pictures tonight. But she'd already been to the pictures this afternoon. With Clooney. Bloody Clooney, cuddling up to her in the balcony seats. Why the hell can't he get his own girl?

The drawing room again: but he was late. They were standing around the fire, about to go. Desperate, he pulled out cigarettes.

"Sally? Tony? Have a cigarette, what's your hurry?"

"Woodbines," Tony said, taking one. "I haven't had a Woodbine since we used to smoke them in secret at the back of Big Field."

Meaning, of course, that he now smoked better cigarettes.

"Woodbines," Gavin said, "are made from the finest of scrapings. They are the true workingman's cigarette and, as such, eminently suited to my present station in life."

"Workingman, did you say?" Tony smiled. "I thought

the A.R.P. was as far away from hard work as a fellow could wish."

"But Gavin's studying," *she* said.

He looked at her.

"I mean Kathy was telling me you're doing your matric this month."

Tony pretended interest. "How's the grind going?"

"I'm scared."

"But the London's easy," Tony said. "Even Donny Gallivan passed it, first time out."

With his pinstripe suit, Tony was wearing a Queen's tie. Gavin pointed to it. "I see you're a varsity buck, nowadays. What are you doing?"

"First med."

"Maybe Gavin will be able to join you next year," Gavin's mother said, with a mother's sure instinct for saying the wrong thing. "Anyway we're all praying for it."

"He'll get it all right," *she* said.

Gavin's mother looked pleased. "Well, I hope so. I don't want him staying much longer in this A.R.P. thing."

Tony Clooney smiled. "There's a warden in our avenue would drive you crackers. He's been in to see my mother about the blinds at least fifteen times."

"Gavin's not a warden," *she* said. "He's in First Aid. I see him sometimes, working in the hospital."

Thank you, Sally, thank you for that assistance. But did you really see me, I didn't see you, why didn't you talk to me, if you saw me?

"Anyway," Tony said, "thanks very much for the tea, Mrs. Burke. We must run. I have to have the old man's car back in the garage before seven."

"Sally, just a sec," Kathy said. "Come into my room, I want to show you a dress I got at Robbs."

Which left him alone with Tony Clooney, left him seeing Clooney out into the hall with no chance at all of talking to *her*. Never mind, he would phone her tomorrow. "I didn't know you were dating Sally," he said to Clooney, as Clooney belted himself into a big rubbery-looking raincoat, all tabs and toggles and flaps.

"Shannon? Didn't you used to take her out?"

"Yes."

"Well, then," Clooney said, "you know the form." He

The Emperor of Ice-Cream • 65

gave a rubbery smile to match his coat. "Nix, nix," he murmured. "Here they come."

"Are we ready, Tony? Good-bye, Gavin. And good luck with the exam."

He wanted to touch her. He held out his hand and, as they shook hands, Kathy opened the front door and there, why hadn't he noticed it before, was a huge Humber, *la voiture de Clooney père*.

"Good-bye, good-bye. Thanks for the tea."

And the door shut. "She's looking well, your former lady-friend," Kathy said. "Do you know, I think she still has a notion of you."

"Mind your own business, Miss Nosey Parker."

At supper that night his father was jubilant. "So Hitler's missed the bus, has he? Remember that, remember Chamberlain saying that last month. I'll tell you a good one. There was a farmer in my office today, an old fellow called Phelemy Friel who's very fond of going to law. Anyway, we were discussing the war, so-called, and he looked at me with the old pipe stuck in his jaw and, said he: 'Mister Burke,' said he, 'sure, and isn't that man Hitler all their daddies.' Wasn't that a grand way of putting it? Hitler's all their daddies. Chamberlain found it out. And his successor, Mr. Turncoat Winston Churchill of Home Rule fame, will find out the very same thing. Churchill. A military incompetent, to boot. Isn't it typical of the English that they'd pick the architect of the Gallipoli shambles to lead them now."

Mary, the Burkes' old maid, appeared at the dining room doorway. "Master Gavin, there's a man here to see you. Will I show him up to the drawing room?"

"No, I'm coming."

"But you haven't finished your supper," his mother said. "Who is it?"

"A man from the post. We have to help a fellow move his digs."

"Moving people's digs isn't studying," his father commented.

"Well, will I leave this man in the front hall?" old Mary wanted to know.

"Wait." He rose, wiped his mouth with his napkin, and fled, grabbing his raincoat off the front hallstand, grabbing

Freddy's arm with a mumbled apology, almost pushing Freddy out of the house. The car Freddy had borrowed was an old Morris, converted into a sort of truck. It bore a legend: FERGUSON. FRESH POULTRY. Freddy told Gavin to sit in front. "We're late, but I'll bet old Gerald won't be on time. By the way, I never asked you. What does your father do?"

"He's a solicitor."

"Is he? What does he think of you pissing away your time in the A.R.P.?"

"He thinks I'm studying for the matric, remember?"

"Ah, yes."

Night came as they drove in a drizzle of rain across the city. At the corner of Stranmillis Road, contrary to Freddy's prediction, a shadowy figure walked toward the car. It was the Captain, wearing a trenchcoat and an old porkpie hat, its edges turned down all around. He seemed both sober and nervous. "Very good of you both to come. I feel relieved tonight."

"It won't take long to move," Freddy said. "And this place I'm taking you to is quite comfortable."

"No, I meant about Churchill becoming P.M. Maybe he'll be able to do something. This way, it's the third house from the corner. Very nice people, my landlords. German refugees, as a matter of fact."

They parked the car outside a tall, narrow house, its ground-floor windows screened by dingy net curtains. The brick work was chipped and, from a broken roof gutter, water sluiced in a steady drip, leaving a slimy green stain on the front steps. The Captain's hand trembled as he inserted his key in the lock. "Have either of you chaps seen a film called *The Mark of Zorro?*"

They had not.

"It's a . . . a melodrama about a swordsman. Sure you haven't seen it?"

They were sure.

"I'd better tell you about it. I mean— Oh, hello, Sigmund."

In the front hall were dark paneled walls, worn linoleum, and a smell of boiled cabbage. A gray-haired man, wearing a gray woolen cardigan, stood by the kitchen door, at the rear of the hall. "Who is that?" he called, in a foreign accent.

"Me," the Captain said. "Some friends are helping me move. Hear about Churchill?"

"Churchill, what's the difference," the gray-haired man said. "It's too late, already. Now, they march across Europe. Now, begins the thousand-year Reich."

"Oh, no. We're not beaten yet."

"We will see."

"Siggie?" A woman's voice called from the kitchen.

"*Ja,* Lili." The man went inside. The kitchen door shut. "He's a first-rate cellist," the Captain told them. "Used to play with the Dresden Guezenich Orchester. This way, my room's on the top floor. They're Jewish, that's why they came here. Ulster must be the end of the earth to people like them. I'm very sorry about this room, I mean the condition."

The room was large, with a skylight window, a bookcase containing many records and music scores. There were a sofa bed and a large cabinet gramophone. There were some bound books and a stack of Penguin paperbacks. The curtain over the skylight was ripped to tatters. The floral bedspread was slashed in a great zigzag tear. The carpet had been similarly defaced and a deep Z was hacked into the plaster of the wall.

"Cripes," Freddy said. "Who was your visitor—Jack the Ripper?"

The Captain hurriedly offered cigarettes. "You see. About that film. I mean, in this film the man's a swordsman, always carves his initial when he ransacks an enemy's place. I had a few drinks the other night after seeing the film, don't remember what happened exactly, but when I got back here I thought of a sword I picked up somewhere, years ago. When I woke up this morning, there was Lili, come in to tidy up. Dreadful scene."

"Z," Freddy said. "Z for Zorro." He looked at Gavin and they went into one of their uncontrollable fits of laughter.

"All right," the Captain said, "but it wasn't funny, this morning. I told Lili I'd pay for the damage, but I'm afraid she misunderstood. Well, shall we start with the gramophone?"

"Z," Gavin cried. "Z for Zorro!"

"Mind that corner."

"Heavy, isn't it?"

As they came downstairs into the hall, Gavin noticed that the Captain's forehead was wet with perspiration. They managed to heft the gramophone into the back of the Morris and were about to go upstairs again when, quite suddenly, the Captain sat down on the running board of the car. "Gavin, old son," he said, "I hate to ask you again, but do you think you could spare another half crown?"

"Now?"

"Yes, dammit, now. Can't you see I'm falling apart?"

Freddy raised his eyebrows. "All right," he said. "Get into the car, everybody. But just one drink, Gerald. Is that clear?"

The Captain nodded. He slipped into the front seat of the car and sat shivering between Freddy and Gavin, all the way to the pub. But once inside the pub door, the smells of whisky and porter seemed to revive him. "There's an interesting combination for half a crown," he said. "You get a bottle of barley wine, a tot of whisky, and a glass of Red Biddy. Horrible mixture, but it seems to work."

Freddy ignored this. "Three half uns," he told the barman.

The Captain's ague started up again as he waited for his drink. When it came, he held it in both hands and managed to drink it down in one gulp without dribbling it. He coughed, smoothed his straw-colored mustache, and turned to Gavin. "Do you mind. That half crown?"

Gavin put half a crown on the bar. "Two Guinness and a large glass of Diamond-X tonic wine," the Captain said. "Guinness all right for you chaps?"

"I said, one drink," Freddy warned. "And anyway, what the bloody hell's the point of borrowing money and then buying drinks for us?"

"Because you're friends of mine. Because you've been very decent, dammit. You know, Hargreaves, sometimes you can be extremely dense."

"Dense?" Behind his spectacles Freddy's eyes widened, magnified. "Did you say *dense?* Do you think because I didn't go to some posh bloody English school that you're somehow better—or cleverer—than me?"

"Now that *is* a stupid thing to say. Of course not."

"Don't you call me stupid, you sodding imperialist

bastard. Don't try that bloody class-system stuff on me, do you hear?"

"Now, gents," the barman said. "Let's keep it a little quieter, *if* you please."

"Do you know what I think about you, Gerald? I think you're a drunk and a bloody liar, that's what I think. I think you have no opinions of your own, I think you just go along, leeching off everyone, telling them just what you think they want to hear. I'll bet any money you were leeching off those poor bloody refugees back there on Stranmillis Road, agreeing with them, right and left. I'll bet you were."

"Yes, of course," the Captain said. "I leech off anybody, as you put it. I'm a drunk, yes. You're perfectly right, I don't like disagreeing with people. Matter of fact, all I really care about is this drink." He held the glass of Red Biddy in his hand, gazed at it for a moment, then drank it down with solemn, drunken dignity. A man down at the other end of the bar came in loud and clear, going on about the British Navy.

"Don't you worry, chum, old Churchill knows ships. He knows the bloody navy, does old Winston, not like that wet mother's get of a German housepainter. Don't you worry, chum, those Huns'll never get across the English Channel, not with the British Navy there. Blow them right out of the water, old Winston will."

"All right." The Captain put down his empty glass. "I'm ready when you are. Sorry about all that."

"Oh, for Godsake," Freddy said, "don't apologize so much."

In silence they returned to the car and drove back to the Captain's digs. As they carried the last load of suitcases and books out onto the pavement, Gavin became aware that a woman had followed them into the street. She was a tall, good-looking woman, her dark hair bound in a turban. She wore a red blouse, an old tweed skirt, and Wellington boots. "I sent for the police," she said. "I sent for them an hour ago. Siggie cannot hold you by force and I am a woman. The police do not come because the police, like you, hate the Jews."

Freddy at once put down the suitcases he was carrying. "Now, just a minute," he said. "I'm a socialist. I'm not anti-Semitic. None of us are."

"None of you. Oh, I laugh. What about Gerald, what about what he did, the swine? J is for *Juden*. *Jude* he scratch on everything when he is drunk. You see his room? I am a liar, no?"

"Look," Freddy said. "It was Z for Zorro, not J for Jew. Don't you know the story?"

"You believe that? Why do the police not come, why can he run away without he pay? I tell you why. Because you are all anti-Semite here. You think not? Then, do you ever listen to what people say here? They say 'don't Jew me' when they mean 'don't cheat me.' Yes, you Irish, you are all the same. Go on, run away, Gerald, remember the nice evenings we had, remember the meals I cook you, remember the music we play together, you don't care, do you, Gerald? Go on, run away, J for *Juden*. I don't want to see you any more."

"Now Lili, dear, that is simply not true," the Captain said. He went toward her, but she slapped his face.

"Drunkard! Go away!"

It was awful, Gavin thought. People across the street had stopped and were looking at them. Behind the black-out blinds of the houses, you could be sure that ears were cocked. There was something foreign and shameless about this outburst. You mean something Jewish, the Black Angel said.

"Go away!" Her voice was a scream.

"Right," Freddy said, throwing the last of the suitcases into the Morris. "Come on, boys."

"Run away, Jew-baiter. Where are the police, I asked for the police?"

"Good-bye," Gavin said to the tall woman. Anything to keep her quiet, but she did not look at him, did not seem to hear him. "Where are the police?" she repeated, looking up and down the street. The Captain, trembling, got in the front seat and sat with his head down. Freddy and Gavin jumped in and slammed the doors. "Run away," the woman cried. "Yes, run away."

Freddy put the car in gear and it shot out from the pavement, going into a long, dangerous skid on the tramlines. "Christ," Freddy said, as he came out of the skid. "That was a near one. Some of these German Jews have a real persecution mania."

"Understandable, though," the Captain said. "You've no idea of what these people have suffered."

"Haven't I? Are you condescending to me again?"

"No, no, of course not. I'm sorry, I didn't mean it in that way."

Come to think of it, the Black Angel whispered, you don't really *know* any Jews. There was that one in school, two years ago, the fat fellow who left to go to the Jaffe School. And Bernstein, who's in the play. You don't know him beyond saying how do you do? That place, just now, is the first Jewish house you've ever been in. And let's be honest about it, she put you off with all that screaming and lunatic behavior and the place had a funny smell of cabbage or something in the hallway. Wasn't there something "Jewish" about her yelling and complaining? Poor old Gerald. Maybe this whole uproar about the German treatment of the Jews is exaggerated. The Jews are certainly terrible moaners. Still, she's right in a way. People here *do* say "don't Jew me." But I don't.

"One thing, Gerald," Freddy said to the Captain. "Just don't go practicing your swordsmanship in my friend's place. He's a big fellow, he might bash you."

"What's he do?"

"He's a parson."

A parson, he was. According to the bulletin board in the carbolic-smelling lobby of the building Freddy led them into, he was:

REV. KENNETH MCMURTRY, M.A., D.D.
CHAPLAIN AND ATHLETICS DIRECTOR
CENTRAL BELFAST YOUTH CLUB

"Ken lives on the top floor," Freddy explained. "But there's a dormitory down in the basement. That's where you'll sleep."

"McMurtry," the Captain said. "Sounds familiar, somehow."

"He played Rugger for Ireland. He used to be known as the Red Reverend. Spoke all over the place, raising money for the Loyalists in the Spanish War."

"Must be another McMurtry, I'm thinking of," the Captain decided.

The top floor of the Youth Club building contained a

small gymnasium, a lounge with imitation leather arm-chairs, much torn at the armrests, a ping-pong table, and a shower room. The Club seemed to be closed. No one stopped them as they went through the lounge and down a corridor to a door marked PRIVATE. Freddy knocked.

Reverend McMurtry answered the door. He had his coat jacket off, but wore his dogcollar and a gray clerical dickey. Big and blond, he met the introductions with a firm handshake and a manly grin. His den, as he called it, was crowded with silver cups and rows of framed photographs, all of them showing teams of boys in foot-ball togs, with Reverend McMurtry in the middle, holding the ball. All of this pleased Gavin. He had never met a Protestant minister, but the Reverend McMurtry fitted his preconception perfectly. Ministers did not pray. They preached. They spent most of their time arranging games and outings. However, the other people and objects in the room did not fit Gavin's preconception at all. For one thing, there was a very strong smell of incense. For an-other, the room contained several Chinese screens, Chinese vases, and painting scrolls. The bed was a divan, covered by a dragon print throw and, in the center of the room, squatting before a cardboard puppet theater, were two young men who were not Gavin's notion of youth club members. They were introduced.

"Freddy, this is Matthew Ware."

"Hello," Freddy said. "I know your poetry."

"How charming of you to mention it," Matthew said. "No one else ever does."

"And this is Maurice Markham. Maurice has just been showing us this splendid puppet theater. Made the whole shebang himself. Marvelous, isn't it?"

"Well, they're not exactly puppets," Maurice said. He wore thick corduroy trousers and a green velours turtle-neck sweater. "They're just little figures in a landscape, arranged into varying tableaux, if you see what I mean."

"Quite," said the Captain. He sat down, very suddenly, on one of the sofas.

Reverend McMurtry pulled aside a curtain, revealing a small kitchen. "Sherry? Or beer?"

The Captain nodded assent to both inquiries. Gavin and Freddy agreed on beer. "Marvelous news about Winston, isn't it," Reverend McMurtry said. "Not that it isn't still an imperialist war. But I've always felt old Winston was a scrapper."

"O Lord," said the young man called Matthew. "Must we? Here we were transported by Maurice right out of this filthy century into the court of *Le Roi Soleil,* and suddenly we're back with beer and bloody old Churchill. Do sit down, everyone. Maurice, please go on. Put the light off, somebody. And let's light another joss stick to kill that filthy stench of pipe."

The Reverend McMurtry brought beer and switched off the light. Maurice placed two pocket flashlamps behind his tiny stage. "Speaking of interruptions," he said, "in the bookshop in which I labor, the most extraordinary thing happened to me today. I was standing at a shelf gazing at a copy of Firbank, when, suddenly, something touched my shoulder. I turned and saw nobody—*nobody.* Then I looked down and there was this most extraordinary creature, an absolutely tiny, little leprechaun of a woman with the longest, most simian arm you've ever seen. And she'd reached up this *long* simian arm to touch me. 'My name is Miss MacMillan,' said she. 'I have an account here.' "

"Oh, MacMillan," Matthew shrieked. "Oh, I know her. Simian, oh, perfect, she's absolutely marvelously repulsive like a court dwarf with a Donegal brogue. O God!"

Freddy seemed to have drunk his beer in one swallow. He stood up and muttered something to the Reverend McMurtry. "I see," the Reverend McMurtry said. "Yes, of course, shove off if you want to. We'll take good care of your friend. Good show."

"Gavin, are you ready?"

"You're not stealing him away, are you?" Maurice asked.

"*Gavin,*" Matthew said. "I have an Uncle Gavin, Gavin O'Kelly. Got mixed up in an awful political scandal some years ago. Do you know where he is now? Spain. Honestly. Sitting in Barcelona, day after day, staring at a nail in the wall."

"What a marvelous image," Maurice said. "Staring at a nail in the wall."

"Yes, I must remember that," the Reverend said. "Freddy, are you still playing for Glentoran Wanderers?"

"Not this season. Ready, Gav?"

"O.K."

But it was not O.K. He didn't see what the rush was. Reverend McMurtry was the first Protestant minister he had ever spoken to, and if that wasn't enough, there were Maurice and Matthew. When he thought of trying to describe those two, words like artistic, poetic, Bohemian floated around in his mind. They reminded him of Sydney Smith's limp portrait of Lytton Strachey, which he had seen reproduced in a little magazine, and, come to think of it, he would not have been surprised if Virginia Woolf or any of that Bloomsbury set walked into this room. To think that people who wrote poetry, burned joss sticks, and built puppet theaters were living here in Belfast, not a mile away from his own home. They were Protestants, naturally. Why was it that no Catholic could grow up in an interesting atmosphere? Most Catholics grew up to be like Tony Clooney. Louts. The thing to do was to become a poet, like Matthew, learn to talk wittily, extravagantly. He could see himself introducing Sally to people like Matthew and Maurice. He'd show her what she was missing by going around with the likes of Clooney.

"Come and see us again," Reverend McMurtry said, taking Gavin's hand, squeezing it between his own large fists. Maurice and Matthew, on their knees, shifting the little cardboard figures around on the tiny stage, turned and smiled their farewells. " 'Bye, Gerald," Freddy said to the Captain. The Captain did not hear him. He was in the kitchen, at the sherry bottle.

"Sorry about that," Freddy said as they went downstairs.

"Oh, that's all right. I suppose you want to return the car."

"That's not why I skedaddled. I was bloody irritated. Ken's all right, he's quite careful, as a rule. But he's an ass to indulge himself on home ground with that pair."

"What do you mean?"

"I mean, supposing one of the elders of First Presbyterian walks in on that scene, joss sticks and all. Ken's getting careless in his old age."

What *does* he mean? the White Angel asked. I think I know, the Black Angel said.

"Anyway, little Maurice Markham is one of the more annoying ones," Freddy said. "He can't keep off. Another five minutes and he'd have been sitting next to you with his hand on your leg."

"You mean they're *fruits?*"

Freddy stared at him, removed his glasses, wiped the glass with his thumb, then put the glasses on again, "Didn't you know?" he said. "What sort of a sheltered life did you lead in that Roman institution? Aren't there any fruits in R.C. schools?"

"Well, no. There are fellows who try to grab you in the jakes. But not real pansies."

"In other words, fellows like old Ken."

The minister too! The White Angel was stiff with shock. *Homosexuals.* I warned you, this Freddy would introduce you to bad companions. And you were charmed by them, you even wanted to imitate them. Think *that* one over.

Freddy started up the poultry truck. "Hop in," he said. "Sometimes I forget how young you are. Fancy not knowing they were fruits."

What did homos *do,* anyway? What repulsive couplings took place between the Reverend McMurtry and Maurice? There was something about the thought which made him feel physically sick. O God, he did not want to be like Maurice or Matthew. How could he ever have admired those effeminate twerps? *He* had never felt homo, never. Still, if you lusted after girls but had never actually slept with one, then how could you be sure you mightn't be homo at some future date?

"One thing," Freddy said, as they drove off. "Matthew Ware is quite a good poet. Funny how many artists are fruits. Matthew has written some good revolutionary poetry, believe it or not."

Yes, said the White Angel. Revolutionary stuff. The stuff you admire.

. . . when the sniggering machine-guns in the hands of the
       young men
Are trained on every flat and club and beauty parlour and
       Father's den . . .

Louis MacNeice. *He* wasn't a homo, was he, of course not. But the lines seemed different tonight, lines for a pansy revolt, sniggering young men, tommy guns in hand, blasting every club and beauty parlor and Father's den.

When Freddy left him off at home, he went up to bed, upset. Jews, left-wing ministers, pansies, poets, boozers, puppeteers: this was a grown-up world, undreamed of in the St. Michan's school philosophy. He lay in bed and looked at Owen asleep in the bed across the way. Owen knew nothing of this other world, this underside. Owen would never know it because Owen was ordinary and would lead a normal, ordinary life. Yet he too wanted a normal life, no joss sticks, no being tossed out of rooms by screaming Lilis. He wanted to live with Sally, he loved Sally.

I am falling over a cliff, I am falling.

Pray, said the White Angel. It's your last chance. *Pray.* But he could not pray.

seven

Queen Victoria, holding an orb of power in her right hand as though she contemplated throwing it, looked down on Gavin as he lit a Woodbine. Rain wet her stone face, streaking the pigeon droppings on her cheeks. Puff away, the Queen said. As a failure, you will never have the money to smoke decent cigarettes. So be it, Gavin told the Queen. Silly old cow, don't you know that failure's not so terrible. Nothing's terrible, once you accept it. But the Queen was not listening. She stared across rainy lawns at her Irish red-brick university, guarding it from the likes of him. You will never get in here, she said. Not after today.

It was the third morning of the matriculation examinations. By now, he knew most of the other applicants, at least by sight. Nervous impostors, they walked the university grounds, exchanging accomplice grins and tentative criticisms of the papers. One of them had just come out of the examination hall, a tall fellow with broken specs, which he had repaired by putting sticking plaster on the bridge. He took out a cigarette and put it up for the loan of a light. "Piece of cake," he said.

"Did you think so?"

"The math this morning? Of course. Listen, did you get sixteen and three-quarters as the answer on the seventh one?"

Gavin had not got as far as the seventh question. He looked up at the old Queen. Math is compulsory, said she.

"No," he said to the tall fellow.

"Didn't you? I think it's right. Well, tomorrow's the last day, thanks be. What are you taking this afternoon, history or chemistry?"

"History."

"Stinks for me. I'm going to get some lunch. Coming?"

"I'm waiting for someone."

On Tuesday, the day I wrote the English exams, the German Army moved in on Abbeville, one million soldiers, one thousand bombing planes, two thousand tanks. Victoria, do you hear me? Two thousand tanks rolling up the avenue there, flattening the university gates, coming across the lawns toward your statue. Blowing your arrogant old head off with a big blast from a tank gun. Maybe you won't have a Queen's University six months from now. The British troops have been cut off at the Channel.

But the Queen was on to him. You'd like that, said she, yes, you'd like to see the whole world blown up just because you're a miserable little failure. It won't, you know, the Queen said. Blow up, I mean. Not bloody likely, said the old Queen.

His brother, Owen, was coming across the quad, wearing a raggedy black undergraduate gown and carrying a clutch of books. His brother seemed to be in a hurry. The time to break bad news was when the other person was in a hurry.

"Well?" his brother said. Gavin made a face. His brother stared at him, then continued to walk toward the lecture halls. Gavin fell in beside him.

"Did you finish the paper, at least?"

"No, I only got it half done."

"You bloody well didn't study hard enough," Owen said. "Laziness, sonny, that's your trouble."

But, it was not laziness. How could you tell Owen, who took exams as normal occurrences, that half an hour before going into the examination hall, a feeling came over you like a disease, a feeling that no matter what you did, it would be wrong.

"Plays and dances and bloody carry on," Owen said. "And no studying. What's going to happen to you now?"

They had reached the lecture hall. Five of Owen's fellow students, fellows older than Gavin, were hanging about outside, wearing raggedy gowns and old tweed jackets. They were smoking, but, as Gavin and Owen came up, they nicked their butts and went inside. "The prof must be in," Owen said. "What have you got this afternoon?"

"History."

"Well, you're good at that. Good luck."

Turn now and go out of the gates and into some tearoom

and eat. You have failed, but you must sit the other subjects. Why? Why go on, when you know it's no use?

The tin toys of the hawker move on the pavement inch by
　　inch
Not knowing that they are wound up; it is better to be so
Than to be, like us, wound up and while running down to
　　know—

I am running down. There is something wrong with me.
I know I'm more intelligent than the likes of Clooney
and other fellows who were in my class. Yet I am doomed
to fail, while they'll go on to become the doctors, lawyers,
engineers, priests, their little hearts desire. I can forget
about Sally, now. There is a certain type of Irish younger
son, ah, yes, indeed there is, Mrs. Mullally, we all know
the type, doless fellows who fail in school and are put out
to pasture in the family business. And if there's no family
business, why they have to emigrate, we hear that they're
in Canada or Australia or someplace, doing something that
nobody knows just what it is. But nothing to write home
about, that's certain sure. Ah, yes, Mrs. Mullally, 'deed
and we all know *those* boyos. Oh yes, he was doing a
line with a girl, a very nice girl, one of the Shannon
girls, the second as I recall, she's married to Dr. Clooney
now, yes, the gynecologist, he's on the staff of the hospital. Yes, I wonder what ever happened to that Burke
boy, wasn't he in the A.R.P. or something? Was he, I
don't remember.
　A girl student ran past him on the path, running toward the university gates, where a fellow waited on a motor
bike. The girl had long, dark hair and a Queen's scarf
furled around her neck. Girls like her will ne'er be mine.
Pillion-riding girls with Hons. English degrees and an
eye for a man with a future, girls who settle in at a fellow's back, putting their arms trustingly around his waist
as the bike roars off, carrying them down arterial roads to
freedom. Not for them, us A.R.P. mates sitting in Crummick Street Post with our tea and slice, waiting for Post
Officer Craig to show us them splints for the umpteenth,
numbteenth time. O Christ. Tonight, back on duty.

　That night everyone listened to the wireless. "One thousand planes," Craig told the post members. "Imagine a thousand German planes over Belfast."

No one could imagine it. Besides, it was not the bombs but the thought of parachutes that filled the mind. Anthony Eden had formed a parachute army. It was invasion, not bombs, that the British feared. Imagine an invasion.

"Hell roast them, do you think they'd ever land here?" Hughie Shaw wanted to know. "Imagine the German coming up Belfast Lough."

"They'll bomb first," Craig said. "They had a thousand bombing planes over Paris last week. Aye, when they drop their bombs here, there'll be a few people in this town will have another think coming. There'll be no more jokes about us."

"Them snotty nurses and doctors over there in the hospital, they'll laugh on the other side of their faces. Aye, they'll need us then, all right."

"Aye."

"No, no," said Wee Bates, "the German will never get across the English Channel. Not with the British Navy there."

"Is that so," Soldier said. "I wouldn't take any bets on it. Hasn't ould Hitler gone through Europe like a dose of salts?"

Weary of the discussion, Gavin went through the scullery to the lavatory in the back yard. Outside, the darkness was total. Listen to them, he thought. They're just like me, they want bombs dropped here so that people will stop making fun of them. Exactly, said the Black Angel. And why not? Heroes can't be heroes without disasters. And First Aid men can't function without wounded and dying. Can you blame them for wanting to show their worth?

In the utter darkness of the lavatory, a small cough sounded. Gavin felt his scalp go tight. Was the cougher inside or outside the jakes? He listened. He heard nothing. He reached out his arms, blindly touching each wall of the lavatory in turn. He was alone in here. The cougher must be waiting outside. "Who's there?" he called.

No answer.

It was Craig, he knew it was, it was that bloody lunatic up to some joke under the guise of its being a drill or practice. "Is that you, Mister Craig?" He was ashamed of his voice, the voice of a scared kid.

He opened the lavatory door and edged out into the blackness.

"Look, if this is some joke, it's not funny," he said, his voice going up now, almost into panic.

The soft cough sounded just ahead of him. He moved swiftly towards it, determined to get to whoever it was, before they got to him. His groping hands met the soft hummocks of a woman's breasts. The woman pushed him off and he heard her footsteps running down the yard. The latch grated on the back door of the yard. Whoever it was was trying to escape into the entry behind the yard. He ran toward the back door and caught the unseen woman by the forearm. She struggled, but he held her. "Who are you? What are you doing here?"

She did not answer. He began pushing her toward the scullery door, hearing himself say, pompously, foolishly. "We're going to see about this. This is private property, you've no right to be here."

She did not resist him. Once inside the scullery, she smiled at him, a weak childish smile, asking his forgiveness. Yet she was older than he, a stout, slatternly girl in a dirty raincoat and a flowered frock. "I was waitin' for me grandda," she said.

"Who?"

"Mr. MacBride."

Did she say "Grandda," the Black Angel wondered. But she's more than twenty, she must be. Soldier's black hair; Freddy said it was dyed.

"What are you doing in here?"

Soldier's voice. He filled the doorway of the scullery, heavy and tidy in his blue battle dress, his ex-service ribbons sewn over his breast pocket.

"This fella pushed me in. It wasn't my fault, Grandda."

Soldier's polished black boots rang on the scullery tiles. His hard, old hand swung in a slap that made a noise like a board breaking in two. The stout girl reeled against the wall. "Get out of here. Go on, get out."

The girl's red, weeping face turned blindly toward Gavin. Soldier's hand smacked her broad rump, propelling her into the yard. "Go on home," Soldier snarled. He shut the door and turned to Gavin, a terrible smile on his face. "That's a wee cousin of mine," he said. "A bit soft on the top, she is."

"Cousin? I thought she called you grandda."

Soldier glanced back toward the kitchen. His boots rang on the tiles again, as he shut the door connecting the kitchen with the scullery. He turned again to Gavin, again with that terrible smile. "Tell us," he said. "You're a Catholic, aren't you, lad?"

"Yes. I suppose."

"Well, so am I," Soldier said. "Us Catholics must stick together. There's a terrible lot of people on this post is bigoted as hell. Do you follow me?"

"No."

Carefully, Soldier packed his briar with shreds of plug. He lit the pipe, still watching Gavin. "Well, then," he said, "let me put it to you straight. I'd be obliged if you'd not mention this to any of the people here. Do I have your word on that, lad?"

"But what's wrong? Nothing wrong with your granddaughter coming here, was there?"

"No. Still, I'd be obliged. Give me your word, there's a lad."

"All right," Gavin said. "Though I still don't think it matters."

"Come on now," Soldier said. "You're not as green as you're cabbage-looking. If some of those Protestant gets, inside there, got the notion I was old enough to have a granddaughter that age, they'd shop me soon as look at me."

"But there's no age limit in this job, is there?"

"How do I know?" Soldier said, bitterly. "I never asked. Besides, my age is *my* business."

Of course it is, the White Angel said. Leave the old fellow alone. How would you like to be him, worried that the authorities will find out you're sixty or even more, far too old to carry stretchers. No wonder he dyes his hair. Wait'll you tell Freddy, the Black Angel said.

"Well, lad," Soldier said. "Will you keep what's happened in this room. Promise me, now?"

"All right. I promise."

"Good lad. I'll make it up to you. Any night I'm on as

deputy officer you have only to slip the word and you can do a bunk for an hour or two. Good lad, so. Give us your hand on it."

They shook hands. But you will tell Freddy, the Black Angel said. You know you will.

"And did you?" Sally asked, a few days later. He shook his head. It was a Sunday afternoon and, mercifully, a warm one, with no sign of rain. They had taken the bus to the top of the Cave Hill Road and were walking among other courting couples along the old quarry and up the paths which led over the mountain. He had told her about Soldier and the girl just to make talk, for his mind was not on Soldier or even on the war, although the latest rumor was that the British were cut off at the Channel and people were saying that the British Army would be evacuated from the French coast, and that Hitler would not stop at the Channel but would invade England at once.

She wore a bright green suit. Her skirt was very short, and, sitting beside her on the bus, he had stared at her rounded knees in their flesh-colored stockings, the Black Angel driving him to such distraction that his sentences no longer made sense. Now, as she climbed up the narrow path ahead of him, he stared at her moving buttocks in the green skirt, silently cursing the other people on the mountainside. There were two little boys up ahead. He knew their game: he had played it himself when he was their age. Foul-minded little cherubim, so innocent-seeming in their short trousers and droopy socks, pretending to play catch with an old tennis ball as they stalked the courtin' couples. Did she know the purpose of this walk, of course she did. She had asked why, on such a sunny day, he had brought his raincoat, and as he mumbled an excuse, he had thought he noticed a smile on her lips. So, she knew. At least, he hoped she did. He was so nervous he was trembling: his palms were damp as he helped her over a stile. On the other side of the stile was a long, sloping stretch of mountainside, its tufty grass spotted with whin bushes. There was no one down there. "Shall we walk that way?" he asked. She smoothed her dark hair out of her eyes and suddenly ran off, as though challenging him to a race. His desire made running a painful thing, but he went after her. Halfway down the slope, she tumbled, accidentally or on purpose, near a large whin bush. He threw himself down beside her.

"I can beat you any day," she said, laughing, rolling over on her back to stare up at the sky. "Oh, I love the country. It's so peaceful."

"But there's a war on. It's coming here. What would you say if the Germans showed up in this field?"

"I'd say *guten Tag*. Is that right? Oh, rocks, stop talking about the war, Gav, that's all I hear these days. Let's talk about something nice for a change."

"Like you."

"You like me?"

"No, I said, 'like you.' You're beautiful."

She rolled over, chin propped in her palm. "I'm not, you know. I'm very ordinary. You're getting to be a great old plaster, Gavin Burke. You never used to say things like that. What girl's been educating you?"

"No girl. No girl at all since you left me."

"I left you. You're mad. You're a looney, do you know that? You get some loony idea in your head and then it becomes gospel truth to you. Any girl would have to be as daft as you are to heed you."

"Are *you* daft?"

"Sometimes."

Go on, the Black Angel said, she's two inches away. Kiss her, you fool.

He sat up and spread his raincoat on the rough grass. "Sit on my coat, it's damp."

"Your coat's damp?"

"You know what I mean," he said.

"Maybe I do, maybe I don't. So, that's why you brought your coat. Oh, you're the artful one."

But she inched over and lay on his raincoat. "Sally, I love you."

"Don't say that."

"Why, does it embarrass you?"

"It's not that. It's just that you don't mean it."

"But I do mean it."

"Then why have you been avoiding me lately?"

He did not answer. She lay back, sighed, and shut her

eyes. Now or never, said the Black Angel. He leaned over her and kissed her on the lips. Her lips parted a little and he tried to put his tongue in her mouth.

"Who taught you that?"

"Nobody. Are you going to let me kiss you, or aren't you?"

She sat up and looked around. "Not in front of those kids."

The two little boys had followed them down the slope. They stood about fifty yards away, silently tossing the ball to each other. Murder rose in Gavin. He jumped up and ran toward them. "Bugger off," he shouted. "Bugger off, or I'll call a policeman."

"Look who wants a polis-man," said the bigger child. "It's you and yon doll or yours the polis will be after."

Riposte delivered, the boys began to retreat, throwing the ball on a longer arc, spreading out, going over the crest of the hill. They might sneak back, but he would have to risk it. He walked down toward Sally, wondering how he could begin all over again.

"I heard that," she said. "You shouldn't use language like that in front of the kids."

"It's the only language that sort of kid understands."

"I still don't like it."

He sat down beside her on the raincoat. "I was telling you," he said, "that I love you."

"So you were."

"What's that supposed to mean?"

"Oh, nothing. You talk a lot."

Do you hear that, said the Black Angel. All talk and no action, she means. Go on. Kiss her again. Lie on top of her.

He held her shoulders and tried to kiss her mouth, but missed and kissed the tip of her nose instead. She smiled, lay back on the raincoat, and closed her eyes. What more do you want, the Black Angel asked. He bent over her, kissing her, and she kissed back, and this time she let him put his tongue in her mouth. Her suit jacket was unbuttoned and, astonished at his boldness, he put his hand inside her blouse and felt her breasts inside their brassiere. There was no resistance. Jesus, said the Black Angel, maybe this is it, this afternoon here on Cave Hill.

She was kissing him and her hands ran up and down his spine, inside his jacket. He began to inch her skirt up over her hips and, suddenly, in a clutch of desire, saw her legs above her stocking tops and put his fingers on her soft, bare inner thigh. His heart thumped. Dizzy, he began to feel for, and find, the waistband of her knickers.

"No, Gavin."

Pay no attention, the Black Angel advised. All girls say that, at first.

"Gavin, please."

Go on, get them off her, the Black Angel ordered.

She pushed him. Hard. She rolled out from under him and stood, pulling down her skirt. "What do you think I am, Gavin Burke?"

"I love you," he said, hoarsely.

"Well, we can't. It's a mortal sin."

"Christ."

"You're developing a very dirty tongue in that A.R.P. job."

"I'm sorry. I just don't think it's a sin for a person to desire another person."

"Who said it was?"

"You did."

"I didn't. I said it was a sin for us to do it."

"But not a sin to feel each other up and nearly drive each other loony?"

"You started that stuff, not me. Besides, that's a sin too."

"Oh, yes, necking's only a venial sin. Well, let me tell you something, Miss Shannon. I'm fed up with this Catholic logic of yours. I've given all that up."

"Don't be silly, you can't give it up, you were born a Catholic and you'll die one."

"Want to bet?"

"Yes, I do. When the time comes you'll be no different from the rest of them, you'll be calling for a priest, screaming for one. Oh, I've seen these hard chaws in the wards, they're all the same, when their time comes, it's confession and extreme unction they want, just like anyone else."

"I won't."

"Gavin, how do you know, you're only a boy. And speaking of sins, it's a mortal sin to deny your religion."

"Everything's a sin to you. Do you know what you are? You're a repressed Child of Mary, that's what you are."

"Is that so?"

You thick, said the Black Angel, now, you've done it. Insulting her, that's no way to get what you want. Kiss her at once.

"Take your hands off me."

"I'm sorry."

"*Sorry*. So you've given up your religion, have you? You make me laugh."

"Tell me, Sally. Would you go on going to Mass and the sacraments if you didn't believe in them? Would that be honest?"

"I'd go and see my confessor, if I were you," she said.

"Oh, great. What confessor? Why should I go and see a priest, when I don't believe what the priest stands for?"

"Because the priest is older than you. Because he would show you where you're wrong. Although, in your case he'd have a hard job, you're so stupid and stuck-up."

"Thank you, Nurse Shannon."

"Not at all. I'm going home now."

"Ah, wait a minute, Sally, let's not fight. I love you, you know. That's what counts."

"Yes, you love me. And when I stop you pulling my pants down, you get as cross as two sticks and start blaspheming and cursing."

"I'm sorry. But I *don't* believe in the Church. I'm fed up with the hypocrisy of the whole damn thing."

"Well, Gavin, *I* happen to believe in the Church. That means I don't have any common ground with would-be atheists. And I don't suppose an atheist would want to go out with the likes of me."

"I don't suppose he would."

"Very well then," she said. "That ends it, doesn't it?"

"I suppose so."

She began to walk away, going back up the slope. Over on his left, he saw a pair of legs in short trousers sticking out from behind a whin bush. Little bastards, they came back. Forget them, White Angel counseled. Run after her, tell her you were only joking. You're not an atheist. Tell her that. Make up. Make another date.

Let her go, the little tease, the Black Angel said. Child of Mary, you were right.

She turned and looked back as she reached the stile.

He began to walk toward her. He wouldn't speak to her all the way home. Blast her.

As he went up the slope, his foot kicked against a stone. He swooped on it, turned around, and they were still there, hiding behind the whin bush. Carefully, he took aim and hurled the stone. It whizzed into the whin bush, flushed the pair of them. He watched them run off. "Go on," he yelled. "Bugger off, you little bastards. Bugger off, before I break your bloody little necks." He was running himself, going after them, but they had a good start on him, it was a dream that he could ever catch them. He stopped, watched them go, then turned back toward the stile.

But she was gone. He ran up the slope, vaulted the stile and saw her far away, running down the path to the glen. "Sally?" he called, but she did not stop. He would never catch her now. She disappeared.

Familiar panic filled him. Oh, darling, come back. Darling, I'm sorry. I love you. Love me, or I'm lost.

But she was gone. Last week he had failed his London Matric, the results would be out any day. Nothing was right. . . .

In the afternoon silence above him, a growl of engines. From a corner of the sky they came, great gray planes of a sort he had never seen before. He stood staring, sure that they were bombers crossing the mountain, bearing down on the city. They roared overhead, rough beasts, their hour come round at last, slouching toward Belfast to be born. Here on the mountainside he would see it all, the explosions, the flames, the holocaust. From here, he would run down to rescue Sally, then on through the smoke and rubble to a hero's job in the First Aid Post. There they go, groaning over the city in the afternoon sunlight, they must be Germans, they *must* be.

But the planes droned on over the Lough, turning in formation as they went out to sea, toward England, toward Europe, far away to that faraway war. German or English, they ignored Belfast. He was left alone on the mountainside.

eight

He turned his key in the front door and the door opened inward, revealing the hall and a flight of stairs leading up to the breakfast room. In the hall were the grandfather clock, which gave the hour as five to ten, a monk's bench jammed with winter scarves and mittens in mothballs, the hallstand with its brass dinner gong and a silver tray for calling cards. At the rear of the hall was a coatrack, which showed that Kathy and Owen had gone out but that his father was still at breakfast. It was dark in the hall, a darkness which reflected the gray, rainy morning outside, the clammy, cold fog which had drifted over the university lawns, the gray morning light in the room where the examination results had been posted. He hesitated in the hall's quiet and then, announcing his return, shut the front door with a slam. At the top of the flight of stairs, a chair scraped back from the breakfast room table and his father appeared in the breakfast room doorway, peering down into the hall. A white napkin was tucked into the second buttonhole of his father's waistcoat and the white folds of the morning newspaper trailed from the fingers of his left hand like a lowered flag of truce. There was no truce. "Well?" his father said.

"I failed."

His father sighed. It was a sigh which said, yes, I expected this, there is nothing more to do now but don the black cap, pronounce sentence, and may the Lord have mercy. His father turned to go back into the breakfast room, saying as he did: "Come up here." It was said without anger, without urgency, in the tone of a parent who knows that duty is stern daughter of the voice of God. And, as it was said, Gavin, looking up at the breakfast room doorway, felt as though he were an actor taking part in a play. His father, high above him, was acting out the role of judge, while he, the youthful transgressor, waited sentence below. As he began to climb the stairs, this unreal feeling persisted. It was as though one scene had ended and a new scene was beginning. He entered the breakfast room. He was almost calm.

His father sat in his usual seat under the window. Above him the canary, Dicky-Bird, hopped from little wooden swing to wooden stand bar, then flew up, claws clutching the thin golden wires of the roof of his cage. Head cocked, Dicky-Bird peered out across the back yard, where, in the window of the house next door, Mr. Hamilton, a dentist, was already at work. Gavin's father reached for and poured a second cup of tea.

"Was it math?" his father asked. Dicky-Bird flew down to the bottom of his cage and perched on a stand bar, head on one side, a tiny golden judge.

"I did well in all the other subjects. I got honors marks in English and French."

His father reached for the milk jug, the signet ring on his little finger winking a golden reflection in the silver surface of the milk jug. "That's the point," his father said. "You did well in those subjects, even though you didn't study them. So it's not a question of studying, is it?"

"What do you mean, Daddy?"

His father sipped his second cup of tea. His mustache, still brown, stained yellow at the edges by tobacco smoking, contrasted oddly with the authoritarian gray of his head. "I mean," his father said, "that these results would seem to indicate something about your capabilities. This is your second failure. I won't go into the fact that you're the first member of this family to fail *any* examination, I won't mention that when I was your age anything but honors marks would have been inconceivable to me. I was, as you know, a gold-medalist, a bursary-holder, and a scholarship-winner. But, as I said, I won't bring that up now. I will simply point out that these results of yours, the bad marks *and* the good ones, lead me to an inescapable conclusion. Do you know what that conclusion is?"

"No, Daddy."

"I have decided," his father said, "that it is not your fault that you failed in mathematics."

Above his father, Dicky-Bird sang, loud and joyous,

applauding his father's judgment. His father's eyes were weary and forgiving. There was no forgiveness.

"You see," his father said, "it's not a matter of application, I'm afraid. It's a matter of ability. You lack ability."

Dicky-Bird, enraptured, shrilled a long throaty solo. His father pulled the napkin from his buttonhole and flapped it backward at the cage above his head. Dicky-Bird, silenced, clung in terror to the roof of his cage.

"So," his father said, "I think, at this point, we must reassess your chances of a career. Do you agree?"

His father, not hearing his agreement, assumed it. "Well, then. This A.R.P. job is a stopgap. With France gone, the war won't last another six months. I don't know what sort of world we'll have under Hitler, but I do know that any country which loses a war faces economic hard times. So, we'd better be realistic. I think your best bet is Uncle Tom."

Uncle Tom was his father's brother-in-law. Uncle Tom was he who handed out pound notes as presents, even to five-year-old nephews. He was he whose suits were made in London, who had a box each year at the Dublin Horse Show, who lived out in Crawfordsburn in a mansion with a driveway a mile long, with greenhouses, stables, and its own electric light plant. He was he who had once gone on a year-long, around-the-world honeymoon with his thin, childless wife; who was friends with people like Lord Down, who could get things done; who spoke often of the market, knowing his advice was heeded; whose relatives hoped for legacies; whose newspaper obituary would be long.

Uncle Tom had thin waxed mustaches, old-fashioned and faintly absurd. Perhaps it was the mustaches which provoked Gavin's father to a smile of condescension, or perhaps it was the fact that, rich as he might be, Uncle Tom was "in trade." In a big way, of course, with twelve pubs to back up his wholesale wines and spirits importing firm, a small mineral water company, which was doing very nicely, and other related assets. Uncle Tom already had two nephews in his employ. Archie and Pat Mangan were their names: they were large, heavy boys, driving large cars and wearing heavy, tweed suits as they went about their uncle's business. Some said the boys would inherit the firm. Others said not: Uncle Tom's thin, childless wife was many years younger than he: she would get his all and hold on to it. But in the meantime, as Gavin's father knew, for other boys who had not come up to snuff, there was always Uncle Tom.

"Between ourselves," his father said, "I know whereof I speak. I handle Tom's legal matters. Anyone lucky enough to be connected with Tom is getting involved in a very substantial concern. What are you grinning at?"

"Nothing, Daddy."

"Wipe that grin off your face. After your performance today, I see nothing to smile about, do you?"

"No, Daddy."

"Very well, then. I'll have a word with Tom next week. Now, supposing he's kind enough to provide an opening for you, how much notice would you have to give these A.R.P. people?"

"I don't know."

"Find out then."

His father wiped his mustache with his napkin and put the napkin in a napkin ring, indicating that breakfast and the discussion had ended. His father, who, until now, had decided on everything—schools, holidays, punishments, plans—was unaware that, this morning, all had changed. He saw the son he had first seen as a baby in arms, the boy he had provided for and ruled. He had decided: it was decided.

"But, Daddy, I don't want to work for Uncle Tom."

His father's eyes, judicial, stared down the criminal. "Just what," his father asked "is that supposed to mean?"

"I want to stay on in the A.R.P. I'll sit the London Matric again next spring."

"Not on my money, you won't."

"I have my own money."

"Ah, yes, quite so. But I doubt that these famous wages of yours will see you through university. Especially since you wouldn't be earning them any more, once you started at Queen's."

"I didn't say anything about university. I just said I'd get my matric."

"Do you know what I think," his father said. "I think you haven't the faintest idea what you want. And frankly, neither do I. Now, for the last time. Will I speak to your Uncle Tom?"

"I'd rather you didn't."

"Very well, then," his father said. He paused, and his eyes were once again weary and forgiving. "I've done what I could. Whatever you do from now on is your own affair."

He rose, went to the breakfast room door and delivered his exit line. "Frankly," he said, "I haven't the heart to tell your mother this morning's news. I'll leave that up to you."

Then left. Was there not, in the malice of that last remark, a hint of the outraged ex-scholarship winner? As he sat listening to his father's footsteps going downstairs, he dared his father. Walk out on me, go on, slam the front door and march down the street, don't come back. Go on. Leave now and I'll never forgive you.

The front door slammed.

Yet why am I crying, I hate him, I don't care about him any more, why should I, when he doesn't care about me. He's not in charge of me any more. I'm grown-up now, this morning was the beginning. I'm alone now. Why didn't he care about me, why didn't he help me?

"What's up?" Kathy, in a raincoat and blue beret, staring at him across the table. "Was it the matric?"

"Yes."

"Oh. Hard luck."

"No, it's not that, it's that dear father of mine. Do you know what he just told me, he told me I'm not worth wasting any more of his precious money on. He warned me to go and work for Uncle Tom. Well, he can go to *hell*."

"Did you tell him that?"

"Damn right, I told him. Then he informed me that he couldn't care less what I do. Just washed his hands like Pontius Pilate."

"Gav, you're always exaggerating. What's Mama say?"

"She doesn't know yet. What's it matter, she always agrees with him, she's completely under his thumb."

"Gavin." Kathy came around the breakfast table, took his head in her arms, and pressed his face against her raincoat. She held him, believing that she comforted him, but there was no comfort, there was no longer the relief of tears. His father, echoing the mysterious judgment of all authoriy, had, this morning, pronounced him a failure in life. The world of misfits, the A.R.P. world, was a world one could enter only if one belonged there. And you belong there, said the White Angel, reprovingly. You have only yourself to blame. It wasn't smoking that stunted your growth, it wasn't smoking that made you stupid, the stupidity your father talked about this morning has its roots in something else. It's no old wives' tale that your favorite indoor sport can affect the brain. It's affected yours. You are alone now, you're nearly eighteen, and, face it, you're one of those fellows, a second son who will never amount to anything.

The Black Angel was silent. As always, the one who egged you into things had no words when retribution came.

nine

In August the Battle of Britain began. But no bombs fell on Belfast. By the end of September, Post Officer Craig had taken to spending long hours alone in his office, staring at the gas fire. He no longer looked at Maggie Kerr. He felt that everyone was laughing at him. Everybody thought it was all a cod, all these drills, all these classes. He had put in for a transfer to England but had been told that the English A.R.P. was different from the Northern Ireland A.R.P. They had no power to transfer him, they said at City Hall. Sometimes he looked up from the gas stove and wondered if Maggie Kerr was laughing at him too. When these thoughts came on him and when he could no longer bear them, he would go out into the hall and blow his whistle.

His drills became lunatic. Screaming, shouting, harrying, he ran among the post members like a mad sheep dog. And, gradually, as his obsession that everyone was laughing at him took hold, he began to conceive of his drills as punishments.

One night, toward the end of October, after hearing on the wireless that the Germans had bombed Liverpool again, he ran out of his office and blew his whistle. "Everybody into he's gas suit." He went back into the office and told Maggie Kerr to get the hospital boilerman on the phone. He and the boilerman were friends. Ten minutes later, he marched the male members of the post, all dressed in their gas suits, across the road and into the hospital boiler room. He shut the boiler room door. "Tonight, lads, we have a new drill. I need three men. Bates, Lynan, and Price, fall in."

Wee Bates was Craig's mascot. He knew he would not be put-upon. But Jimmy Lynan and Big Frank Price, two of Craig's favorite butts, exchanged uneasy glances.

"Now, you see this wee room in the back. Now, in this

exercise we're going to suppose that this wee room is contaminated by gas. We want to use it as a dressing station. Price and Lynan will take buckets and wash down the walls, ceiling, and floor. But, seeing as how this is just a practice, youse can use plain water, no chemicals."

"Excuse me," Freddy said, "but isn't that sort of a job a job for the special squad?"

"Supposing it's an emergency, supposing we can't get a hold of the special squad? There's a war on. I said, there's a war on."

"Not here."

"Who said that? Did you say that, Burke?"

"No, sir."

"All right, sonny boy. Smart alec. You'll be next on this drill. Lynan and Price. Get your buckets and mops."

"What's Bates going to do?" Lynan asked suspiciously.

"Bates and me will provide the debriss."

"The what?"

"Falling debriss. We're pretending there's an air raid on and you fellows is working under bomb conditions. O.K., Bates, follow me."

The other men on the detail loosened their oilskin jackets and sat down in the outer part of the boiler room. Price and Lynan found the buckets and mops. The door shut in the small storeroom and, after a few minutes, a whistle blew. Craig's voice bellowed from behind the closed door. "O.K. First man in."

"Go ahead, Frank."

"No, you go, Jim. I'll follow directly."

Lynan tightened the chinstrap of his steel helmet and went toward the door. "Come on in," Craig's voice called. "And shut the door behind you."

Lynan went in. The door shut. There was a clanging sound, loud as a hammer on a forge. "Mother of God," said Big Frank Price.

Again, a clanging sound. The whistle blew. Craig's voice bawled out. "Come on, Price. Don't let Lynan do all the work."

Ponderous and uneasy, Big Frank picked up broom and mop and advanced on the shut door. Freddy nudged Gavin and, together, they edged toward the door, behind Frank. When Frank opened the door, they caught a glimpse of Wee Bates, a few feet inside the room, blocking Frank's path. Between Bates' knees was a bucket of sand, and, as Frank stepped over the threshold, Bates threw a handful of sand into Frank's eyes. Someone tried to kick the door shut, but Gavin caught it and held it open. The someone was Craig, standing on a kitchen chair behind the door. As Big Frank stumbled forward, blinded, Craig raised a fireman's axe over his head and brought the blunt end down with a clang on Frank's steel helmet. "Falling debriss, watch out!"

Stunned, Big Frank went slowly down on his knees. "Get Lynan," Craig yelled. The dwarfish Bates obediently threw a fresh handful of sand into the face of the second stumbling figure. Gavin, watching from the doorway, felt the shock of one who witnesses a serious accident.

Blinded by the sand, dazed by a previous blow, Lynan blundered out into the danger area, beneath Craig's chair. The axe scythed up.

"Cut that out!" Freddy shouted.

But the axe scythed down, banging off the edge of Lynan's helmet, sending him reeling into a corner. "Come on in, Hargreaves," the mad voice yelled. "Want to have a go?"

At the sound of his master's voice, Wee Bates hurled a fistful of sand into Freddy's face. The axe scythed up once more. But Freddy bulled through in a blind Rugger charge, reaching the far corner of the room before the axe could complete its swing. "Put that axe down," Freddy ordered. "Just what the hell do you think you're doing?"

"I'm testing tin hats. I'm testing men. I want to know how these fellows will stand up to danger."

"Gavin," Freddy said, "you're a witness to this."

Craig's pale gull's eyes picked out Gavin in the doorway. "Young Burke. Want some advice? Get out of here. Go on, get out. Shut that door behind you."

"Pay no attention, Gav."

"Countermanding an order. O.K., Hargreaves. That goes on the charge sheet. I'm the one has witnesses. Burke, Lynan, Price, Bates. Youse all heard that."

Lynan, his face mottled and sweating, sat in the corner where he had been felled. Big Frank Price knelt on the floor, his forehead touching the ground. Something in his posture infuriated Craig, who hopped off his chair and stood over Frank. "Come on. On your feet."

But Big Frank did not move. The small room was quiet. The rest of the shift began to crowd in at the doorway, as Craig knelt and shook Frank's shoulder. Frank raised his head: his breathing was stertorous, his face was wet with sweat, his color ghastly. His eyes reminded Gavin of the eyes of a dog he had once seen, lying in a roadway, its leg amputated by a passing car.

"Come on, Frank, cut out the play-acting. Help him up there, lads."

"Mister Craig?" Big Frank's voice was a whisper.

"What's that, Frank?"

"I'm sick, Mister Craig. You nearly broke my skull."

"Ah, you're codding me, Frank? It was just a wee tap."

"No, Mister Craig."

"Frank, them helmets can stand a blow from a shell. That's a fact, now."

Frank slowly got to his feet. He put his hand, palm flat, against the wall, steadying himself. After a moment, he bent his head, resting it on his outstretched arm. He vomited.

"Some wee crack," Freddy said, angrily.

"Lynan's all right, and he was hit too," Craig said. "It's Frank's own fault. He's not fit."

"How do you know who's fit?" Freddy said. "Are you a doctor?"

"That's enough of your cheek, Hargreaves. Frank isn't well. I seen him taking pills earlier on. Isn't that right, Frank?"

"No, Mister Craig, those pills were nothing. Just for indigestion."

"Indigestion. Then that's what made you sick to your stomach. You're all right, now, though, aren't you, Frank?"

"Yes," Frank said, wearily, "I'm all right."

"I told you. He's all right. Tell you what, Frank, we'll let you have a wee lie down when you get back to the post. O.K., Frank?"

"That would be good, Mr. Craig."

"Fair enough, then. Everybody back to the post. You, Hargreaves, and you, Burke, clear up that sand. If youse wants to be cheeky, I'll give youse cheeky."

"You needn't think you're going to get away with this," Freddy said. "Whether Frank complains or not has noth-

The Emperor of Ice-Cream • 99

ing to do with it. The rest of us can complain. Eh, Gavin?"

Gavin, said the White Angel, you heard the man. In the long list of your failures are we to add a new category tonight? Failure of nerve?

He looked at Freddy, who waited, confident of his support. "That's right," he said, finally, hating the tremor in his voice. "I'll back a complaint."

"Oh, you will, will you. We'll see about that. Get that mess cleaned up. The rest of youse, form fours. By the right—quick march!"

As the rubber-booted marchers squelched out of the boiler room, Gavin turned to his friend. "Think he'll really put us on a charge?"

"I'd like to see him try. Clouting people with axes. I'm not bluffing. We'll see the inspector the next time around. The man's mad. Are you on?"

"O.K."

"What?" said Mr. Harkness, the inspector, as they followed him out to his ancient Morris Minor. "Complaint? I've no time. I'm late on my rounds."

"Now, just a minute," Freddy said, in a voice which made Mr. Harkness turn in surprise. "This is a serious matter. That man in there is not right in the head."

"There's none of us right in the head," Mr. Harkness said. "Or we wouldn't be mixed up in this carry on."

"Do you think it's normal to hit a man over the head with a fireman's axe under the pretext of testing steel helmets?"

"Did he hit you?"

"No, he hit another man."

"Where's the other man? Has he made a complaint?"

"No. He's afraid to make one."

"If I had my way," Mr. Harkness said, "I'd hit every one of you over the head. There's men being killed across the water. I hear no complaints from them."

"Does that mean you're not going to do anything about this?"

"Too right, it does. Good night."

The Morris Minor coughed, started up, and went off down the street. "Well, that's that," Gavin said.

"Oh, no, it's not. The thing we need now is collective

action," Freddy said. "We need a petition, signed by at least half the people on this post. Let's see Soldier."

Soldier was doubtful. "Craig, off his head?" said he. "Ah, now, I wouldn't say that. There's them that likes drink and them that likes fights. But your man Craig is different. He likes only one thing, and that's shoving it into his fellow man as often and as hard as he can. But, off his head? No, he's not. He's just one of nature's bastards."

"We can still sign a complaint."

"Not me," Soldier said. "One thing I learned in the service. Never sign nothing that's not a paysheet."

Miss Albee signed. So did Mrs. Clapper and Mrs. Cullen. The Captain signed and so did Hughie Shaw. But Lynan and Big Frank Price, the men who had been stunned, simply shook their heads. "No sense wasting your time," Lynan said. "The higher-ups will never listen to the likes of us."

"But that's the point," Freddy told him. "Unless the workers take collective action, the bosses always win."

"Who are you calling a worker?" Lynan said. "I'm not a worker, I'm a workingman."

"I'm sorry."

"I know your sort," Lynan said. "Communists."

"Well, that's that," Gavin told Freddy, when they were alone. Surely Freddy would give up now?

"Sodding proletariat, they'll let you down every time," Freddy grumbled. "You watch. That lunatic will murder us all without anyone lifting a finger to stop him."

Freddy was wrong. On Craig's night off, Soldier Mac-Bride held forth in Deegan's Crown & Anchor Lounge. "Speaking of Craig," said he, as five hands reached for five fresh pints of black Guinness porter, "you know, 'tis a terrible dangerous thing to be put in charge of your fellow man. I mind in the last war, many's an officer or sergeant never knew where the bullet came from."

"Aye," said Hughie Shaw, "there was officers I knew, it was as much as their lives were worth to be first over the trenches in an attack."

Soldier lit his pipe and stared over the burning match at Freddy Hargreaves. " 'Tis pure supposing, of course," said he, "but the exact same thing could happen in an air raid."

The Emperor of Ice-Cream • 101

"True enough," said Jimmy Lynan, the ex-hod carrier who had been stunned by Craig. "If a few bricks was to fall on him, he could be let out quick enough."

"But that's just wishful thinking," Freddy objected. "Because there won't *be* any air raids. I still say a petition is the only answer."

"Petition, my arse," Soldier said. "About what, are we going to complain? About hitting men on their tin hats? About tightening up bandages until a man's blood stops, or drawing the red line in the book on the dot of seven? Have sense, Hargreaves. Men get promoted for things like that. Not sacked."

"Aye," said Jimmy Lynan, "Soldier's way is the right way. Let him out with a brick on the noggin."

Gavin found himself staring, first at Lynan, then looking over at Freddy for reassurance. Surely, this was some joke? He looked at Soldier, who winked a brilliant black eye. "Mind you," Soldier murmured, "I said nothing."

"No, you said a mouthful, mate." Lynan leaned into the circle, lowering his voice. "In the old days, down in the yards, I mind a man was let out. It was this foreman, see? He was always sticking it into us. Well, one day there was six of us on this tanker hull and this get of a foreman come by, right beneath us. So a man on the bench, Barney Ross, he just nudges a wrench off the edge. Down it goes, right on this foreman's noggin. Aye. They had to send for the morgue wagon. Now, mind this. There was six of us on that bench. Any one of us could have shopped old Barney. But nobody opened he's beak. The whole thing was wrote off as an accident."

There was a moment of silence. Soldier went to the bar and ordered a round of pints. He returned to the circle. "And no one was any the wiser, eh, Jimmy?"

"Right. There was no stoolies in that yard."

"Aye," Soldier said. "If a thing is done right, it's best done among friends."

Again, there was a silence. Lynan looked around the group, his consumptive face flushed with a sudden excitement. "Are youse with me?" he asked.

It *is* a joke, the White Angel insisted. It has to be. But you never know with grownups. There's no telling what lengths they'll go to, pretending they're in earnest.

Wait a minute, said the Black Angel. You're grown-up yourself now. You're eighteen.

"Right," said Hughie Shaw. "I'm with you. If Craig was let out, I'd not weep."

"Me neither," said Soldier. "What about the rest of you? Freddy?"

Freddy took off his thick-lensed glasses and wiped them with his handkerchief. His eyes, oddly naked, stared blindly at the group. "Look here," he said, "killing a man is a bit steep."

"And you, young Burke," Lynan asked. "Are you as yellow as Karl Marx here?"

"No need to get hard," Freddy protested. "I just draw the line at murder."

"I'm not speaking to you, you Russian. I'm speaking to the young lad here. Well, Gavin. Are you with us?"

This is the way that sins are committed, the White Angel warned. You have to make a stand somewhere, do you hear me, Gavin?

But Soldier's black eye was upon him. Lynan leaned forward, his crooked teeth showing in an anticipatory grin. Come on, the Black Angel urged. Stop being a wet-nosed kid. Uneasily, Gavin nodded.

"Good lad," Soldier said. "Aye, a slate off a roof, a brick off a wall. Oh, in a raid there's all kinds of ways to let a mean gaffer out. And even on maneuvers. Eh, Jimmy?"

"Right, Soldier," Lynan was breathing heavily. "My hand on it, Soldier, I'm your man."

"Aye, Jimmy's our man," Hughie Shaw said. "Let's have a drink on that."

Pints were raised. Everyone turned toward Freddy. "Well, Karl Marx?" Lynan asked.

"All right," Freddy said. "Bugger Hitler. We'll do it ourselves."

"Do what?" Soldier asked. "Bugger Hitler?"

Everyone laughed.

Later, walking back from the pub, Freddy and Gavin moved ahead of the others. "Freddy? Were they serious?"

"God knows. I think Lynan was. I tell you, the minute Lynan sees his chance, Craig is a corpse."

They walked on in silence. What was there to say? Even Gavin's angels were silent. The angels said nothing. The angels only spoke when there were two sides to a thing. But there were no two sides to this: it could not be dismissed or belittled. Yet, paradoxically, it was so frightening that it must be belittled. It *had* to be a joke.

"Damn Soldier," Freddy said. "It was all his idea."

"Let's go and talk to Lynan," Gavin said. "Let's tell him we'll have nothing to do with it."

"Pontius Pilate Burke," Freddy said, bitterly, "washes his hands of the blood of this man."

"Ha, ha."

"I mean it. We can't escape this by pretending it hasn't happened."

"What'll we do, then? Tell Craig that Lynan's after him?"

"What good would that do? If saying you wanted to murder your boss was grounds for the sack, then half the men in Ireland would be out of a job. We couldn't prove anything, and Craig wouldn't listen, anyway."

"Well, what *do* we do?"

"We keep an eye on Lynan. That's all we can do."

"All right, from now on, in every exercise, one of us will always be watching Lynan."

"O.K.," Freddy said. But, as they entered the post, they did not look at each other. They knew it was no solution, a conscience-saver, a lie.

ten

He woke from a confused dream of girls into late afternoon in a house where the loudest sound was the clock ticking in his bedroom. His eyes opened on the Divine Infant of Prague, perched on the mantelpiece, waiting, as ever, for a chance to preach. He shut his eyes on the Infant's leaden stare and, a moment later, heard footsteps on the landing below. His father, Kathy, and Owen would all be out, but his mother and old Mary were probably at home. That was old Mary coming upstairs to tell him that a police sergeant was waiting to see him. The police sergeant, large and patient, waiting now in the front hall, had come to inquire about the circumstances of a certain fatal accident. Of course, that wasn't true; there could be no police sergeant in the hall, because there had been no accident. Not yet. He listened as the footsteps went past his bedroom, going upstairs toward the maid's room. False alarm.

Or perhaps, said the Infant, a forecast of things to come. Amazing isn't it, the compound interest of sin. A year ago, any sin *you* might have committed would have been minor, a schoolboy's sin. But sins beget sins. It didn't seem much of a sin to go into a pub and have a drink, but going to pubs and having drinks led you into what happened yesterday. And *there's* a sin for you, a great iceberg of a sin, punishable, here and now, by prison and, possibly, death. From masturbation to muder, in a month. Compound interest, all right.

The Infant was a born exaggerator, of course. First of all, there was very little chance that Craig would be killed, unless there were an air raid. And now, in November, after Coventry and other raids all over England and Scotland, still no sign of a single bomb here.

It could happen, though, the Infant warned.

Well, supposing there is a raid. There'd be such confusion no one would notice it if a man was hit by a falling brick.

Is that so, the Infant said. Interesting how, when people lose their religion, they lose all sense of right and wrong. It becomes all right to murder someone, as long as you're not caught. Oh, you're mixed up, my lad. You *are* mixed up. You're a mess. Stuck in a dead-end job, drilling under a lunatic for a raid that will never come. As for studying, why, you've given up all pretense of it. Acting, did you say? Come off it. The Grafton Players have disbanded for the duration, and nobody ever saw you in that part. Sally Shannon? Oh, you love her, do you? Why, you haven't seen her for ages.

For once, he had no answers to the Infant's taunts. He couldn't even pretend he enjoyed being a failure. He was a flop, even at that. Despite all his boasts of great scarlet whores, he hadn't even succeeded in losing his virginity. All he could say about this present life of his was that he was sleeping some ten hours out of each twenty-four, getting up just in time to go down to the boring old, bloody old A.R.P. post to play ping-pong with Freddy. His ping-pong had improved. He could say that.

The clock, ticking away his life beside the bed, said five minutes to four. If he hurried, he could be at the hospital by four-thirty, when she came off duty. They would have to talk in the crowded lounge of the Nurses' Home, no place to say anything private. Still, he had to talk to someone. She might send word that she was busy and couldn't see him. She might be doing a steady line with some clot like Clooney. Maybe it would be better to stay here in bed, where it was warm, commit a sin with himself and drift off to sleep.

He looked at the Infant. Was the Infant right about him?

"Gavin, where are you going, don't you want something to eat?"

His mother came from the kitchen, staring at him, as he buckled on his raincoat in the front hall.

"No time. I have to be someplace at half-past four."

"Then, what about your sandwiches for tonight? Will you come home to pick them up?"

"I'm not sure. I'll ring up later and tell you."

He went out. How long had it been since he had any real conversation with his mother? Not, he thought, since he was fifteen and reading about the Spanish Civil War. His mother had told him then that General Franco was a saint and should be canonized, just as, later, she announced that Cardinal McRory, the Primate of Ireland, was the one man in the world who could stop this war, if only he were given the chance. She said she loved her children, but Gavin wondered how she could love him who did not know him at all. When he thought of his mother, he heard a voice parroting worn prefatory phrases, such as, "Your father says," or "Children, nowadays, don't seem to realize," a voice which nagged gently about opening doors for ladies, changing socks, brushing teeth, folding table napkins, picking up clothes, saying prayers, and having some consideration for other people. His mother was fond of saying that God is good, but God, if there were a God, did not seem to have been particularly good to her. She was forced to endure her husband's taunts about the natural irrationality of women, yet obliged to side with him in all disputes with her children. If she attempted to tell a story, he cut her short or contradicted her. Nor did God bless her with health: she suffered from bronchitis, sciatica and varicose veins. Her missal was stuffed with black-edged Mass cards, in memoriam of the many friends and relations God had taken from her. Her life was not her own. As Owen once said, in a joke, bereft of the opinions of her husband and her parish priest, their mother would be a mute. How could you love a person like that? How could a person like that love you? Gavin wondered if his mother would ever speak to him again if she could spend just thirty seconds inside his mind. He doubted it.

Still, he wished she had not let him down by siding so completely with his father over the London Matric. His father had gone into a three-month sulk after Gavin's failure, a sulk more daunting than a dozen angry lectures. His mother, Greek chorus to his father's thumping silence, offered vague, disapproving remarks about how, goodness knows, they had done their best for each and every one of you children, it was a nice thing to see them repaid like this, the least you'd think a boy could do was listen to those who had his interests at heart.

Stuff like that. But said in a sort of past tense which exactly echoed his father's decision to write Gavin off. Talking of love, wasn't a mother supposed to love her children, no matter how they turned out? Not *his* mother. Not Mrs. Deirdre Burke.

A nun in starched white headpiece and rustling black veils stopped Gavin in the main corridor of the hospital. "What are you doing here? You're not supposed to come in here without special permission from the hospital superintendent."

"I'm sorry, Sister. I came to give a message to Nurse Shannon. I'm a friend of hers."

The nun, worn white face that no lover had ever kissed, small hairy mole on the edge of her upper lip, made an impatient sucking noise with her tongue to show how put-upon she was, turned her head abruptly, as though she heard someone behind her, and called down the corridor: "Dolan?"

A frail old man in a green porter's coat came from a doorway marked X-RAY. "Sister?"

"Tell Nurse Shannon, I want her."

The nun turned back toward Gavin with a great rustling of veils. "Follow me." She led him around a corner into the front entrance hall and opened the door of a room. "In here, please." She shut him in.

The room was small. The sofa and chairs were black buttoned leather, the circular mahogany table was bisected by a blue brocade runner, on which was placed a vase containing red artificial roses. There was an unlit gas stove in the grate, and over the fireplace, a crucifix. The floor was of polished wood, with two small, patterned rugs. It was, in fact, a typical convent parlor, except for the large sepia photograph on the wall. Two rows of men, one standing, one sitting, all in white coats, stared across the room at the muslin-curtained window. Underneath the photograph was a legend: MEDICAL STAFF & INTERNS. 1930. He looked at this photograph and felt uneasy. Nothing had changed in this room since 1930. Nothing would change. Out there, in the world, governments might be overthrown, capitals occupied, cities destroyed, maps redrawn, but here, in Ireland, it made no difference. In convent parlors, all was still. Why, in years to come he would become a drifter, he might even be

sentenced to jail for his part in Craig's death. He would
serve his long sentence, age and be released, a tottering
old man, to wander the streets and perhaps be knocked
down by some great flashing car of the 1980s, and, at
last, be brought back to this hospital after all those years,
to die in an upstairs ward. And this photograph would
still be here. The doctors of the staff of 1930 would continue to face the muslin-curtained window, contemplating
futures they had long since lived. A nun would arrive
each morning to dust the furniture and polish the floor.
Each evening, another nun would come in to draw the
blinds.

Nothing would change. The care of this room would
continue, as would the diurnal dirge of Masses all over the
land, the endless litanies of evening devotions, the an-
nual pilgrimages to holy shrines, the frozen ritual of Irish
Catholicism perpetuating itself in *secula, seculorum.*
Yeats was wrong in '16 to think that he and his country-
men,

> Now and in time to be,
> Wherever green is worn,
> Are changed, changed utterly:
> A terrible beauty is born.

This room denied that boast. Even Hitler's victory
would not alter this room. Armageddon would bypass Ireland; all would remain still in this land of his fore-
fathers. Ireland free was Ireland dead. The terrible beauty
was born aborted.

"Gavin, what's up, has there been an accident?"

The same rustling, starchy sound as the nun had made,
the tiny, absurd probationer's cap held by some invisible
magic on the top of her seal-smooth mass of black hair.
And those black-stockinged legs, so often an occasion of
his sins of intent. Yet she had changed since that day
she ran away from him on Cave Hill. She was older, somehow, more grown-up. The word "accident" jumped ir-
rationally in his mind. What telepathy told her that, when,
my God, it hadn't even happened yet?

But he was wrong. There was no telepathy. "Is it your
mother?" she asked.

"My mother?"

"Oh, I thought. I mean when they put people in this room, it's usually because one of the doctors is going to talk to them."

"No, some old crab of a nun grabbed me in the corridor."

"That was Sister Mary Frederick. As a matter of fact, I'm a pet of hers. That must be why she let us use this room."

"Sally, there's something I want to talk to you about. If you're off duty, can we go somewhere, somewhere private?"

"It's private here," she said. She went to the sofa and sat. "What's up?"

"Well, first of all, I want to apologize about that Sunday on the mountain."

"Never mind that. What's wrong?"

"Oh, Sally," he said. "Do you know—it's funny—I mean, no matter what ever happens between us, you're the only person I can talk to. It's been bloody awful, lately. You've no idea."

"I think I have. You and your father are barely speaking to each other. You're not studying any more, and the family thinks you might be drinking. Everyone's worried about you."

"Who told you all this?"

"Kathy."

"Wait'll I get my hands on her."

"You won't mention a word to her," Sally said. "I wormed it out of her. I wanted to know."

If she wanted to know, that meant she was still keen on him, maybe she loved him. Maybe they could run away, he and Sally, run away from his father's sulks, the A.R.P. and all that, find jobs in some other town and live together . . .

Come off it, said the White Angel. Tell her about Craig and the plan. That's what you came for, isn't it?

He told her. He told her all about Craig's mad drills and how the men hated him. He told her about the pub and what was said. He found himself standing up, acting different parts, imitating voices. When he had finished, he was quite pleased with his performance.

"When did all this happen, did you say?"

"In the pub? Yesterday."

She began to laugh. "Really," she said. "You're such a kid. Do you mean to say you don't know those men were pulling your leg?"

"They were serious. Freddy thought so too, and he's ten years older than I am."

"Age has nothing to do with common sense. He's as big an ass as you are, if he believes that guff. You said this old fellow, Soldier, is a Donegal man. Well, let me tell you, Gavin, Donegal people are all the same, they'll go to any lengths to make a fool of you. He put the others up to it, getting a rise out of you and your pal, Freddy."

If only she were right, she must be, she was sensible. Of course! He reached across the sofa and hugged her. "Stop it," she said. "What if one of the nuns comes in?"

"Oh, Sally, why did we ever fight, what's the matter with me. Listen, would you go out with me again? I swear I won't put a finger on you. Word of honor."

"All right," Sally said. "But on one condition. Will you promise me you'll stop drinking. And that you'll start studying again. Will you?"

"All right."

"A year from now, Gav, you could have your matric and then, you'll see, your father will come around and send you to Queen's. Kathy thinks he would and I think she's right. Oh, Gav, don't you see, all you have to do is get a grip on yourself. Stop being so gloomy about everything and stop making a tragedy out of every blessed thing that happens to you. Will you?"

"Yes," he said. "Yes," he repeated, almost shouting the word. It was like confession in the days when he had believed in confession. The priest said the words of absolution, and you made an act of contrition and came out of the box, washed clean of sin, pure and holy, half hoping you'd be run over by a bus and die in the state of grace and have your soul go straight to heaven. There was a great joy, a sense of your burdens being lifted. In this talk with Sally there was that same confessional relief. Sally was right, he could reform if she helped him. They would go out together to the pictures and to dances, they would go on long walks, and theirs would be real love, nothing to do with the dirty sex thoughts which teemed in his mind, but real love, pure love. Then, later on, they would marry and have a family . . .

And in the meantime, the Black Angel asked, what about the little devil between your legs? Do you expect him to lie down and die altogether? And Miss Holy Catholic Virgin here, who won't go out with anyone who isn't religious and sober, won't she lead you back to Mass and the sacraments and all the rest of it? Some agnostic you've turned out to be.

He told the Black Angel to go to hell, where he belonged. He went out of the hospital parlor, happy, walking with Sally, making a date with her for her next day off, a cured boy, a pure boy, a boy who had seen the error of his ways. He would study, he would make peace with his parents, he would listen to Sally's advice. O God, it was such a relief to give in, to be welcomed back.

eleven

Two nights before Christmas, the telephone rang in the front office. Shortly afterward, Craig rushed down the hall, blowing his whistle. He stood in the center of the kitchen, waiting for the post members to assemble, his pale face glistening with excitement. "This," he told them, "is it."

Old Mrs. MacCartney made the sign of the cross. "A raid?"

"Raid, nothing. Royalty is coming."

Royalty? Confused, they turned questioning stares on each other. Royalty did not come to Ireland. It was simply not safe to do so. True, the Duke of Windsor had risked it once, but had returned to England on a warship that same night. It had long been assumed that an overnight stay in Ireland, even in Loyal Ulster, was an invitation to assassination.

"Yes, royalty," Craig said. "No less than H.R.H. the Duchess of Gloucester will be visiting the hospital to-morrow morning. A.R.P. is to be there. Boy Scouts is being sent in to act as mock casualties. Now, I want every-body, except Maggie Kerr, who'll mind the phone, to get their gear, stretchers and all, and march straight over to the hospital for a practice drill."

"Three cheers for Her Royal Highness," said Mrs. Clapper. Nobody took her up on it.

"Government ministers will be present," Craig warned, "and all heads of the A.R.P. Mind that. I want youse spic and span. I said, spic and span."

Well, now, said the Black Angel. So you're going to kow-tow to a member of the house of Windsor, are you? Think of the Famine, Cromwell, and your uncle shot by the British. Never mind, said the White Angel. Who'll see you? Nobody you know, that's certain.

"The day shift will also be on hand," Craig said. "And Post 204 will be here too. I want us to put Post 204, not to mention the day shift, I said, I want us to put them in the halfpenny place. In the halfpenny place, I said. Now, over to the hospital, on the double."

"No rest tonight," Soldier commented.

"What did you say, MacBride?"

"I said God bless their Majesties, Mr. Craig. It's a great honor for all of us, isn't it lads?"

"Well, see you're up to it," Craig said, with a sour look. "Get your helmets and follow me."

So nobody will know, will they? said the Black Angel. It will be in all the papers. With photographs. Sally will be there. The nurses will come to watch.

On the following morning, when Gavin reported to the extern department of the hospital, not only the nurses were there. Outside, in a drizzling rain, grimy hands held aloft a waving chain of little paper Union Jacks. Faces stared through the iron railings at the front entrance to the hospital, heads turning as cars drove up to disgorge, disappointingly, a doctor, or yet another official of the Royal Ulster Constabulary. Policemen in black uniforms, their revolvers holstered, stood in a protective line within the railings, their faces turned toward the crowd who, restless, excited, moved and shifted, jostling for position. District inspectors of police, military in their black great-coats, consulted wristwatches. Royalty was late.

In the extern department, the wooden benches which occupied the large waiting hall had been stacked at the rear. The outpatients, who normally waited on these benches for treatment, had been sent home, except for a sampling of minor injuries, told to hold themselves in readiness for demonstration purposes, should royalty pass by. Boy Scouts clustered around an A.R.P. official, who daubed them with soot and false wound stripes, in preparation for their roles as raid casualties. Stretchers had been neatly arranged in long rows in the center of the hall. Groups of First Aid personnel stood in whispering circles, waiting to be called to attention. Interns in white coats offered cigarettes to probationer nurses. The atmosphere, reminiscent of backstage preparations for amateur theatricals, emphasized that this was a charade designed to show royalty how ordinary life was lived.

Soldier MacBride, his battle-dress jacket bright with ribboned campaign medals, marched smartly up to Gavin.

"Craig says you're to fall in with Stretcher Party Number Six."

"Right, Soldier. You're looking very grand today."

"The old ribbons." Soldier winked a brilliant black eye. "Ah, that goes over well with royalty. They always stop a man with ribbons. 'Where did you get that, my man?' Not that they give a curse."

"Well," Gavin said. "Those medals are certainly impressive."

"Oh, not all of them is here," Soldier said, grinning. "And we know why, don't we, Gavin lad? Some of the old ones is left off." He turned and saw a gangling Boy Scout standing directly behind him. The boy was staring at Soldier with the open-mouthed interest which children sometimes display when a grownup has caught their fancy. Soldier smiled kindly at the boy. "Tell me, lad," said he, does your cock stand in the morning?"

"What, sir?"

"You heard me, sonny boy. Bugger off."

He turned back to Gavin. "Have you seen the Captain?"

"Not yet."

"Well, if you do, tell him he's on Number Six, same as yourself."

"Right, Soldier."

Soldier marched off. In the center of the extern hall, Craig faced Bob Greenwood, head of the day shift, rival commanders united in a temporary truce against the officers of Post 204, who, with loud cries and much counterordering, were assembling their male and female personnel in two long inspection lines. There was no sign of Sally.

Gavin went outside. Under the ambulance awning, half in and half out of the rain, he found Captain Lambert. The Captain seemed down. His straw-colored mustache, soaked, drooped into the corners of his mouth. His eyeballs were touched with red, worm-like streaks, and he appeared to be having some difficulty in breathing. However, on turning toward Gavin, he gave some sign that the restorative process had been applied. His speech was thick.

"Ah, Gavin. Bloody awful time of morning to be out of bed, eh?"

"Soldier says you're to go on Stretcher Party Six. I'm on it too."

"Six," the Captain said, nodding, as though he had enunciated a meaningful solution. He yawned. "Bloody royals. Always late."

"Are they not here yet?"

"Just showed up. Look."

Four large black Daimlers were parked outside the main entrance to the hospital. Several figures, male and female, were hurrying up the steps under the protection of umbrellas. The crowd, silent, pressed close to the iron railings. A ragged cheer arose, then died.

"Which is the Duchess?"

"Probably the one in the silliest getup," the Captain said. He drew from his greatcoat a green bottle and took a long swallow. "They dress as if life's a garden party. It is for them, I suppose."

"I think we'd better report to stations."

"What's our hurry? She's got the whole damn hospital to inspect."

"Well, I think I'll go in, all the same. Number Six, remember."

"Six," the Captain said.

Inside, Gavin met Freddy Hargreaves, who seemed similarly irritated at royal tardiness. "Feudal bloody caper, this. Standing around like a bunch of serfs. Come the revolution, boy. No more parades."

"What about those dos in Red Square with all those Red generals standing around with thumping big gold epaulettes on their shoulders?"

Freddy looked hurt. "We'd better get back in line."

Big Frank Price, who was number one on Number Six Stretcher Party, looked apprehensive. "They're here already. Have you seen the Captain?"

"He's outside. He'll be in in a minute."

"There's to be no demonstration, thank the Lord," Frank said. "We just stand to, four men, one at each stretcher pole."

Captain Lambert, unbuttoning his greatcoat, came across the hall. His step was telltale. "Jayus," Frank said. "He's lit."

"No. Just recovering, I think."

"Mother of God, I hope he can stand up straight."

"He'll be all right," Gavin said.

The Captain, having tossed his greatcoat on a bench

in the corner, came downwind, lighting a cigarette. At that point, Craig, wearing a newly painted white steel helmet, ran across the hall to intercept. *"No smoking.* Put that out."

"Sorry."

There was no sign of Sally among the cluster of watching nurses. The hall was quiet. The word had got around that Her Royal Highness had started the tour of inspection. Bob Greenwood came past, whispering, "Stand to: she's coming." He glanced down at the stretcher, neatly blanketed and with a clean pillow at its head. The bearers stood stiffly to attention. A few minutes later, Mr. Kilvert from A.R.P. headquarters passed by, accompanied by two lieutenants. Again, the party passed muster. After some fifteen minutes, the atmosphere of the room lost its tension, as though the A.R.P. personnel, so often on alert for raids which never came, again sensed a deception. Half an hour passed. There was a sudden flurry to attention as two uniformed police inspectors entered from the main hospital building, coming from the direction in which the Duchess' party was expected. The inspectors, grim-faced men, walked all around the hall, staring into out-patient rooms and surgeries as though they expected to flush an I.R.A. terrorist at any moment. This was a Roman hospital, run by Roman nuns. The police inspectors' manner made it evident they considered it lunatic for royalty to venture into such a place. After a final round, they went back the way they had come. Again, there was a feeling of letdown. Some of the Boy Scouts began to wander from their positions, but were brought to heel by a threatened cuff from their scoutmaster.

Ten minutes later, by telegraph of whispers, it became apparent that royalty was at last on the way. The actual entrance was sudden, coming on the edges of the whispers, shocking the room into rigid attention. Royalty was accompanied by Dr. MacLanahan, medical superintendent of the hospital, a stiff old Corkman, wearing a white surgeon's coat over his brown tweed suit, a suit which in its informality proclaimed that, like a man forced to meet his wife's relatives, he would do his duty, but no more. On Royalty's left side was the Lord Mayor in chain of office, wearing a somber director's coat and wide-striped morning trousers, his cheeks the color of Brighton Rock with pleasure and embarrassment. A naval commander, an aide-de-camp of some sort, trailed negligently at the rear, his eye on the clock at the back of the hall. With him walked two ministers of the Northern Ireland government. There were were also a lady-in-waiting, the Lord Mayor's wife, and a district inspector of police, all of whom seemed exceedingly anxious for the tour to end.

Gavin, at attention, watched Royalty come up the main aisle, dressed, not quite as though to attend a garden party, but very gala in a suit of pale blue, trimmed with fawn fur. Royalty's voice, murmurous and discreet, could be heard making appropriate response to Dr. MacLanahan's gruff *Te Deum* of praise for the hospital's efficiency. With the pleasure one feels from winning a bet, Gavin watched Royalty stop at Soldier's stretcher party. Her voice, quiet, yet penetrating, floated in the morning air.

"Iniskilling Fusiliers?"

"Yes, your Highness," Soldier bellowed. "Served with the Regiment. India. Yes, your Highness."

Royalty smiled, passed on. The royal head turned in the direction of Gavin's party. For a moment, she seemed to look directly at Gavin, but then, as though noticing something, or someone, directly behind him, she paused, smiled and said: "Good morning."

"Morning, ma'am." It was the Captain's voice, slurred and imprecise.

"Are you a volunteer?" This, with a hopeful smile.

"No, no, ma'am. Just in it for the money." This, followed by a sudden, very drunken chuckle. "We're all in it for the money, you know, ma'am."

Gavin, no longer able to hold his pose of attention, risked a quick look sideways and saw, in a frozen tableau, the statue-like stillness of the men behind him. All save one. The Captain, his teeth fillings showing in a loose grin, his body shaking with amusement. Royalty smiled wanly, moved on. But the Captain's convivial chuckles did not cease.

"*Lambert,*" Big Frank Price whispered.

"Right," said the Captain, loudly.

Royalty, hurrying on, had now stopped by the surgery to shake hands with a young intern. The police inspector sprang to the door, holding it open, with a half bow to Royalty as the party went out. The Mayor and the Mayor's wife glared back scandalized looks and, as he exited, one of the government ministers hooked a finger. Mr. Kilvert, the deputy A.R.P. head, went hurrying over. The minister said something. Mr. Kilvert nodded. The door banged shut.

For a moment, like the moment after the detonation of a bridge, when it remains improbably suspended over the river, for that unreal, dreamy moment, no one moved. Then, dogs to the attack, Craig from one direction, Mr. Kilvert from another they came in for the kill.

"Do it for money, do ye?" said Kilvert's grating Ulster croak. "Aye, well you'll not do it for the money much longer." He turned to Craig. "You, there. What the flaming hell did you let this man come on parade for?"

"Sir, I reported this man, many's the time, nobody took no heed. I said, nobody took no heed, it's not my fault. I said, it's not my fault. I shopped him to H.Q."

"You thick, stupid porridge, you let him come drunk on parade, didn't you? You're not fit to be in charge of a nursery, let alone a post."

"*You.*" This, to the Captain. "Wipe that grin off your mug. You're sacked. Get your cards and clear off this post."

"And *you.*" This, to Craig. "You'll hear from me, later."

"It's not *my* fault, sir."

"Shut your gob," Mr. Kilvert said, coarsely. He wheeled and walked away. He could be seen gesticulating to his aides. They made for the door. The door shut.

twelve

"The streamers," said Miss Albee, "should stretch from each corner of the ceiling and join in the center. Then we'll put the paper bell at the center join."

"And the mistletoe?" Mrs. Clapper asked. "Will it hang on the bell?"

Gavin, holding one end of the paper streamer, winked at Freddy, who was holding the other. "That wouldn't do," Freddy said solemnly.

"And why not?" Miss Albee wanted to know.

"Because how could we kiss under the mistletoe? The table would be in the way."

"Oh," said Miss Albee. She looked down at the paper bell, twiddling it in her hands. Freddy and Gavin affixed the streamer and put the mistletoe over the door. Wee Bates came in with paper and pencil. "Soldier says I'm to lift five bob off everybody for the party."

"But I'm teetotal," Miss Albee objected.

"It's two bob for teetotals," Wee Bates said. "We'll have orange crush and ginger ale for them as wants it."

Miss Albee and Mrs. Clapper went to get their purses. Freddy and Gavin paid and their names were entered on Wee Bates' sheet. Soldier MacBride and Jimmy Lynan arrived, carrying a large cardboard box. "Gather round," Soldier said. "Wait'll you see this." He began to unpack the box, revealing paper hats, favors, a big fruitcake, a plum pudding, several bags of toffee, and some oranges. "Courtesy of the Ladies' Red Cross Auxiliary," Soldier said. "I went around there this afternoon. Comforts for the troops."

"But why should they give them to us?" Miss Albee asked. "We're not the Forces."

"And are we any different from some young conscript sitting in front of an antiaircraft gun in Lurgan?" Soldier wanted to know. "Aren't we in the front line of Home Defence?"

Miss Albee, who was Loyal Ulster and who knitted socks for the soldiers, shook her head, disapprovingly. "I'd hardly say that. I think it's a disgrace, giving comforts to the likes of us."

"Maybe so, maybe so," said Soldier. He began to repack his box. Your Man Mick Gallagher came in from the yard, carrying a scuttle full of coal. "Five bob for drinks for the party," Wee Bates said, holding out his hand. Your Man stared at Bates, then unbuttoned his battle-dress jacket and showed a tiny Sacred Heart button pinned to his undershirt. "This, here," he said, looking at Soldier, not at Bates, "do you know what this is?"

"Indeed I do," Soldier said. "The Pioneer Total Abstinence Association, a grand organization, founded by Father Matthew, R.I.P. Ireland sober is Ireland free."

"Correct."

"Right then," Soldier said. "Just pay two bob for minerals."

"But I don't want no minerals. I don't want no party."

"Get away with you," Soldier said, jovially. "Sure, Christmas comes but once a year."

"Aye, and I'll have my Christmas dinner at home. Not with outsiders."

"But we'll all have our dinners at home," Soldier said. "This is just a bit of jollification on the premises. And how can you call us outsiders, us that's been cooped up in this wee house together, day in and day out for a whole long year?"

"Youse are still outsiders to me," said Your Man.

At that moment, Post Officer Craig entered the room, followed by Old Crutt, his stoolie. Wee Bates, sheet in hand, went up to them. "Collecting for the party, sir. Five bob for the drinks, please?"

"What drinks?" Craig said.

"Christmas Day, sir."

"Minerals only. I said, minerals only."

Soldier looked at Freddy, who looked at Gavin, who looked at Jimmy Lynan. It was as though they passed the remark around to make sure it had really been uttered. "Minerals, of course, for them that wants them," Soldier said. "And a few dozen of stout and a bottle of whisky for the rest of us. Right, Mr. Craig, sir?"

"You heard me the first time, MacBride."

"But surely to God. It's Christmas Day."

"Minerals only."

"But even in the trenches, sir, in the last war, I re-member—"

"I don't care what you remember."

"It's allowed in the other posts," Freddy said. "In Post 204, for instance."

"What Post 204 does is Post 204's business. What this post does is my business. No drinking on duty."

"Ah, it's that business of the Captain," Soldier said. "Ah, I don't blame you one bit, Mr. Craig. But we're a cut above the Captain, sir. We're sensible men."

"I've had enough trouble," Craig said, darkly. "None of youse knows the trouble I've had."

"Ah, but a few stout, sir—"

"No. There's a war on. I said, there's a war on."

There was a long moment of silence. Craig moved over to Miss Albee and Mrs. Clapper. "Well, ladies, and how is the decorations coming along?"

"Rightly, Mr. Craig."

"That's good. I want to see a good turnout of decora-tions. Something nice, and in keeping."

"Yes, Mr. Craig."

"Right, then. Carry on."

He left the room. The men turned and looked at Old Crutt, the stoolie. Old Crutt, comprehending, followed in his master's footsteps.

"That man," Soldier said, "is not Christian. Eh, Jimmy?"

Look at Lynan, said the Black Angel. *That* man is ready to kill. Remember the pub. It was no joke, that threat. No joke, no matter what Sally says.

Lynan, breathing heavily, turned toward Freddy. "One brick," he whispered. "One brick, right between he's eyes."

Uneasily, Freddy nodded. Soldier, smiling, took the paper bell from Miss Albee and pinned it at the center join of the streamers. Big Frank Price came in from the front office. "Yellow warning," he said.

"Not again." There were groans. In the past month there had been three yellow, or preliminary, warnings, fol-lowed by siren alerts. Nothing had happened. It was a sour joke around Belfast that the sirens were sounded at night to wake the A.R.P. personnel from their slumbers. After the second false warning, few citizens bothered to go down to the shelters, for now, reading about the mounting count of raids on Britain, everyone knew that the Germans had decided to ignore Northern Ireland. So, when the sirens wailed, people turned over in their beds. Usually, the all clear was sounded within fifteen minutes.

The sirens sounded shortly after Big Frank's announcement. Ten minutes later, the all clear was given. Freddy and Gavin, on their way upstairs to play ping-pong, met Your Man Gallagher coming down from the attic. He was wearing his steel helmet and carrying his gas mask rucksack. "Bloody Germans," he muttered. "Bloody Germans."

thirteen

Mrs. Burke made an excellent trifle which was always served on Christmas Day as a first pudding. So, when old Mary entered the dining room, holding aloft the plum pudding ringed by brandy flames and decorated with a sprig of holly, there were groans of mock protest from the family and guests. Canon Wood patted the convexity of his black waistcoat, shut his eyes, and shook his head slowly from side to side. Mrs. Sullivan, a widow, who had been a bridesmaid at Gavin's parents' wedding, said that only on Christmas Day and in this house did she believe she committed the sin of gluttony. However, Mrs. Burke, Gavin, Kathy, and Owen, knowing how easily old Mary was offended if one did not eat her puddings, politely nibbled on small portions. Mr. Burke declined. A few minutes later, when the ladies had retired to the upstairs sitting room, he broke the seal on a box of cigars and, going to the sideboard, brought out a decanter of port.

"Try this, Malachy," he told the Canon. "And, in honor of Christmas, I think I'll let you boys try it too."

"Is this Tom's stuff?" the Canon asked, peering at his glass. The Canon had been to school with Gavin's father and with his Uncle Tom. Mr. Burke nodded and passed around the box of cigars. "Probably the last decent port we'll have for a long time," the Canon decided.

"No, no," Mr. Burke said. "This war's as good as over. In fact, I wouldn't give it another six months."

"I wouldn't count the British out just yet, if I were you," the Canon warned. *"Gott mit uns* is a sight more applicable to British history than ever it was to the German Reich."

"Oh, come now," said Mr. Burke. "The Luftwaffe's bombing the britches off them. You heard about the riots in Liverpool last week?"

The Canon had not heard a thing.

"John Sherry's wife was over, saw it with her own two eyes. People were marching around in the streets, carrying placards asking Churchill to make peace and stop the bombings. Mounted police charged them. There was quite a panic, she says."

"Is that so? In Liverpool. Well, well."

"And in other places too, I'll bet," Mr. Burke said. "Oh, the English are going to find out that their troubles are only beginning. Mark my words, Hitler won't be an easy master. He won't spare them, not after the way they turned down that perfectly reasonable peace offer he made last summer."

"Lord knows, these bombings of women and children are sickening, no matter which side does it," the Canon said. "We're very lucky over here. Ah, I forgot. We have an air raid expert, right at this table. Eh, Gavin?"

"Some expert," Owen said. "Never saw a bomb in his life."

"Or will see one, please God," the Canon said. "That's one advantage of living in a backwater, I must say."

"What did they do at that post of yours today?" Mr. Burke asked. "Did they have a party?"

"Sort, of, but it fell flat. Craig, our leader, forbade any booze. The men were furious."

"It must be a very tiresome job," the Canon said, "sitting around all the time."

"It gives me time to study," Gavin said, looking at his father. His father caught the look and told the Canon, "Yes, Gavin's trying the London Matric again. I think he's decided to put his back into it this time."

"Then he'll have no trouble passing," the Canon said. "There's no shortage of brains in this family. How are *you* doing, Owen?"

"Oh, Owen's doing very well," his father said. "I've never had any trouble with Owen. He wasn't always off to dances like some boys I could mention."

"Well, I hope there's one dance he goes off to, very soon," the Canon said. "And that's the school Old Boys' Dance on New Year's Eve. I hope you'll all buy tickets for it."

"I never go to dances, Malachy, you know that," Mr. Burke said. "But the boys will go."

"With fair damsels, I trust," the Canon said, winking at Owen and Gavin.

"Like Sally Shannon?" Owen said to Gavin.

"And the beauteous Miss Cooke for you?" Gavin asked.

"She'll do," Owen said.

"Excellent." The Canon raised his glass. "As chairman of the Dance Committee, I'm delighted to hear that the girls will be up to snuff."

"Did you listen to the King's speech today?" Mr. Burke said.

"I had something better to do," the Canon said, "than listen to that idiot."

"On the contrary," Mr. Burke said. "I wouldn't miss it for anything. He's great value. What an orator. They must be sitting on eggs at Windsor Castle, waiting for him to trip up."

"Ah, poor devil," the Canon said. "What can he say, even if he's fit to say it? It's been all bad tidings this last year. The only hope for them now is if the Americans come in on their side."

"Too late," Mr. Burke declared. "Wasn't that what somebody said in a speech in the Commons last spring? 'It's always too little or too late, or both, that's the road to disaster.' No, Malachy, I'd not give them another six months. Bet you a pound."

"A pound," the Canon said. "All right. Imagine *me* betting on England."

In the washroom of the school gymnasium (the same washroom where, aged thirteen, he had been held immobile by two older boys while a third squirted urine from a water pistol into his face), Gavin walked toward the mirrors, admiring the sight of himself, a grown-up stranger in his first dinner jacket. He stopped in front of the washbasins (those same washbasins in which, after science classes, he had washed off dyes) and, from an inside pocket, took an old silver cigarette case of his father's, extracting a cigarette, tapping it on the back of the case in a film-star manner, before lighting it. As he struck a match, he glanced instinctively at the door (that door he had always had to watch while smoking surreptitiously) and marveled how a simple thing like a rented dinner jacket made one, at last, the compleat grownup. He

eased the white handkerchief a little farther out of his
breast pocket, and then, his main worry, fiddled with the
black tie—tied for him by his mother—which had an
ugly trick of twisting lopsidedly, one bow up, one bow
down.

He was ready. But Sally wouldn't be ready: she always took ages in ladies' cloakrooms. He had no intention of going into the gymnasium-turned-ballroom without her. Some priest would be sure to nab him and ask
what he had been doing since he left St. Michan's. If he
had to mention the A.R.P., he preferred to do it with
Sally beside him. Toss it off, then sweep her into his arms
and tango away like George Raft.

It would be better to wait for her in the bar which had
been set up in the gym master's office. But when he and
Owen came in tonight with their girls, he had spotted
Tony Clooney in the bar. Clooney was the sort would
come off with those A.R.P. warden jokes at the drop of a
hat. No, better not wait for her in the bar.

But why should Clooney worry you, the White Angel
asked. Didn't you take her away from Clooney? Did you,
really? the Black Angel wondered. You fancy yourself in
this dinner jacket, but let me point out that Clooney, as
a future M.D., will wear dinner jackets all his life, as a
matter of course, while you, *acushla*, have no similar
guarantee. Pay no heed to the black scoundrel, the White
Angel chided. Pass your matric next time, and everything
will be all right. You've lost eighteen months that's all.
It's not a lifetime.

"Burke? On my soul. I'd never have recognized you in
those glad rags of yours."

It was Father Mallon (Latin and Greek), one of the few
half-decent priests, a sad, blond man, untidy, even now,
with traces of chalk dust on his dark clerical suit and
nicotine stains on the hand he offered Gavin. "Well, and
what are you doing with yourself, these days?"

"I'm with the A.R.P., Father."

"I see." Plainly, Father Mallon did not understand. "I
suppose you're up at Queen's?"

"No, Father, I failed my senior. Don't you remember?"

"You did well in Latin, I remember that. Failed? Well,
that's not the end of the world, Burke. You must study
hard and pass it next time."

"But I have a job. Actually, I'm working for the London Matric in my spare time."

"Ah, the London." Father Mallon said. "Quite so. The London. And then you'll go on to Queen's, of course?"

"Perhaps."

"Yes, of course," Father Mallon nodded, as though he had finally made sense of a bad translation by an inept pupil. "Law, like your father, no doubt. Yes, I hope so. Well, good luck, Burke. I'm sure you want to go on inside and trip the light fantastic, eh? Good-bye, now."

"Good-bye, Father."

Father Mallon left. Ronald Colman Burke, inspecting himself again in the mirror, remembered that a source of his recent nervousness in the conversation with the priest was the cigarette in his hand. It was hard to believe that this room was now a room like any other: that he might smoke if he wanted to. He thought of Father Mallon in class: the groaning of heating pipes, the damp green walls, the creak of bare floorboards as the priest paced among the row of boys, the swirl of his soutane as he turned, pointing a finger at random, asking a boy for translation. The boy would stand and, in halting sentences, try to give, in English, the dry prose of Caesar. Other boys, huddling forward, would slip their *Kelly's Key to the Classics* from the underside of the desk, trying to memorize a few sentences in the following pargraph, in case their turn came next. Poor Father Mallon: he had no taste for caning boys. A priest or master who did not cane regularly soon lost his usefulness. By senior year, the boys, no longer fearing Father Mallon, had come to ignore him. Fear, said the Black Angel. That is the only thing which drives boys like you to effort. Fear. And now that there is no more caning, you have given up. Undriven, you will drift.

Undriven? asked the White Angel. There are more things to fear than a caning, my friend. School may have been frightening, but the grown-up world is more so. Go into the gymnasium and find out. Go in and meet your former classmates and discover what the grown-up world thinks of you now.

Sally in a pink dress, coming out of the ladies' room, gliding up to him with a smile, Sally was somewhere between the world of school and the world of grownups.

As a student nurse, she must deal with sickness and sores, must hear foul language in the wards, must even handle naked male limbs. And yet, despite the womanliness of her bare white shoulders coming out of that pink dress, she remained girlish, a virgin eponym who inspired his lust, making him stiffen with embarrassment as her silken-sheathed thigh innocently touched between his legs, making him pull back, hold her a little apart as they danced past Canon Wood, Father Fremont, and Mr. Tushingham, who had once taught him science—all of whom looked at her, watching her whirl in, and out, and past them. Canon Wood waved, winking at Gavin, a worldly cleric, watchful. Dancing with Sally, dancing past boys who were now becoming grownups, boys in university or in their fathers' businesses, Gavin felt that he danced away all the years of humiliations and punishments that were school; danced, smiling his Ronald Colman smile, his rented dinner jacket effectively disguising his true status as a lowly stretcher-bearer in life's race, a slave to a slave called Craig, who would be surprised, wouldn't he, to see Gavin, so elegant, dancing here in this ballroom. Sally. He held her tight, forgetting his lust, held her as though she might faint and fall. Sally was his answer to the Black Angel's taunts that he would never amount to anything in this grown-up world of ball gowns and dinner jackets. Sally believed in him: if one person really believed in him, he knew he could do anything.

At the end of the fourth dance, they met Owen and Peggy Cooke, Owen's girl. "What about a drink?" Gavin said.

Owen did not drink. As a student, he had no money to buy drinks for girls. He looked at Gavin with distaste.

"Well, maybe a lemonade," Sally said.

"It's New Year's Eve, for goodness' sake. Aren't we going to have a real drink?"

"It's up to you, Gavin. I'd like a lemonade. What about you, Peg?"

"Lemonade would be grand."

"Owen? It's my round," Gavin said.

"Ginger ale."

This'll be the gay evening, the Black Angel said as he went to the bar. The look she gave you, you'd think you were the biggest boozer in Belfast. Well, Sally darling, much as I love you, I'm going to sneak a big double whisky in here, before bringing back all that damn lemonade.

He drank the double whisky in one long swallow, although it made his eyes water. He lit a cigarette so that she wouldn't smell the whisky. He need not have bothered. When he went back to their table, carrying three lemonades and one ginger ale, Sally wasn't there.

"Where is she?"

Owen pointed to the dance floor. A great sack of a man well over six feet tall and dressed in the uniform of a British Army captain, glided on the fringe of the crowd, easing Sally through the intricate steps of a hesitation waltz. He held her tight, his head a good two feet above hers, his face, staring out above the crowd, a curiously unreal face, like a store dummy's, with shiny black hair lacquered to his skull, a pencil-thin mustache, rouge-red cheeks, and staring blue eyes, round and false as the weighted eyes of a china doll.

"Who the hell is that?"

"That's the famous John Henry," Peggy Cooke said.

"I didn't know he'd joined up," Owen said. "I thought he was still working in the hospital."

"No, he resigned last month," said Peggy Cooke, who, like Sally, was a student nurse.

"After the court case?" Owen asked.

"Yes. The word was he was asked to resign. That's why he went out and joined up."

"Well, God help the British Army," Owen said.

"What court case, what's all this, will somebody please fill me in?" Gavin said. Jealousy nipped at him as Sally glided past in the monster's arms.

"You mean you never heard of John Henry? Dr. Moriarty, the most dangerous man in Belfast, they used to call him."

"Yes, he was a legend up at Queen's," Peggy said.

"I never went to Queen's."

"Oh, anyway," Owen said. "John Henry was one Queen's sight worth seeing. He used to go to the student hop every Saturday night and pick fights. He's a terror."

"He doesn't look it."

"That's just it. He looks like a big sissy."

"And you should hear him thpeak," Peggy Cooke lisped. "He'th tho ni-ithe."

"Part of his act," Owen said. "He'd start lisping away with some insult and some big Rugger Blue would look him over and decide he'd be a soft fall. The Rugger Blue would swing at John Henry, and that would be the end of it. Half an hour later, the Blue would wake up in the cloakroom, never knowing what hit him. I saw it happen once. John Henry just ducked this fellow's punch, then took the man by the throat, backed him into the wall, and hit him so hard on the jaw that the fellow's head banged against the wall. The fellow went down, poleaxed."

"That's what the court case was about," Peggy said. "Seems he hit some commissionaire in a night club and fractured the man's skull."

"And he's a doctor?" Gavin said.

"And a good one," Peggy said. "You'd better watch out, Gav. I think he has a great notion of Sally. He was always hanging around our ward when she was on night duty."

"Oh?"

"Mother Carmel was on the prowl one night, and John Henry came up the back stairs—" Peggy began. She stopped. The music had stopped and John Henry was bringing Sally over.

"John, this is Gavin Burke and Owen, his brother. This is John Moriarty."

"How-dou-dou," said the huge man.

"What do the priests think of you in that uniform?" Owen asked him.

The huge man smiled and touched his pencil mustache in an affectionate manner. "It'th getting very popular," he said. "I mean the medical corps. I jutht hope they don't thend me to Coventry." He laughed, his shoulders shaking. "Thay," he said. "How about a drink? Come on, Thally, I'll buy you a drink."

"I already have a lemonade."

"Oh, come on, jutht one. I mean, all of you," the huge man lisped. "Come on, chapth."

"Thanks, but I promised Peggy this dance," Owen said, rising as he spoke and nudging Peggy toward the dance floor. John Henry, smiling, watched them go, then linked his arm in Gavin's, and, with his other hand, took hold

The Emperor of Ice-Cream • 131

of Sally's elbow. "Jutht a small one," he said, and led them into the room which was being used as a bar. Two boys in ill-fitting dinner jackets stood aside for him at the door, and, as he passed, one whispered something to the other. The second boy sniggered. A third boy, standing a few feet away, made a frantic shut-up sign, warning the sniggerer. John Henry did not seem to notice. He went up to the bar, secured a stool for Sally, and called to the barman. "Three Thcotcheth, pleathe." Then turned politely to Gavin. "Are you up at Queen'th?"

"No."

John Henry smiled and nodded as though this were an interesting answer. Then turned to Sally, presenting Gavin with a view of his buttocks, big as full potato sacks. Sally asked something about somebody called Dennis, and John Henry began a whispered, giggling tale. Whatever it was, it made Sally laugh. "Oh, John!" she said.

Now why, said the Black Angel, just why does she consent to have a Scotch with this big tub of lard, after flatly refusing to have one with you? And just what did Peggy Cooke mean, he's got a notion of Sally? Coming up the back stairs. Christ, she couldn't kiss that monster, could she?

"And what did old Jack D. do then?" he heard Sally ask. She seemed to be in fits of laughter. The fat man smiled and giggled. "He thaid, 'Take that man downthtairth at onthe and have him thtomachpumped.' "

"Oh, John! Honestly?"

"And the betht of it wath, Dennith didn't even wake up."

"No!"

Would you mind sharing the bloody joke? Bloody rude, turning your bloody back, like that. George Raft Burke, small but deadly, mentally swung this big villain around, planted a George Raft downward left to the chin, watched him spin and topple, to fall face down on the barroom floor.

"A tango," the monster said. "Hear the muthic? How about it, Thally?" And turned, at last, to Gavin. "Excuthe uth, will you?"

Go on, Thally. Go on out there and let that bloody big killer squeeze your lovely breasts against his belly, let him paw your naked shoulders with his banana fingers, let him lisp and smile and hug you, Nurse, and it's all right because he's a medico and doctors are your aim in life, they're the men in white, you look up to them, God help you. Or maybe it's the army uniform that does it, Thally, the Tham Browne belt and the tunic that they wore to kill your ancestors. Why did I ever come here, I always hated this damn school. I'm not a member of the Old Boys' Society, nor never will be. I'm going home.

But, of course, he did not. He had another whisky instead, his third, no, his fourth, he realized, for the first one had been a double. A fellow called Fitzpatrick, whom he remembered as being a year ahead of him in school, came, sat down on the stool vacated by Sally, ordered a bottle of stout and offered him a Player's cigarette.

"Well, Burke, how does the old charnel house look to you now?"

"The same, if not worse."

"Well," Fitzpatrick said, "one thing I've learned since I went out into the great wide world. There is no place worse than school. This school. Did you know, I've joined up?"

"Why aren't you in uniform, then?"

"Didn't think it would be appreciated here. Anyway, I'm on leave. I'm going to England next week to train as a pilot. Jimmy Gilroy and I."

"Wasn't Gilroy bloody nearly an I.R.A. man?"

"Yes, but he's a good Rugby player, you know. That counts with the R.A.F. selection people. Both he and I tried out for Ulster last year and both of us were put up for commissions the minute we let that slip."

"But why did you join up, Fitz?"

"Don't know. I was fed up at home. Besides, I hear the women over in England are man-starved and hot as coals. When Jimmy and I are covered in Air Force blue, we plan to be bloody great studs up and down the land."

"So you joined up just for intercourse?"

"It's a clear-cut motive," Fitzpatrick said. "I mean, do you think anyone ever joins up for purely patriotic motives, even the English? Fellows join up because they want to leave home, see some excitement, stuff girls, and so on. All of them."

"But you could get killed. What about this Battle of Britain caper?"

"At least," Fitzpatrick said, "I won't die wrestling to get my man in between the thighs of some cold Irish virgin. This uniform's going to liberate me. Nobody will notice my acne or my bad teeth, because I'll be Pilot Officer Fitzpatrick, an officer and a gent. The uniform works miracles, believe you me. Look at that slob, Moriarty, tonight."

"What do you mean?" What *does* he mean, the Black Angel hissed.

"Look what it's doing for *him*. Nix, nix, here he comes."

"Excuthe me. That's our theat."

Fitzpatrick, smiling in fright, slid off the bar stool and backed away. John Henry settled Sally on the bar stool. "Where'th our drinkth? Oh, we drank them, I thuppothe." He signaled to the barman.

"No more for me," Sally said. "And Gavin, I don't think you want another, do you?"

"It's my round," Gavin said, looking at John Henry, not at her. Who did she think she was, his nurse?

"Then let's have two ginger ales," Sally suggested.

"Three Scotches," Gavin told the barman.

"Gavin, I don't want a Scotch."

"Oh, stop being such a damn wet blanket."

A hand, heavy as a hammer, came down on Gavin's shoulder. It gripped the cloth of his dinner jacket and he was spun around to a close-up of John Henry's weighted doll's eyes, rouge-red cheeks, baby mouth. "That'th rude," John Henry said. "If I were you, I'd thay I'm thorry to Thahlly. And thay it damn quick."

As he spoke, his thick fingers shifted grip on Gavin's shoulder, expertly settling into position. A firm hold, one terrible punch and the Rugger Blue's head hit the wall, fracturing his skull as he slid unconscious to the floor. Gavin looked up at the round doll's eyes, at that small, smiling mouth, and fear, shameless, trembling fear, made his legs weak. He saw that Sally saw his fear, for, at once, she stepped between them. "Now, look, John," she said. "Gavin didn't mean anything, honestly, he didn't. And it wouldn't be fair for you to hit him, he's not your size. *Please,* John."

John Henry let go. He let go, Gavin imagined, the way a tiger backs off from a goat when the animal trainer fires a blank in the tiger's face. But, as he let go, John

Henry gave Gavin a little push. That little push sent Gavin thumping against the makeshift bar, jarring his spine, jiggling the liquor in glasses all the length of the bar, causing people to turn and stare. Faces looked into Gavin's face: they saw his fear.

A priest, Monsignor O'Malley, who was having a drink farther down the bar, left his whisky and his friends, and walked up. "Good evening," he said, in a voice which knew its own authority. "Is anything wrong?"

"No, Father," John Henry said, smiling his deceptive doll's smile.

"Good evening, Dr. Moriarty," said the Monsignor. "Are you enjoying the dance?"

"Yeth, very much." John Henry picked up his whisky and drank it in one careless toss, hurling the liquor back into his throat. He put his glass down, smiled at the Monsignor, then turned to Sally. "I wonder," he said, "would it theem a terrible impothition if I athked you for one more danthe?"

"Not at all," she said. "I love rhumbas. Gavin, I'll see you back at our table."

The Monsignor, assured that order had been restored, nodded and went back to his friends. John Henry escorted Sally toward the ballroom. The fellow called Fitzpatrick moved up and slapped Gavin on the back. "What happened, sport? I thought you were due to be stiffened."

His heart thumped: he felt sick. He turned to look at Fitzpatrick, only half hearing what Fitzpatrick had said. "I wasn't afraid of him," he heard his liar's voice declare. "I'd have hit him, so I would."

"John Henry? Well, and, if you did, it would have been your last dance tonight. What did you do, say something to his girl? I heard him tell you to apologize."

"She's not his girl, she's *my* girl." He was shouting now and people were listening, but he didn't care, he was going straight into that ballroom to take her out of the arms of that fat pig.

"Shh," Fitzpatrick said. "Easy there. Forget the girl. No girl's worth getting yourself crippled for."

"You owe me ten shillings," the barman said, coming up.

"Give me another whisky."

"You've had enough, sir. No offense meant."

"I said, give me another *whisky*."

"I'm sorry, sir. Father Redmond just sent the word up, you're not to be served any more."

"Where's Father Redmond? Who does he think he is?"

"Now, take it easy, Burke, old boy," Fitzpatrick said. "Let's skedaddle out of here. Come on."

"Where's Father Redmond?" But, as he repeated his challenge, he suddenly felt woozy, it wasn't just the drink, it was the adrenalin of fear, anger, and self-disgust. He remembered that Sally had promised to meet him at their table, and so he let himself be led away from one more confrontation, this time with Father Redmond. Coward, said the Black Angel. A coward twice over in the short space of fifteen minutes. Admit it.

As he and Fitzpatrick entered the ballroom, the band finished its number. The dancers began to break up and he saw her walking across the dance floor with the monster, saying good-bye to the monster, and then, turning, going alone among the tables toward their table, where Owen and Peggy Cooke sat, holding hands. "Excuse me," he said to Fitzpatrick. "There's my girl."

"Good luck," Fitzpatrick said.

He went among the tables, aware that his dizziness was making him just a little bit unsure on his feet. He didn't want Owen to know he'd had all those Scotches, and that reminded him that he'd better get there, to the table, he meant, before Sally gave her version of what had happened. Her version might not sound very complimentary. It was all her fault, after all, but girls forgot those things—

"Oh!"

Someone had rammed two fingers into his rear. Goosed him, stiff fingers driving at his rectum, making him jump like a silly nun. Outrage flooded him as he turned—was it that fellow there or was it—he turned a little more, and there, smiling down from his great height, was John Henry, the colored lights from the ballroom kaleidoscope playing yellow and blue over his monster face. The weighted doll's eyes blinked and the baby mouth pouted in a smile, infuriating, a smile which said yes, it was me, you little twerp, and what, may I ask, do you intend to do about it? The Rugger Blue, provoked, hit out and was felled, the commissionaire was hurled through a

136 • *The Emperor of Ice-Cream*

doorway, his skull cracking on the pavement, the remembered little push was stiff enough to set all the bar glasses rattling, and now that smiling dollface waited, waited to be challenged, waited to smite. He stared at that hated face and, as he did, felt his own face flush with shame. The moment had passed, he knew it, John Henry knew it, and anyone who was watching would know it too. But, no one was watching. The ballroom lights spun, changing John Henry's yellow and blue face to a devil's red. The red devil grinned in contempt as Gavin, afraid, went away among the tables toward Owen and Peggy and Sally. He who fights and runs away. A coward's excuse. The grown-up world was no different from school, it was a world where bullies came out best, where excuses satisfied no one, least of all one's self, where cowardice corroded one's soul and left one sick. Sick, he went toward Sally. In his heart, he had already lost her. Sooner or later, some more powerful male would take her from him. He knew, as Yeats knew, that the rough beasts, the John Henrys, are always with us. They, not he, would prevail.

fourteen

It was Aunt Liz who brought the news. She had heard it on an early morning broadcast and came by the Burkes' with it on her way home from seven o'clock Mass. It was in the *Irish News,* of course, but none of the Burkes had been downstairs to get the paper, and, when Aunt Liz rang at half-past seven and was let in by old Mary, the family were in their dressing gowns, taking turns in the bathroom. There was a rule in the family: no one spoke before breakfast.

But there was Aunt Liz, in her sensible rubber mac and her tweed hat which might have been made for Sherlock Holmes, shouting up the stairs in a voice you could hear at the far end of the avenue. "Is anyone up? James? Are you there, James?"

"Damnation," said Mr. Burke. He and Owen were shaving in the same mirror. He went out onto the landing, lather on his chin, and looked down at his sister. If looks could kill, Aunt Liz would have fallen.

But Aunt Liz ignored his glare. "James, have you phoned Agnes, yet?"

"What would I telephone Agnes about? She's not sick, is she?"

Agnes was Mr. Burke's and Aunt Liz's older sister.

"Well, after the bombing," Aunt Liz said, "I just thought you'd want to be sure she was all right."

"What bombing?"

Gavin's mother and Kathy had both come out of their bedrooms and were listening. Gavin's mother put her hand over her mouth. "Gracious God. What are you talking about, Liz?"

"Dublin was bombed last night. I heard it on the six a.m. news."

"Dublin? Don't talk balderdash, woman," Mr. Burke said. "Dublin is neutral."

"It's not balderdash. They say it was German planes."

"Mary," Mr. Burke yelled. "Mary."

Old Mary appeared from the scullery at the foot of the stairs. Mr. Burke leaned into the stairwell. "Bring the *Irish News* up here," he shouted. He turned to his family. "Utter nonsense. Eire is neutral. What sense would there be in bombing a neutral country."

But Gavin noticed something in his father's voice, something he had not heard before. His father was afraid. Of course, said the Black Angel. It's hitting close to home, now.

Old Mary, holding the paper in front of her, trying far-sightedly to read the headline, came in from the front hall.

"Come along there," Mr. Burke said, sharply.

"Yes, sir."

Old Mary began to ascend the staircase. The family watched, figures in a tableau, caught in a moment they felt to be history. Mr. Burke took the newspaper, shook it out, and began to read snatches, muttering to himself. "Unidentified planes, possibly German—what do they mean 'possibly'?—dropped two bombs on the city of Dublin last night. The first bomb . . . hm, hm . . . second . . . oh, it's all right, Liz. They were nowhere near Agnes' place."

"Still, we should give her a ring," Aunt Liz said. "Merciful God! *Bombs.*"

And what of all the bombs that fell on England these last months, the Black Angel said, weren't *they* real bombs?

"Came up the river Liffey," his father said. "Now, how the blazes could they mistake a neutral city, all lit up, for part of England?"

"They thought it was Belfast," Owen said. "They were one hundred miles off course, that's all."

"They'll have found out their mistake, by now," Kathy decided. "They'll probably come here tonight."

"Nonsense, girl," Mr. Burke said.

"Has it ever occurred to any of you," Aunt Liz said, "that this bombing might *not* be the work of the Germans? It could be the work of *agents-provocateurs*. Remember the Troubles. The Brits could be doing it as a dodge to frighten the Eire government into coming into the war."

"By George, that's right," Mr. Burke said. "Aha, yes, a damned, clever dodge. And one I wouldn't put it past them to use."

"Oh, not killing people, surely?" Gavin's mother said.

"Has that ever stopped the Brits in the past?" Aunt Liz wanted to know.

"These bombs *didn't* kill anybody," Mr. Burke said. "That's the fishy part of it."

"Well, will we telephone Agnes?"

"No. No need. Let's have our breakfast."

At breakfast, Aunt Liz grew more convinced. "Why it's as plain as the nose on your face. The Brits want the Yanks to come in and save them, the way they did in 1917. And what better way, than to pretend the Germans are bombing Ireland. It's well known the Americans are far fonder of the Irish than they ever were of England."

"That might be," Mr. Burke decided. "But if they think they'll force Eire into the war, they have another think coming. Any Southern Irish government that voted to join the British in a war might as well resign the same afternoon."

"And right, too," Aunt Liz said. "In twenty years, is a people expected to forget the brutality of their butchers?"

They were whistling in the dark, Gavin decided. They might try to blame this bombing on the British, but, secretly, they knew the Germans had done it. Now, for the first time, his father would have to put his principles to the test. Would Hitler still be a great fellow, if Hitler bombed one's house?

At the post that evening, the mood was one of suppressed excitement. There was little discussion of the Dublin bombings, but Gavin noticed that, for the first time in the year he had been on the post, there was no grumbling when a practice drill was called. Each time the telephone rang in the front office, ping-pong, knitting, draughts, all stopped. Everyone listened. Faces were grave.

But no raid came. In the morning, the day shift people, coming on duty, were similarly expectant, although, until then, there had been no news of daylight German raids. That night, the excitement was still present when Gavin and his shift took over. But, again, no raid came.

In the morning, the B.B.C. announced that Dublin had been bombed a second time. Again, the bombs had done little damage. This news, announced by Miss Albee, who had been listening to the wireless, produced a reaction which seemed close to rage.

"On my soul," said Hughie Shaw, throwing down his gas mask, as though he would stamp on it, "what do them Germans want? Do they expect us to switch on the lights and send out a welcoming committee?"

"It's the blackout," Wee Bates said. "They can't find us in this blackout."

"They know rightly, it's Dublin, they're bombing," Mrs. Clapper said. "Hasn't the Irish government sent a protest to Hitler through the German embassy in Dublin?"

"What's the matter with them, the idjits?" Jimmy Lynan complained. "Why don't they come on up here?"

"God forbid," said Big Frank Price.

But Big Frank seemed alone in his moderation. The faces around the fire were cheated and cross. In the voice of a person who announces a great loss, Miss Albee told them that, in her opinion, the Germans had some secret reason for ignoring Belfast. "Politics, maybe," said she, darkly. "Anyway, it's plain to see, they'll *never* come here."

Post Officer Craig had entered the kitchen as Miss Alice spoke. He walked to the center of the room and stared around at these unbelievers, his face pale with suppressed emotion. "Miss Albee is wrong shipped," he announced. "The Germans know this place. Gerry will be up in them skies above us, any night now. This is just target practice, this bombing of Dublin. Target practice. When Gerry comes here, don't youse worry, it won't be no two bombs he'll let drop. It'll be Coventry."

"Aye, better no raid at all, than a wee cod of a raid," Hughie Shaw said.

"A raid like Dublin had, we'd never be called out," Craig said. "The ordinary ambulance service could do the job. Nobody was hurted."

"Aye, nobody was hurted."

Old Mrs. MacCartney, who rarely engaged in discussion when men were present, being of a generation of Irishwomen who sat down to eat only after the men had been fed, suddenly rose up from her seat by the fire, wagging a finger in malediction. "Youse should everyone of

The Emperor of Ice-Cream • 141

youse be ashamed," she said. "Youse should be down on your bended knees asking God's forgiveness. The Almighty has seen fit to spare us, yet you sit here, wishing that ould Hitler will drop bombs. And why? For the glorification of your own selves, that's the why."

"Hold your tongue," Craig shouted. "There's nothing wrong with people wanting to do their duty."

"No one wants an air raid," Miss Albee said, crossly. "Whatever gave you that idea?"

"That's right, quite right, of course not," other voices chorused.

"I just want us to do our duty," Craig said. "Carry on." He turned and left the room.

"Back to his lady friend," said Soldier. "Skirt duty."

"It's a mortal disgrace," Miss Albee said, obliquely. "Would you ladies care to help me tidy the upstairs room?"

The ladies left. The group of men around the fire broke up. Some began to play darts and others went into the scullery to wet some tea. Jimmy Lynan, in the scullery, turned and winked at Gavin. "*He* wants a raid," he whispered.

Soldier, lighting his pipe, puffed up a thick blue cloud of plug. "Aye," said Soldier. "There's them that wants what's not good for them. Eh, Jimmy?"

"That's right, Soldier," Jimmy said, and both began to chuckle. "Eh, young Burke?"

"What's the joke?" asked Old Crutt, the stoolie.

"Sorra the joke," Soldier said, chuckling. "Sorra the joke that's in it. Eh, Jimmy Lynan?"

"Coventry," Jimmy shouted. "Your man Craig wants a Coventry. What do you say there, young Burke?"

Yes, what *do* you say, the White Angel asked. Dublin's been bombed. There's every chance that Belfast is next. Craig's death is no longer a pub daydream. Look at Lynan. A murderer if ever I saw one.

Nonsense, the Black Angel said. Don't heed him. Lynan is watching you. Don't act the scared kid. Smile at him. What harm will it do to smile?

He smiled at Jimmy Lynan. The smile froze on his face. A Judas smile, whispered the White Angel. A Judas to yourself.

fifteen

Rain began to fall as Sally and Gavin turned the corner of Windermere Street, coming home from a Fred Astaire and Ginger Rogers film. Ahead of them, a young couple began to run, disappearing into a brick air raid shelter, halfway down the street. A moment later, looking embarrassed, they came out again. Giggling, the couple fled on in the rain.

Sally, not hurrying, for she and Gavin were wearing raincoats, watched this scene and said: "There was someone in there."

"In where?"

"In the shelter. Same thing happened to us last week, Moira Casey and me. We went in to get out of the rain, and there were two people canoodling on a blanket inside. It's ughy, the things that go on in those places. They ought to tear them down."

"They might be needed some day."

"Oh, come on, Gav. Do you think so?"

"I don't know."

He didn't know. It was over three months since those false-alarm raids on Eire. At the post, the mood was one of complete disillusion. The volunteers—wardens, firewatchers, and first-aid people—who had shown up in large numbers after the Dublin raids of January, had, by March, dwindled to a thread of lonely people, willing to put up with any charade in order to spend their evening hours in the company of others. The raids on Britain continued.

"Yet, dammit to hell," as Hughie Shaw said, "the shipyards here are working day and night, building tankers and warships. And there's factories all over the place doing war work. Belfast is a first-class target."

"But, too far away," Soldier said.

That was it. Everybody seemed to agree. The boredom of the twelve-hour shifts became intolerable.

"Do you know something," Gavin said to Sally. "I have a good mind to join up. Anything's better than sitting around like this."

"Is it? Is it better to go away now as an army private and, when the war's over, come back to no job and no security? Have sense, Gav. You've got to settle down and study for your London. This is your last chance."

His mother agreed with Sally. "If you ever so much as mention a thing like joining the British Army, it will kill your father. After what the British did to his family—"

"For goodness' sake, Mother, I *know*. But I'm fed up being a laughingstock."

"Then, get your London this spring."

What was the use? It was always the same when he tried to talk to his mother. Come to think of it, Sally was beginning to sound very like her. Women were great for security. *Your* security, so that you'd be a better bet when *they* decided to marry you.

"Who ever said a word about marriage?" Sally said. "Marry you, for goodness' sake, you have years of university ahead of you. Marry you, would I be mad altogether?"

"But supposing I don't go to university. Supposing I join up and get a commission?"

"The answer is no, doubly so. Why would I want to marry some mad kid who joins up and goes off to get killed, just because he's bored."

She didn't understand, girls never did. After all, he wasn't the only one who was fed up. Even Freddy was talking of leaving.

"Sometimes," Freddy said, "I wonder if people realize just what I'm giving up by staying in this job. Most people don't realize that, for me, it's a political decision. Imagine trying to explain to my parents, for instance, that this is an imperialist war and that the best thing all around would be for England and Germany to go under so that the U.S.S.R. can take over. My parents are pro-British. It would be a damn sight more pleasant for me if I joined up. Don't you see?"

No, he did not quite see. Freddy was rationalizing things, because, perhaps, Freddy was afraid to join up.

But he, Gavin, wasn't afraid. He was fed up. Here it was, a year and four months of sitting around, and all they had ahead was more of the same, more Craig, more drills, more ping-pong. My God, in October he would be nineteen. *Nineteen.* Wouldn't it be better to join up? At least, after the war he would have a chestful of ex-service ribbons when he stood on the street corner, begging, or sprawled on the pavement, his empty jacket arm pinned to his shoulder, making untalented chalk drawings on the pavement, like the First World War ex-soldier who used to sit in Donegall Street, coloring in horrid childish landscapes, then lettering the legend: EX-SERVICE MAN, GOD BLESS YOU. Or the other favorite of that beggar, a loaf of bread done in white and brown chalks, white for the bread, brown for the crust, with the legend: EASY TO DRAW, BUT HARD TO GET.

"What are you grinning at?" Sally asked, taking hold of his arm. "Come on, what's the joke?"

"I was just wondering how many pavement artists this war is going to produce."

"What are you talking about?"

"Nothing, it's too hard to explain."

They had come to the gates of the Nurses' Home. The shower had stopped, and there were a few fellows saying good night to nurses up and down the street. If he joined the army, *he* would be the one going into barracks, kissing some girl good night before passing the sentry. Instead of which, here he was, kissing Sally, who wouldn't let you do anything, who seemed to think that a fellow could be eternally content with kisses. He thought of those English girls, man-starved and hot as coals, remembered some Manchester factory girls he had seen on holiday in Bangor, girls who laughed and liked it when their fellows put their hands up the girls' legs. Remembering, he got excited. She eased back. "I'm late. Sister will be standing in the hall, counting off the minutes. Good night, Gav. Give me a ring, will you?"

"Good night," he said, turning away abruptly to show her his disappointment. Bloody Catholic girls! He walked off into the wet night. Country girls were different: he had seen them in country places going off up the fields with their fellows. But city girls, the girls he had always known, were nuns in mufti, every damn one of them.

Across the water, in England, there were girls, hot as coals, not a Catholic virgin among them, girls like that Mrs. Luddin he had met last year at the Plaza Dance Hall. England must be full of girls like Mrs. Luddin. What if a fellow *did* join up?

Blacked out, almost invisible in the night and rain, was the front entrance to the Crown & Anchor Lounge. A fellow needed a drink after being fobbed off like that. Having a drink meant defying Sally, so having a drink was a very attractive proposition at the moment. Just one. He must not be noticed when he got home.

Inside was bright-lit, blaring with talk, crowded with fellows who seemed to have come from some football game, with, here and there, a woman or a girl. There was one woman who seemed familiar, a woman standing at the bar with a man, their backs to him as he went in their direction, their faces still hidden from him as he ordered a small whisky. But when she turned to pick up her cigarettes, a tall, good-looking woman in a turban, he recognized her: the Jewess who had screamed at Captain Lambert the night they moved the Captain from his digs. Lili something. She looked at him, but did not remember him, so he pretended not to remember her. But then, looking past her at her escort, he was startled into speech. *"Gerald."*

"Hello, there, Gavin." It *was* the Captain. Shabby trench coat, porkpie hat, yellow chamois gloves lying beside his cigarettes on the bar. His smile was drunk. "Lili, a friend of mine, Gavin Burke. Mrs. Rosen."

"Yes, Mrs. Rosen, we met once. When we moved Gerald from your place, do you remember?"

"Funny coincidence," the Captain said. "Tonight, we moved me back."

Lili smiled, leaned across the bar, and kissed the Captain's puffy cheek. "And welcome home, my dear," she said.

"By the way," the Captain said, "I'm back in the service. Post 268. I'm post officer there, as a matter of fact."

"Post officer? I thought you were sacked."

The Captain took a mouthful of whisky and pursed his lips. "Yes," he said, "I was. But, there was a technical hitch. I wasn't officially on duty that morning I dirtied my slate with the royals. Technically, I was off duty, you see.

So I went down to headquarters and put my case to a man I know. He's pretty high up in local government. He reinstated me. With a little promotion, you see."

"Wait'll Craig hears this," Gavin said, delightedly.

"You two," Lili said, leaning forward into the conversation. "You make me sick. All this talk of victories, when all you do is hide from the war in your little back streets. If I were a man, I would be fighting."

Her eyes searched the pub ceiling as though some deity would appear to change her sex. She sighed. "You," she said, fixing her attention on Gavin. "You are young and you are healthy. Why don't you fight Hitler?"

"I've been thinking about it," Gavin said. "I mean, joining up."

"There is nothing to think about. It is your duty."

"Now, hold on a sec," the Captain said. "Gavin may not feel, I mean people should have free choice, Lili."

"You are a coward, Gerald. You and your pacifist talk." She turned to Gavin again, jabbing a finger against his chest. "You. Don't you think to fight Hitler is a just war?"

"Just war, unjust war," the Captain said. "Dammit, in every war, each side considers it's fighting on the side of the right. That's the trouble, you see."

"You can say that, because you don't suffer. Because your people are not going into camps and being killed like animals."

Here we go again, the Black Angel warned. Admit it, my liberal, socialist friend. These Jews are desperate moaners. Shame on you, the White Angel said. She makes you feel guilty, that's why you're cross with her.

"Quite right, Lili, quite right," the Captain said. "One can't tell what one would feel if one were someone else. I mean, that's why one mustn't lecture young Gavin, here. Matter of fact, Gavin, old son, I do think A.R.P. seems the wrong thing for a fellow like you."

"The wrong thing?" Gavin said, his voice breaking in that damnable way it had when he was flustered.

"Well, a boy of your age should be thinking about the future," the Captain said, signaling the barman for a refill. "Something with a future to it, you know. What about private secretary, for instance?"

"Private secretary?"

"Yes, you know, be a Man Friday to some important figure. You're young, presentable, and so on. You might do very well at that."

"What is a Man Friday?" Lili asked, but the Captain shook his head, dismissing the interruption. "Not a bad job, you know," he said. "Find the right person, some bigwig in politics or in business. That's the thing."

"You mean you can see me as a *secretary?*"

"Why not?"

And why not indeed, the Black Angel wanted to know. It's better than your present occupation. Even the Captain, broke, boozy, old Captain, sees you as a future flunky. Even the *Captain*. Chew on that, Gavin, old son.

"That'll be eight and sixpence, sir," said the barman.

"Lili, do you have ten bob?"

"Gerald, I told you that was my last pound."

"I say, Gav, could you help a fellow out."

The barman waited. The barman did not have a kind face. Gavin produced a pound.

There was music, unfamiliar and not at all soothing: strings, drums, and flutes. It came from a gramophone behind the man in Merchant Navy uniform, who danced, stately, grave, and solitary, across the carpet. The Merchant Navy man had olive skin and a black mustache, curled at the tips like a pantomime pirate's. A glass of Guinness, held aloft in the Captain's hand, moved metronomically in tune to the music. From the kitchen, Lili came, carrying a tray with still more Guinness and a bottle of Vat 69, all of this provided by the Merchant Navy man, who, Gavin now remembered, was a Greek. The trouble was, unless Gavin kept his left eye closed, the Merchant Navy man became two Greeks, dancing in overlapping unison. Faint and fuddled, from the edge of an earlier anxiety, came the voice of the White Angel, cautioning, too late, a return to temperance.

"What time is it?" His voice sounded loud over the strange gramophone music.

"Shh," the Captain murmured. The Greek Merchant Navy man did not break step, but came around in a little circle, head on one side, listening to the music, creating his own choreography. Gavin set his Guinness on the floor. The events of the last few hours ran disconnectedly through his mind: Fred Astaire singing "Smoke Gets in Your Eyes"; Sally refusing a second kiss; Lili staring at him through the smoke of the pub as he told her he felt guilty about the Hitler camps but, to his father's generation, the British were Hitler. Lili saying it was all right, not to worry; and then a bus ride across the city, sitting with Lili and the Greek Merchant Navy officer who wept about Mykonos; a man outside an off-license pub arguing with the Captain about the price of a bottle of Scotch; narrow, dark stairs on which Gavin had stumbled, Lili holding his head, lifting him up, saying no, Siggie was *not* her husband, he was her brother, so that was all right. Lili on his knee, laughing at him as he told her that he loved her. The Captain at the gramophone. Guinness and Scotch.

Father and mother, semaphored the White Angel.

This time, laddie, the Black Angel warned, there's no question about it, you're stiff as a board, worse than you ever were in your life before. You're beyond the salvation of throwing up, you're away with the band, entirely. Asking Lili to sit on your knee, telling her you love her.

But I do love her. She's nice.

You're drunk. *Do you know how late it is?* What will your parents say when you go home in this condition?

You can always say that there was some emergency at the post, the Black Angel decided. Tell your parents you slept the night at the post.

What if they've rung up the post already?

The gramophone record came to an end, the needle stuttering repetitiously as the Greek came around in a last half-circle. The Captain and Lili raised their hands to clap, but the Greek's stare was disapproving. His dance was private. The Captain, accepting this rule of etiquette, rose and poured some whisky.

"What time is it?" Gavin asked.

From the kitchen came a voice, guttural and disconsolate. "It is three o'clock."

"Ah, Siggie, not asleep yet?" the Captain said.

"Who can sleep?"

The Captain, nodding as though he understood the symptoms, rose once again and went towards the kitchen, a tumbler, half-filled with Scotch, extended in his hand. "Here, old son, have a nip,"

"Danke, no. Please, Gerald, it is very late."

"Yes, of course."

Drums and cymbals clashed. The Greek Merchant Navy man had turned the record over. A stringed instrument gave off a high, twanging note. The Merchant Navy man stood, his head cocked to one side, listening for his cue. "Poor chap," the Captain told Siggie. "Hasn't been home in more than a year. Misses Mykonos."

The Greek began to dance. Siggie, sighing in exasperation, came to the kitchen door and watched, his darned woolen cardigan bunched like a blanket about his shoulders. Three o'clock. The Black Angel suggested going in over the wall of the back yard, opening the scullery window, and tiptoeing past parents' room with shoes off. It seemed a sensible solution.

"But the buses stopped hours ago," the Captain warned. "It's a long walk, you know."

The Greek Merchant Navy man wanted to go back to his ship. Lili knew a man who had a taxi. He lived up the street. The man, a cross Scot, was not at all pleased to be wakened at that hour. "Nearly four in the morning, four in the morning, what do you take me for, a bloody owl?"

The Greek offered two pounds. While the taxi, a 1935 Austin, was being brought around from the garage, the Greek kissed Lili's hand. She asked him to sink a German ship. He said he would. She advised Gavin to join up. He nodded, not saying yes or no. Their taxi was the only car abroad in the night streets. It was stopped by a policeman in Donegall Square. The policeman asked if they would give a soldier a lift. The Greek said yes, but the taxi driver wanted an extra five shillings for the new passenger. The soldier offered to stuff the driver, free of charge. They drove first to the avenue where Gavin lived.

"Good night," Gavin told the Greek. "Sink a German."

"Him, sink a German?" the soldier said. "Why, he's only a bloody sparks."

"Yes, a bloody sparks," the Greek agreed.

"What's a bloody sparks?" Gavin asked, and was told it was a ship's radio operator. "Bloody Merchant Navy," the soldier said. "They get bloody good pay and bloody good grub, not like us service blokes, you know."

"Yes, I'm just a bloody sparks!" the Greek roared suddenly into the night.

"Shh, you'll wake my parents."

"*A bloody sparks!*"

Jesus, he'd wake the whole avenue up. Gavin made a stumbling getaway, going up the entry between the houses, coming to the back door of the yard. His father, who locked up each night, had not forgotten to bar the door. He would have to climb over the wall.

The wall. On top of the wall, he took a sudden notion to stand up, no hands, no fear. He stood on top of the wall, his arms outstretched like a tightrope-walker's. What if he threw back his head and bayed to the moon? But in sickening suddenness, he swayed, almost fell, crouched on the rim of the wall, then lowered himself down into the yard. There was a three-foot drop. He dropped, missed his footing, and rolled over. Amazing, how drink relaxed one.

"Gavin?"

"Shh."

"What the hell are you doing?"

"Shh."

Owen, looking down from a bedroom window. His head disappeared. The kitchen door was unlocked, and Owen came out into the yard in his bare feet. "Get up. What the hell's wrong with you, did you hurt yourself?"

"No, no. I'm O.K. Shh."

"Jesus, you're *tight*."

"Just a bloody sparks, mate."

"You're all wet and filthy. Get up off the ground."

"Shh."

"Come on, you'll wake the whole street."

Owen's arm around him, guiding him, Owen's hand closing the kitchen door. Pitch bloody dark in the kitchen.

"Put the light on."

"No," Owen said.

Owen's arm around his neck, Owen's face touching his, as they went into the shadows of the front hall. "For Godsake, Gav, take it easy. The old man only put his light out an hour ago. Shh. Easy does it."

Easy did it, easy, and be careful at the turn of the stairs. Amazing how drink relaxed one. Up the second flight, past his parents' bedroom, mother's snores. Amazing how—

"Amazing, do know, Owen, how a few drinks relaxes one."

"Christ, *will you shut up!* Mind the step, now."

What step? And then, O God, the whole house was falling, Owen's hand slipping from his, and down, head over heels. He found himself lying on his back, staring up into darkness, probably blinded for life, amazing how drink relaxed one, no bones broken, he was sure. Lights on. Not blind. His father in plaid dressing gown, like God the Father, at the top of the stairs. "Is he hurt?"

Owen's voice: "I don't know, Daddy."

They were lifting him up. He saw Kathy there, in her nightgown, damn near transparent it was, somebody should mention that to her.

"What's the matter with him, is he concussed or what?" His father was puzzled. His father had never seen him drunk, his father always thought of him as a child, little Gavin, dandled once on Daddy's knee. His father would have no idea that little Gavin, tonight, had dandled a thirty-year-old Lili on *his* knee. But, tonight, at least, such parental ignorance must be protected. Actor Garrick Gavin Burke arose, pretending severe concussion. "Bumped my head, feel dizzy."

"He looks green," Kathy said. "Maybe, we should get the doctor?"

"Where *were* you?" His father said. "It's nearly—on my soul, it's nearly four o'clock in the morning."

"Come on," Owen said, gently. "He'll be all right. I'll take him up."

"Just a *minute*, sir," his father said. "Gavin, what's the matter with you? Are you *drunk?* Have you been drinking?"

"No, no. Bumped my head, that's all."

His father's face came close, his father's authoritarian gray head becoming two heads, overlapping. "My Lord, he *reeks* of whisky. How dare you, you young pup!"

His father slapped him. The pain of the slap was dulled by drink, amazing how drink relaxes one. But, in Kathy's watching face, in Owen's turning away, the stinging humiliation of becoming, once again, a child, cuffed by Daddy.

"Leave me alone."

"Leave you alone, I've got a good mind to put you across my knee and lather the hide off you, you pup, you miserable, disgusting young ruffian, who were you with, who taught you this, those A.R.P. layabouts, I'll wager, well, let me tell you, sir, that's the last time you'll come into this house in this condition, do you hear me, sir? I've been far too easy with you, far too easy, believe me. But, not any more."

That was grownups, all over, who did they think they were—Gods? Just because they'd sired you, they assumed they were Roman patresfamilias with the power of life and death over you and your actions, well, sod that, as Freddy would say, yes, sod that. I can leave home. Don't you forget it.

"Your poor mother," his father said. "Thank God, she's asleep. This will kill her, she'll never get over it."

"Oh, there's no need to be so dramatic."

"What did you say, what *did* you say, don't you dare talk to me in that tone of voice, you pup. How dare you."

"Gavin," Owen's voice, pleading. "Come on, Gavin. Let me put him to bed, Daddy, he doesn't know what he's saying."

"Oh, yes, he does."

"Yes, I do."

"Exactly," his father said. "He knows what he's saying, all right. *In vino veritas,* yes, indeed. Well, I suppose every family, even this one, has its black sheep."

Kathy was weeping. She stood at the turn of the stairs, weeping. She believed his father, of course she did. Black sheep. That's what they all thought.

"Go on, get him out of my sight," his father said.

"Come on, Gav," Owen said. They started up the stairs.

"That's what comes of not studying." His father's voice pursued them. "Drifting and loafing, well, drifters soon get stuck in the weeds, let me tell you that. I don't know what's going to become of that boy, but I can tell you I have no hopeful prognosis. No hopeful prognosis."

"Daddy, please come to bed," Kathy said.

"Your poor mother, what's this going to do to her?"

In their bedroom, Owen sat across from him on the other single bed, helping him untie his shoes. "Come on, get your trousers off. Do you want to be sick?"

"No."

"You'll feel better, if you can."

"Can't."

"All right, then get into bed. You'll feel better in the morning."

But would he? Shivering between the cold linen sheets of his bed, staring into the darkness, he felt the unseen room whirl, then grow still. His life, since leaving school, had been a seesaw, going up to the height of the grown-up world, a world where Lili sat on one's knee and nobody thought it odd, then down with a bump to being a child again, slapped by Daddy, lectured about exams, sent to bed in disgrace. Yet both worlds ran on the same old moral lines: although he had left God behind in the dusty past of chapel, confessional, and classroom, the catechism rules prevailed. In both worlds, lack of purpose, lack of faith, was the one deadly sin. In both worlds, the authorities, detecting that sin, arranged one's punishment. All of life's races are fixed and false. You stand at the starting line, knowing you can run as well as the others, but the authorities, those inimical and unknown arbiters, have decreed that you will not get off your marks. They know, those authorities, that your place is with the misfits, that your future will be void.

A dawn light discerned, on the mantelpiece, the statue of the Divine Infant of Prague. The Infant, as usual, was eager to catch Gavin's eye. Well, said the Infant, you can't say I didn't warn you. You've been leading up to this for a long time. It's happened now, you know: it's all up with you. Over, finished, done. Do you hear me, Gavin?

Gavin turned toward the wall.

sixteen

Mr. Burke, wearing the earphones of his crystal wireless set, sat by the sitting room fire, plainly excited by the six-o'clock B.B.C. news. Old Mary had just brought in a full scuttle of coal and Gavin's mother, using the tongs, was rebuilding the dying fire. Kathy, home from work, was stitching the hem of a dance frock, and so, when Gavin ventured his head around the sitting room doorway, no-body noticed him, at first. He had stayed in bed all day, hungover, and also to avoid the row he foresaw as certain. In half an hour, he would leave for night duty.

His father was the first to notice him, but his father, listening to the wireless, did not seem to be thinking of the previous night's happenings. "Wait'll you hear this," his father told the others, loosening his earphones, but still listening to the announcer's voice. "The Germans have just marched into Greece. They went fifty miles in their first day. And the British are camped on Mount Olympus—isn't that marvelous—camped there, preparing for another of their 'tactical withdrawals,' I'll wager. You mark my words, what day is it—Tuesday?—well, by the end of the week, they'll be running for their ships, leaving another of their allies in the lurch. God help the poor Greeks."

The Greek of last night danced, stately, grave, and solitary, into Gavin's mind. The Greek had wept on the way to Lili's. He must have known this news.

His father was listening again. "Aha, the Yugoslavs," he said.

Mrs. Burke rose from her fire-making labors and turned to look at Gavin in the doorway. Her eyes threatened tears. "I'm just going to pick up my sandwiches," Gavin said hurriedly. "Good night, everybody."

"Don't you want any supper?" his mother asked.

"I'm not hungry."

"You look like death."

The Emperor of Ice-Cream • 155

"I'm all right."

He fled, escaping explanations and recriminations, knowing they were merely postponed, but sure that, in his present state, he could not endure them without a collapse into childish, hateful tears. Out into the rainy avenue, the day fading to night, running past the old waterworks where, as a child, he had spent long hours sailing his toy boat. Grownups, forgetting the servitude of children's lives, were fond of saying that one's school years were the happiest years of one's life, a statement which no child believed. But now, perhaps, he *was* becoming a grownup, for, looking back at the bleak St. Michan's days, he saw them in the fond forgetful light of an easier time. Life as an adult could be more terrible than anything a schoolboy might imagine. The Greek of last night danced into his mind, the weeping Greek whose mother, sisters, brothers, might even now be falling under Nazi guns. He felt sorrow for the Greek, and yet there was a shameful, guilty comfort in knowing that if he, Gavin Burke, was facing an ominous future, the rest of the world, whole countries, even, was in the same boat.

On the post everyone was excited by his news of Captain Lambert's comeback.

"On my soul," Soldier said. "It just shows that what I always said is true. The gents look after their own. Ah, wait'll we slip this to Craig. 'Twill be a grand kick in the arse for him."

"Which post is the Captain on?" Freddy asked. "God, if only I could wangle a transfer."

"Ah, the Lord love him, can you see him," old Mrs. MacCartney offered. "Himself dead drunk in he's office, and every man and woman on the post asleep on their stretchers."

The thought of the Captain's being in charge of others was irresistible. In a world where nothing happened, where the only battle was against sleep and Craig's drills, the Captain's elevation to power seemed a triumph against all those higher-ups, post officers, Local Authority inspectors, Control Centre and headquarters muckymucks, who, until now, had defeated the personnel as regularly as Hitler beat the Allies. A real excitement preluded the ten-o'clock drill. Wait'll they told old Craig.

"Bandages has not been folded properly. I said, bandages is a disgrace. Mister Bob Greenwood was in to see me tonight, and he has put the shaft in me. I said, he has put the shaft in me. He tells me his people is folding all bandages according to regulations, but that, when his people comes on duty in the mornings, the bandages left by our people is not properly folded.

"Now, I am not saying Mister Bob Greenwood is right, no, I am not saying that at all. But I address this, especially, to the ladies. I want them bandages just perfect. I said, perfect. I am excusing the ladies from drill tonight, because I want youse girls upstairs, folding the bandages. I want the bandages all correct and ready for inspection by me at eleven. I said, at eleven.

"Now, the ladies can fall out. The men, fall in."

The whistle blew. Soldier, at the head of the line, squared off, straightening the line with an old soldier's efficiency.

"Now, tonight, we'll just run over the casualty clearing procedure."

"Slip it to him, now," Soldier whispered to Gavin.

"Hargreaves, I am asking you, what would you do if you had a casualty with his left wrist fractured and, at the same time, a temperature of one hundred and five?"

"Excuse me, sir," Soldier said. "I just thought you'd be interested. Have you heard about Captain Lambert?"

"MacBride, I am asking Hargreaves a question."

"Sorry, sir. But 'tis an extraordinary thing. Him getting that job."

"What job?"

"Ah, you'll not credit this, sir. But the Captain's been appointed a post officer, the very same as yourself."

"Your head's cut, MacBride."

"No sir, 'tis true. Post 268, it is. Young Burke here met him last night."

"He has no advanced certificate," Craig said, his voice suddenly failing. "You can't get no job like that without advanced certificates."

But he did not sound sure. They watched him, delighted to be able to stick it into him.

"Ah, well," Soldier said, "it's different for gents. He knows a lot of higher-ups, so he does."

Maggie Kerr, sallow-faced at the kitchen door. "Mister Craig. Red alert."

"Red alert," Craig shouted. He blew his whistle.

"Ah, for crying out loud," Soldier grumbled. "Will they never let up?"

"Red alert, stand to your stations."

Craig dashed back to his office. "Well," said Jimmy Lynan, lighting up his pipe, "we got out of a drill, but, still and all, it spoiled the crack."

"Did you see his face?" Wee Bates asked.

"Did he say *red* alert?" Big Frank Price asked. "Why was there no yellow alert?"

"Red or yellow," Freddy said. "What does it matter? They just forgot to put the yellow through. No wonder. They're sick of these capers."

Down the hall, the phone rang loudly in the office.

"All clear," Soldier said, taking off his steel helmet.

"Right," said Hughie Shaw.

Craig's voice, screaming: "Burke and Hargreaves! In here, on the double."

"Well, that's a new one," Freddy said as he and Gavin left the kitchen.

In the office, Craig paced up and down. "They're evacuating the Nurses' Home. The doctor in charge is short of firewatchers, and H.Q. has ordered us to fill in until replacements is sent. Youse two—over there and up on that roof. Incendiaries is expected."

"It'll be nice to get a breath of fresh air," Freddy said.

"Just a *minute*." Craig's eyes were manic. "This is no joke. German bombers is over the Irish Sea, they'll be here any minute."

"Are you sure?"

"I have it straight from H.Q.!"

"In a pig's eye," Freddy said, as he and Gavin went into the blackout.

Searchlights swept the sky. "Look," Gavin said, "I never knew there were so many."

"Maybe something *is* happening."

In the blackout, they began bumping into nurses who were being evacuated from the Nurses' Home to the main hospital building. Harried by shouting old matrons, the nurses, some of them in their night clothes, some carrying suitcases and parcels, laughed and called to each other like schoolgirls on a picnic. Gavin went among them, hoping to find Sally, but in the darkness and in the rush of women, he could not discern individual faces.

"Come on," Freddy said. "Maybe there's some skirt still asleep up there."

The thought of Freddy discovering Sally in her night clothes set off an instant rage. Keep your paws off her, do you hear? He found himself half running after Freddy, unwilling to let that old Plaza Dance Hall rake out of his sight.

"We're the firewatchers," Freddy told the matron on the main door.

"You can go up the back stairs to the roof. And keep out of the dormitories. I have more girls to get out."

"I'll bet we're the first men ever allowed in here at night," Freddy decided, as they started up the back stairs, two at a time. "Wonder which floor the dorms are on?"

"Oh, knock it off."

"What's the matter with you? There's not going to be any bloody raid. But we might get a bit of a cuddle."

"Jesus." Gavin stopped on the landing. "What's that?"

Over the noise of footsteps and the giggling sounds of girls, a sudden cough of explosions.

"Bombs?"

"Guns," Freddy said. "Ack-ack, behind Cave Hill."

"Let's get up on the roof and have a look."

For a moment, coming up through the trap door onto the flat roof, they were blind mice, unsure in every direction. The first thing they discerned were two searchlights, circling across the semicircle of sky, intersecting, then falling, great white columns, down behind the black horizon. Tiny and sudden, flashes of light appeared on the far off hills, followed by the stammer of guns, which, like firecrackers, went off all around the perimeter of the city. Then, silence.

"Listen," Freddy said. "What's that? Do you hear?"

Did he? At first Gavin could not be sure. But as he and Freddy approached the parapet of the roof, he heard it again, a distant grumble like the growl of a lion, a growl which grew to a loud, snarling roar: the sound of huge engines.

"Where are they?"

"Coming up the Lough."

"Going for the shipyards, I'll bet."

The first bomb dropped. The explosion, far different from the harsh cough of the guns, preceded the faint red sheen which arose in the sky above the place of impact, then faded, leaving in the eye's retina a momentary after-image of rooftops and church spires. The guns chattered like chickens.

"That was a bomb," Freddy said, redundantly.

Two more explosions boomed on the far side of the city. The guns were silent. Then, beautiful, exploding with a faint pop in the sky above them, a magnesium flare floated up in the stillness, lighting the rooftops in a ghostly silver. Freddy was revealed, a few paces away from Gavin, his face uptilted, his glasses silvery opaque as they searched the sky. And in that moment, within Gavin, there started an extraordinary elation, a tumult of joy. He felt like dancing a Cherokee war dance on the edge of the parapet. The world and the war had come to him at last. To-night, in the Reichschancellery of Berlin, generals stood over illuminated maps, plotting Belfast's destruction. Hit-ler himself smiled in glee, watching the graphs of the planes' progress. Tonight, history had conferred the drama of war on this dull, dead town in which he had been born. And what about your parents? asked the White Angel. What about Kathy and Owen, down there in the darkness. And you. You too can be blown to smithereens.

But there, there was the joy. He had no fear: he did not care. He was actually smiling, impervious to his danger, enjoying the bombing as though it were a military tattoo, put on for his benefit.

"We'd better find some sandbags," Freddy said. "It looks as though they're dropping incendiaries."

On a rooftop across the street, flames grew with startling suddenness, licking across the slates, exploding from an upper-story window. In the reflected light of the flames, Gavin saw that Freddy seemed nervous.

"Hey, see over there." His own voice was elated. "Look. That one's on the Ormeau Road, I'll bet."

"Maybe on Reverend Batshaw's house," Freddy said. "Go on. Blow up old Baldy Batshaw."

The Reverend Batshaw, an archenemy of Freddy's, had once threatened to put the police on Freddy for going around with the Reverend's underage daughter.

"Do you hear me, Batshaw?" Freddy shouted. "This is the bloody revolution, Batshaw, you praying mantis, you.

It's the end of your whole bloody world. Come on, Hitler. Blow up his bloody church."

"Yes, and blow up St. Michan's," Gavin shouted, prancing in his war dance on the roof.

"Blow up City Hall."

"And Queen's University."

"And Harland and Wolff's."

"Blow up the Orange Hall."

"And the cathedral and the dean."

"Jesus, what a show."

But the next bomb fell quite close. The roof shook. Gavin was thrown to his knees.

"Are you all right, Gav?"

"O.K."

"Let's find those sandbags."

"I saw some behind you."

A high, ominous whine sounded above them, and, instinctively, the heroes of a moment ago crouched down, hands over their necks. A second explosion shook the street, and they heard, in delicate counterpoint, the tinkling, rending smash of windows in their own building. They stood, ran to the parapet and looked over. "Blew out every window in the place," Freddy announced, triumphantly. "That was close, let me tell you."

"I wonder are all the nurses out?"

"Maybe we'd better look."

Back down through the trap door to the sound of the ack-ack guns. The lights had gone out inside the building and, instead of the giggles and footsteps of ten minutes ago, there was the black silence of an empty loft.

"Hey, nursies," Freddy shouted down the stairs. "Nursies," echoed back. A bomb fell. The staircase shook. "Let's go back up," Gavin suggested. Somehow it seemed safer on the roof than in here, in this black emptiness, knowing that bricks and marble and concrete could tumble down and bury you.

Up on the roof again, they had a clear, fire-lit view of the city. "Flaming, by Jesus, all over the place," as Freddy put it. "Except here and in the Antrim Road."

Gavin's house was in the Antrim Road.

"Blow up a few capitalists," Freddy shouted, suddenly.

"And the Bishop of Down and Connor," Gavin yelled.

The Emperor of Ice-Cream • 161

"And Stormont Castle and Lord Carson's statue and the houses of bloody Parliament."

"Not with a whimper, but a bang."

"Right you are, Gavin boy. A big bang."

They stood for a moment, drunk with the bombers' power. "Say, Gavin, do you smell something funny?"

Smoke drifted over the parapet of the roof. "Maybe the hospital's on fire. Let's have a look." Gingerly, they approached the parapet. The hospital was invisible in the blackout. But two streets away, a house blazed with flames, illuminating smaller fires all along a row of working-class dwellings. The smoke, however, came from somewhere closer. They began to cough and choke. They moved to the other side of the roof. "Hey, Freddy?"

"What?" Freddy's myopic eyes blinked and watered as he peered out across the city.

"Look down below. Do you see?"

Two floors beneath them, smoke and flames were coming from one of the windows of the Home.

"Christ, we're on fire."

"Get a couple of sandbags."

Carrying two sandbags, they went down through the trap door into the blackness of the building. Gavin led the way, his hand on the stair rail. The fire was on the fifth floor, in a room at the end of a long corridor. They approached it through a thick swirl of smoke and, when Freddy opened the door, saw that it was a nurses' dormitory, its window frames, beds, chairs, and rugs all garlanded by long ribbons of flame. They retreated at once, pulling the door shut.

"An incendiary must have come in through the window," Freddy said. He dropped his sandbag.

"I suppose we should phone the fire brigade."

"O.K."

Freddy remembered that there were telephones in the lobby. Down on terra firma was where they both wanted to be. To ease their conscience, they stopped on each landing on the way down, calling out: "Nurse? Nurse? Anybody there?" Luckily, no one answered. They reached the lobby and struck matches to find the phone booths.

The phones were dead.

"What'll we do now?"

"Better tell them at the hospital. No point in hanging around here any longer."

"Anyway, every fire engine in the city must be out on call."

"O.K., then. Let's cut on over to the hospital."

They went out, leaving the front door open. "Makes it easier for the firemen," Freddy said, although, as he spoke, they both sensed their failure and avoided each other's eyes. They stood in the courtyard of the Home and looked up. The whole of the fifth floor was ablaze. Above them, in the cloudy night sky, they heard, once again, the dull roar of bomber engines. The roar was ominous. Aye, said the White Angel. You know what I'm thinking, don't you? Say an act of contrition, and be quick about it. You may not get another chance.

"Come on." Freddy had found and opened the court-yard gates. A magnesium flare burst in the sky, lighting the street. A policeman in a steel helmet was coming to-ward them, helping an old woman in a black shawl. The old woman's face was bleeding. "Hey, you," the police-man called. "Are you First Aid?"

"Right."

"This woman needs to go to the hospital."

"Come on, missus," Freddy said, putting his arm around the old woman's waist. The policeman let go and, turning, hurried back across the street. "Our first job," Freddy said. "Gav, get on the other side of her."

Half dragging, half carrying the old woman, they set off up the street. The antiaircraft guns set up a fresh chat-ter.

"Them sons of whores," the old woman groaned. "Them bastards done it on purpose. They brought the German."

"Who?" Gavin asked, staring at her bleeding brow, mater martyr, a face from a Dürer triptych.

"The Fenians, the I.R.A., them's the ones who done it. They should be hung, every one of them, aye, and a fire lit beneath them."

"Come on now, missus," Freddy said. "Save your breath."

"A fire lit beneath them, hell roast them."

"Let's take her over to the extern department."

"I can't see a thing," Gavin said. The flare's light had

died. Two cars passed, their masked headlamps almost invisible in the blackout.

"I suppose everybody's trying to get out of town."

"Wouldn't you, if you could?"

The old woman, her feet dragging, her breathing stertorous, rallied herself and began to sing:

> "Do you think that we would let
> A dirty Fenian get
> Bespoil the Royal Orange Lily-O!"

"Shut, up, mother," Freddy said. "Come on now, we're nearly there."

"Nearly where? Is it the papist hospital youse are taking me to?"

"Yes, mother."

"Well, youse can let me die in the street, so youse can. If you think I'm going into any Fenian hospital run by them nuns to get myself poisoned and kilt, then youse have another think coming. Take me to the Royal Victoria, boys."

"But that's on the other side of town. Now, come on, have a heart."

"Let go of me. Are youse Fenians?"

"Come on, Gav," Freddy said. "Lift her up."

Arresting officers, they carried the old woman, kicking, through the extern department entrance. The waiting hall was crowded, mostly with people who had come in to take shelter from the bombs. A young girl, her face smeared with dirt, came running out of the huddle of people in the doorway. "It's my gran! Oh, Gran, what cut you?"

"Fenian gets," the old woman muttered. Weeping, she put her arms around her granddaughter. Freddy and Gavin, glad to be shut of her, went into the extern surgery to report on the fire. A bomb fell close by, a big one. At the sound of the explosion, the herd of people in the extern hall crouched down, heads bowed. Some made the sign of the cross. Doctors and nurses paused in their work of bandaging and suturing, as though arrested in some private moment of reflection. It was as though everyone waited for the next bomb, the one they would not hear, the one which would bury them. Gavin and Freddy, nonchalant, kept on walking, officers going along the top of a trench. They spotted old Dr. MacLanahan, the medical superintendent, coming down the corridor from the main hospital building, accompanied by a staff sister. He wore slippers, tweed trousers, a white coat over his striped pajama top. A stethoscope dangled from his neck. "What, what?" he snapped, as Freddy went up to intercept him.

"Sorry, sir. The Nurses' Home is on fire. We couldn't get the Fire Brigade."

"Any nurses there?"

"No, sir."

"All right. You men help with those stretchers."

"Excuse me, sir, but shouldn't we report back to our post? We're supposed to be on ambulance call."

"There's plenty of work for you here."

The staff sister whispered something in Dr. Mac-Lanahan's ear. "Hmhmhm," he hummed, impatiently. "All right."

"You two follow me," the staff sister said. "Pick up a stretcher over there. I have a job for you."

Carrying the stretcher, they went into a small rest room behind the surgeries. An old man sat on a straight-backed chair, his head lolling against the rest room wall. His face was a purplish color: his eyes were open.

"Heart attack," the sister said. "Cover him up and take him around the back to the morgue."

Clumsily, they took hold of the corpse and carried it to the stretcher. As they laid the old man's head down, his mouth opened and his false teeth fell out. Freddy put the teeth in the old man's jacket pocket. They covered him up in a blanket, then carried him out, past the crowds. At the back entrance, a policeman held the door open for them. "Where's the morgue?" Freddy whispered.

"Up the yard, mate."

At the morgue entrance a light shone, defying the blackout. A man in a long rubber apron held the door open for them. "That a corp?" the man asked.

"Yes."

"Bring it in here."

There were several morgue tables inside but only one of them contained a sheeted body. The morgue man beckoned them on, into a back room, bare as a garage. There, on a concrete floor, a middle-aged woman, a young girl, a baby, and a sailor lay in the lax postures of death. "Put it down there on the end of the line," the morgue man said. "Do you have his name and address?"

"No. He died in the extern."

"That's all right, then. He was admitted."

The morgue man lit a cigarette. "Did you notice?" he said. "The bombs have stopped."

"Have they?"

"Listen."

An ambulance backfired in the yard outside. Somewhere, a child wailed. Then there was silence, the silence of death. The morgue man puffed on his cigarette. "I hope it *is* over," he said. "We only have room for fifteen bodies in here, that's why I'm stacking them in the back. I expect we'll have fifty before the night's out."

Outside, in the main morgue room, a familiar voice bellowed: "First Aid party with one dead."

Freddy pushed open the swing doors. Craig, his battle dress chalky with dust, stood at attention among the morgue tables. Behind him, lowering their stretcher, were Wee Bates and Jimmy Lynan. Freddy explained about the fire in the Nurses' Home.

"And youse didn't put it out?"

"We couldn't."

"Right then, youse will have to fill in a report. Get back to the post on the double."

"A report. Now? Dr. MacLanahan told us to help with stretchers."

"Dr. MacLanahan has no call giving youse orders. I'm in charge here. Who does he think he is?"

"Simmer down, will you," Freddy said.

The morgue building shook. "I was wrong," the morgue attendant said. "They're still at it. O.K. Put that corp in the back room."

As Bates and Jimmy Lynan passed by with their burden, Jimmy favored Gavin and Freddy with an exaggerated wink and jerked his head meaningfully towards Craig. For a moment, his mind confused by the excitements of the night, Gavin found himself puzzled as to the meaning of the wink. Then, in a brutal image, he saw Craig lying on the concrete floor in the back room, blood congealed on his brow. No, that was rubbish, there was enough real death around here without giving in to schoolboy fantasies.

Yet Lynan looked serious. You've got to separate Lynan from Craig tonight, the White Angel warned. Otherwise—

"Come on, get the lead out," an ambulance driver called, coming in at the main door. "I have a call up the Antrim Road."

The Antrim Road. "What about me and Freddy taking a turn on the ambulance?" Gavin said.

Craig, flustered by the ambulance driver's shout, nodded agreement. "All right, get moving."

Outside, in the hospital yard, the clouds had parted, allowing a sinister moon to shine down on the city. "Antrim Road," Freddy said. "Isn't that where your people . . . ?"

"Yes."

The ambulance raced out of the gates, turning into a deserted street. The moonlight showed broken window glass, glittering like rhinestones on the pavement. There was no noise, other than the sound of the ambulance motor. "The bombing's stopped," Freddy decided.

"You should have seen the one I seen," the driver said. "The soldiers told me they call it a land mine. It come down on this parachute and blew up a whole row of houses in one go-off."

"Whereabouts?"

"Over in the Shankill."

"Where else have you been tonight?"

"No place. This is only my second call."

The ambulance swung into the rotunda of Carlisle Circus, passing the pigeon-spattered statue of a Protestant divine. As it turned into the Antrim Road, Gavin saw three boys coming out of Mullens' Sweet Shop. The shopwindows were broken, and the boys carried boxes of chocolates, which they were eating in gluttonous haste. When they saw the ambulance approach, they ducked back into the shadows of the doorway.

"Whereabouts in the Antrim Road is this call?"

The driver had no time to answer Gavin's question. The ambulance shook violently and, without any of them being aware how it happened, the ambulance was on the far side of the street, but still moving.

"Holy God."

"A bomb?"

From behind them came a sudden, deafening roar. They looked back and saw a huge sack of dust swell up behind the dwellings in a nearby side street. Fragments of brick and glass fell on the ambulance roof.

"Did you see that? That bomb blew us right across the street."

"And we kept going."

"Suffering J.," said the driver. "Wait'll I tell about this, nobody'll believe me."

"The Germans are still on the job."

"Too right, they are. We're not home yet."

Guns rattled defiance off the slopes of Cave Hill. Gavin, sitting between Freddy and the driver, looked in turn at each of their faces. Was Freddy afraid? There was no question about the driver's fear. He said, "Let's pull in a minute. We don't want to be blown off the road."

"Keep going," Gavin said. Freddy looked at him strangely.

"What's your hurry, Gav? It's bloody dangerous driving in the middle of these bombs."

"We're getting paid for it."

"Aye, paid heroes," the driver grumbled. "And dead heroes." But he kept the ambulance moving.

The driver was afraid. Freddy was afraid. Why wasn't *he* afraid, then? Why was he filled with excitement, with a feeling that, tonight, nothing could kill him, that, like the knight in some ancient romance, he carried a shield which stood between him and all harm? He did not know: he *did* know that, given the chance, he was capable of dashing into a burning building, snatching a girl from beneath a tumbling wall, walking among explosions, anything.

As they reached the Lyceum Cinema, people began appearing from the streets which converged there, people who tried to flag the ambulance down, calling. "Hey, wait a minute. We have a sick woman here."

"Are youse going out of town? Give us a lift, please."

"Hey, mister, take these kids and me as far as Glengormley."

"Please, mister."

The driver, his finger jabbing at his horn, kept the ambulance moving through the crowd. Gathering speed once more it turned up the Cliftonville Road. At the corner of the road was a Presbyterian church which Gavin used to pass each day on his way to and from school. Tonight, all was changed. The church was without its steeple. Bricks and rubble were strewn on the lawn of the adjoining manse. The steeple lay, like a great tree, amid the headstones of the old church graveyard.

Light shone from the windows of a pub called The Swan. There was the sound of a shot. The light went out. A policeman came out of the pub into the moonlit street, holstering his service revolver. He waved at the ambulance as it passed. He was smiling.

A moment later, the ambulance passed the avenue where Gavin lived. All seemed quiet. Had his family taken refuge in the shelter in the street, or were they huddled in the coalhole beneath the stairs? Was his father still appaluding Hitler's deeds?

And then, turning into an avenue, two streets up from his own home, the ambulance was flagged down by a stout old warden, who waited in the middle of the road. "There's two casualties in the back entry," the warden told them, as Gavin and Freddy jumped down, carrying their folded stretcher. The warden's torch guided them. Arms straining, they lifted a very fat man onto the stretcher. The warden's torch showed the fat man's left leg, broken below the knee, turned sickeningly around so the the man's shoe seemed to be on back-to-front. Arms straining, stumbling in the rubble, they carried the fat man to the ambulance and, returning, were guided toward an injured child. Gavin applied the first real tourniquet of his life in an effort to staunch the bleeding from the child's mangled arm. Uneasily, he remembered his inattention in all those months of first aid classes.

Two old ladies had climbed into the ambulance, believing it to be leaving the city. They wept as Freddy and the warden forced them out. As the ambulance turned back down the Cliftonville Road, a bomb fell two streets away, the force of its explosion spinning the vehicle around in a wild skid, ramming its bonnet against a lamppost. The motor stopped. The driver stamped on his dead accelerator pedal, pulled out the choke, hammered his fist in anger against the dashboard. "Holy God!"

Gavin and Freddy got out and pushed the ambulance bonnet free of the lamppost. "If I could get her on the hill, going down," the driver said. "I might get her running. We need a shove."

Just then, two English air force sergeants emerged from a doorway. They had been taking shelter on their way home from a dance. They offered to shove, in exchange for a lift. With Gavin and Freddy, they ranged themselves behind the ambulance and, all four straining, managed to push the ambulance back onto the road and point it downhill. The driver called out: "All together now. Push hard!"

They pushed. The ambulance began to gain momentum, but the motor did not catch. Suddenly, the engine began to splutter, and, at that moment, Freddy and the two air force sergeants jumped on the tailboard. The engine caught, the ambulance accelerated, and Gavin was left alone in the middle of the road. He continued to run, expecting that, once the engine was firing properly, the driver would apply the brake and wait for him to climb aboard. But the ambulance did not stop. Gathering speed, it shot off down the Cliftonville Road, turned a corner and was gone forever. He was stranded.

seventeen

Hail Mary, full of grace, Mrs. Burke prayed, not saying the words out loud, but thinking them to herself as she crouched under the dining room table, her knees drawn up to her chin. Why didn't James hurry up, what about Gavin, would they go past the A.R.P. and pick Gavin up, or what? Would the car start? *The Lord is with thee, blessed art thou amongst women,* how many Hail Marys have I said since this started, I've lost track of the decades, the wind would cut you, is every window in the house broken, if we're away in Dublin, it will rain in and ruin the carpets, what if robbers come in and steal the silver, I should put it away, lock it up in the pantry, oh, what's the use, I haven't the strength, we could all be dead before the night's out. *And blessed is the fruit of thy womb, Jesus.* Supposing Gavin refuses to come with us, he always was a stubborn wee boy, he'll not heed James, James never knew how to handle the children. Merciful God, do you hear that? That must be close. I wonder how many people are killed already? *Holy Mary, mother of God, pray for us now, and in the hour of our death, amen.*

Hail Mary, full of grace. I have a whole roast of beef in the meat safe in the yard, would it be any use to take it with us, no, it would just go bad, besides there's plenty of meat in Dublin, no rationing, Agnes will put us all up, she has room, but what'll James do, he'll have to come back sometime, he can't let the office go to pot, and Owen, maybe we could transfer him to National University, what about Kathy, oh, what matter, won't it be saving our lives, isn't that the main thing. Do you hear that, is it guns, James said guns, or is it some sort of bomb. *Holy Mary, mother of God, pray for us now and*—who's that? James?

"James, is that you?"

"No, mother, it's me. Gavin. Where are you?"

"Here. Under the table. Come on in, for the love of God, there's glass breaking everywhere."

"Where's Daddy and the others?"

"They're out in the garage getting the car ready. Are *you* all right?"

"Of course I'm all right."

"Is it terrible out? Will it be safe to drive?"

"Drive where?"

"We're going to Dublin, to your Aunt Agnes. We were going to come by the A.R.P. and pick you up."

She could see him now. In the moonlight, she saw his face, he was still only a child, it was a crime seeing him dressed up in that steel helmet like a soldier and him only a wee boy, just a year out of school. Oh, this war.

"I got stranded over on the Cliftonville Road," he said. "The ambulance took off without me."

"Wasn't that an act of God," she said, "them leaving you off so near here. Now, we can all go together."

"I'll go and see Daddy."

"Tell him to hurry."

Gavin went into the kitchen. The kitchen windows were broken. He let himself out the back door and went down the yard, through the entry and across the allotments to the shed where his father garaged the family Austin. The car, old and frail, was put up on blocks each winter, for his father, who hated to drive, used it only on holiday. He could see an oil lamp burning in the shed, in defiance of the blackout. Inside, Kathy was holding one of the car wheels while his father tightened bolts. Owen, out of breath, was pumping up another tire with a hand pump. His father looked pleased to see him. "Ah, there you are Gavin. Grand, grand. Now we won't have to make a detour. How are things downtown?"

"Pretty bad."

"Are the roads clear? Are there lots of cars on them?"

"No, not many cars. I don't know about the roads."

"Gav, give me a hand with this pump," Owen said. "I'm fagged out."

"Daddy," Kathy said, "while you put the last wheel on, do you want me to try the engine?"

"Is the petrol in? Will we have enough to get to Dublin?"

"We'll get petrol across the border," Owen said. "O.K., Gav. You have a go at this wheel, now."

When the tire was inflated, Gavin rolled the wheel across

the shed and held it while his father tightened the bolts. As they worked on the last bolt, the shed rattled and shook. "Another bomb," his father said. "Somewhere over by the docks, I think. The shipyards must be a shambles. Ah, well. I've said it before and I'll say it again. The German jackboot is a far crueler burden than the heel of old John Bull."

"When did you say that?" Gavin asked. "You never said anything of the sort."

But his father chose to ignore him, turning to watch Kathy at the wheel of the car. "Ah—good girl, good girl."

The old Austin's engine, after several misses, caught in sudden, shaking life.

"Owen, go and get your mother. Tell her to bring my heavy coat. Gavin, are you ready, have you pajamas and so on?"

"I'm not going to Dublin. You can drop me off at the post."

"Oh, Gavin, have sense," Kathy said. "We're not going to leave you here."

"I have a job to do. There are people injured out there. They need stretcher-bearers."

"Let the British carry them," his father said. "Come on, Gavin, I've had enough of this nonsense. Get your pajamas."

"No."

"Gavin," Kathy said. "Think of Mama. It would kill her, knowing you were left behind."

"We'll have enough trouble making our way to Dublin, as it is," his father said. "I may need you boys to stop people trying to commandeer the car."

"You might," Gavin said, sourly. "I've seen a lot of rats out tonight."

"Oh, stop playing the twopenny hero," his father said. "Get in the car."

Again, the shed shook. His father got behind the wheel and tried out the gearshift. Kathy was right: his mother would make a drama if he tried to get off at the post. In fact, knowing his father, he knew his father would go nowhere near the post. There was no sense in waiting around for a lift, then. He might as well go.

A searchlight's beam probed the sky above him as he ran out of the shed. He turned toward the allotments, hearing Kathy's voice over the noise of the car motor. "Gavin, wait!" His feet sank in the freshly spaded soil of a lettuce patch as he went uphill, planning to cut across the allotments and come out at the end of the avenue. It would be a good twenty-minute walk to the post.

I didn't even say good-bye to them, any of them, I've finished with them, let them run off to Dublin, I can live here alone. When the raid is over, I'll come back to the house, board up the windows and live alone. I don't need them, I don't want to see them ever again.

"Gavin."

Daddy's voice.

"Gavin, wait for me, I want to talk to you, sir."

I can go faster than he can, I can lose him in this allotment. I can hear his breathing, it's hard on him, running, like that, especially with his heart.

He looked back over his shoulder and saw his father, in the moonlight, running uphill toward him. "Hold on," his father shouted. "Wait a minute, son."

Son. His father had never said that before. His father called his children sir, or miss, or you, or Gavin. For his father to say *son* was tantamount to another father's calling out that he loved you. You could not continue to walk away after that.

"Please," his father said. His father came close, his breathing harsh and winded, his gray hair disarranged, a thin lock falling across his brow. His father's hand, with its familiar, heavy gold signet ring, caught at his sleeve, not in command, but in entreaty. "Wait, son," his father repeated. "Please, listen to me."

"I have to get back."

"I know, I know, you feel it's what you—what you should do, I understand that, it's very commendable, of course, but, after all, your mother and I are very fond of you, we wouldn't want to see anything happen to you, don't you see that?"

"Yes, Daddy."

"Then, come along. We're all ready. Let's keep together. We're a family, after all."

"I have to go back. I'll telephone you at Aunt Agnes'. Don't worry, I'll be all right."

"But, you could be killed," his father said. "Don't you see, we can *all* be killed tonight. This thing isn't over, they'll flatten this city, it'll be just the same as Liverpool or Coventry. I know it. My God, haven't I enough trouble, without having to stand here arguing with a silly young pup, so puffed up with his own importance, he can't even see he's breaking his parents' hearts?"

"Good night, Daddy. Good luck in Dublin."

He pulled his arm away, knocking his father's restraining hand up in the air, making his father reel as if he had been struck. He ran across the allottment, ran as fast as his legs would carry him. To the north, the guns chattered again. A new wave of bombers approached.

The whole of the city seemed to be on fire. All around the night bowl of sky, from Cave Hill to the Lough, from Antrim to Down, a red glow eddied and sank, the reflected light of hundreds of burning houses, shops, factories, and warehouses. Yet the streets were strangely empty. Occasionally, as Gavin half walked, half ran toward his destination, people in twos and threes would appear from some side street, glancing up at the sky as they hurried toward unknown destinations. Twice, he came upon small groups of men and women moving, dirty and dulled, among the crater ruins of their homes. People could be heard calling out the names of relatives, as though trying to summon the dead to rise. There were few police about and, as yet, no sign of fire engines. And, always, the rumbling crash of a new explosion would drive these forlorn victims to take shelter in doorways and in other houses, sending them stumbling over broken water mains, bricks, and planks, like figures in a Biblical scene, fleeing from terrible retribution.

He hurried on. In a side street, not far from the hospital, an old truck, loaded with some twenty people, had broken down on the corner. The driver, swearing foully, was trying to lighten the truck's load. Men and women cursed at each other, exchanging blows, and, as Gavin passed, an old woman and a girl were pushed off the truck's tail gate, the old woman receiving a cruel kick from a heavy man in a cloth cap and a white cotton muffler. The adjoining street was almost invisible. A bomb or land mine had fallen here, blowing up twelve houses in a row. Fires set up a heavy pall of dust and smoke.

Voices could be heard, crying, cursing, comforting each other. Gavin avoided this street, taking the longer way around, going down a silent avenue, past rows of shut, fearful doors, keeping to the middle of the road to avoid falling bricks and slates. He forgot his father, forgot his own feelings of anger and grief. He walked, caught in a cold excitement, feeling himself witness to history, to the destruction of the city he had lived in all his life.

Two men, tough corner boys, in caps and neck scarves, came out into the moonlight from the doorway of a shop. One carried the shop's till, the other a sackful of stolen articles. They looked up the street, stiffening on point at sight of Gavin, whom—in silhouette, wearing his steel helmet—they mistook for a policeman. They stared at him as he came closer, uncertain whether he might intervene. They waited until he was safely past them and then, jaunty again, set off in the opposite direction.

He fell down. He did not hear the bomb, felt no pain from the fall. He was lying face down in the road, his helmet knocked off, his eyes smarting, his nostrils filled with the acrid stink of smoke. Tiny bits of debris fell all around him. He got up onto his knees, his heart pounding, and, wonderingly, discovered himself to be unhurt. The bomb had fallen somewhere in the road behind him. He did not look back. He no longer felt detached and invulnerable. He began to run and did not stop running until he reached the front door of Crummick Street Post.

Fat Mrs. Cullen sat in the front office with Maggie Kerr, the telephonist. The post seemed silent and deserted.

"The phones are all mixed up," Maggie Kerr said. "The whole thing is broken down. Control Centre has ordered all our personnel to work directly from the hospital."

"Most of them's over there now," Mrs. Cullen confirmed.

"What about ambulance calls?"

"The ambulances are going out directly from the hospital. Mister Craig was told to take his orders from the hospital doctors."

"He'll love that," Gavin said.

"Ah, it was always a cod," Mrs. Cullen said. "The idea of treating casualties in this wee bit of a house. You'd better get on over to the hospital."

Before he left the post, he went upstairs to the lavatory and discovered Soldier MacBride, lying down on a stretcher in the front room. "Is it over?" Soldier called out to Gavin. His voice was a whisper of its normal tone.

"No, they're still at it."

"Bad cess to them."

"How are you, Soldier? You don't look well."

"It's them stretchers," Soldier said. "I took a bad turn on the stairs of the hospital a while back."

"Soldier, have you heard any word of Jimmy Lynan and Craig? You know what I mean."

But Soldier did not seem to be listening. "I should have stuck with my service pension," he said. "I was too greedy. I'm seventy-two years old, boy, did you know that?"

"I met your granddaughter once, do you remember?"

"Aye, aye, so you did. You're a good lad, young Burke. A good lad."

"What about Lynan? You didn't answer me."

"Aye," Soldier said. "Well, there's no telling with a man the class of Jimmy Lynan. Some of them Orange fellows is bitter. Very, very bitter."

"So, you think he might?"

"I'd not put it past him."

"Shouldn't I warn Craig? There's been enough trouble tonight, without a thing like that happening."

"I wouldn't concern myself, lad, if I was you. There's nobody likes an informer."

Gavin went out. As he came out of the lavatory, he heard a sound on the attic stairs. Your Man Mick Gallagher put his head around the corner of the banisters. "Who's there?"

"Me. Burke."

"I was just getting some bandages," Your Man said. He disappeared.

Or hiding up there, Gavin thought. It was funny the people who turned out to be cowards. Perhaps Lynan was a coward too, perhaps his talk of killing Craig was just a windy boast. God, wasn't it ironic that his mother, Sally, or any one of the people he loved might be killed this minute, and here he was worrying about Craig?

But the sight of Craig, in the hospital extern, was enough to dispel any worries. And the sound of him. "Where were you, where were you?" he shouted at Gavin.

"I was left behind in the Cliftonville Road. I had to walk back."

"Left behind, there's some of youse would leave your heads behind if they weren't screwed on to your necks. Go on, get stuck in over there. We're short of men on stretchers."

The hall of the extern reminded Gavin of field hospitals he had seen in films of the First World War. Stretchers lay everywhere among the waiting room benches, and, moving among the prone bodies, were men, women, and children, almost all of them dirty, wandering distracted, their ears tuned to the sound of distant explosions. Doctors and nurses rushed about, bending over patients, calling out to A.R.P. stretcher-bearers, who, staggering under their loads, carried the more seriously injured casualties out of the extern and into the main buildings of the hospital, climbing many flights of stairs to reach the wards, for the lifts had broken down. Priests and ministers moved in the crowds, trying to comfort the bereaved. From time to time, the buildings shook, arresting all movement within them. When the danger passed, the hubbub recommenced.

Gavin found himself helping Freddy Hargreaves carry an old woman up to the maternity ward, which had been pre-empted for raid casualties. In the effort of lifting their burden, of climbing the steep flights of stairs, maneuvering the stretcher around landings, and waiting, like mules, for the nurses to decide where they should deposit their load, they had little breath left for talking. No sooner had they deposited the old woman than they were ordered to carry a pregnant girl downstairs to the operating theater. Then, back to the extern for another patient. The minutes became an hour, then two hours, stretching into three—hours during which they became uncomfortably aware that the waves of German bombers were still coming in over the city, hours during which they had little time to snatch a rest or a smoke until, moving up the main corridor of the hospital, they heard a British-accented voice call out. "Steady, lads. Steady. Must talk to these chaps. Freddy? Gavin? How are you."

The Captain, wearing a white steel helmet, symbol of his new authority, stood at the head of a group of stretcher-bearers who were off loading patients from an ambulance at the hospital's main entrance. His face blackened like a commando officer's, his straw-colored mustache streaked with soot, he came forward to them with a drunken, convivial grin. Over his shoulder he carried a green musette bag, which he patted meaningfully. He opened its flap. "Take a peek."

The musette bag contained some twenty half-pint bottles of Powers' Irish Whiskey.

"Baby Powers'," the Captain said. "Lovely little things." He produced two, stuffing one each into Gavin's and Freddy's battle-dress blouses. "Now you'll be like big Saint Bernard dogs."

"Where'd you get them?"

"Luck. There's a pub quite near my new post. Bomb dropped in the back yard of the place just as we went past on ambulance call. So, thinking of a free drink, I led the charge inside. Owner's wife was laid out, poor woman, leg broken, so we put her on a stretcher and brought her here. The owner fellow was most appreciative. Forced these on me."

"Well, thanks very much," Freddy said.

"Not at all." The Captain turned back to his stretcher party. "All right, chaps. Get her to bed."

"God bless you, sir," said the pub owner's wife, as the Captain's men carried her toward a ward. The Captain took her hand, tenderly, drunkenly, walking beside the stretcher. And at that moment, watching this scene, Gavin and Freddy erupted into their first laugh in hours, a laugh cut short by the tearing crump of an explosion, so close that the terrazzo floor underneath them seemed to shake. People cowered down in the corridor. Surely, this one had hit some part of the building?

A priest rose amid the cowering figures. "It's all right," he said, nervously. "It's quite all right. I don't know what religion all of you are, but I think we should give thanks to our Lord for our deliverance."

There was a confused murmur, much like the mumbling at an official luncheon when the speaker has voiced some indisputably patriotic sentiment. The priest seemed heartened by this reception. "Very well, then," said he. "If you'll all kneel, for just a moment, I'll recite the Lord's Prayer."

He knelt in the corridor, and, following his example,

doctors, nuns, and orderlies knelt too. Stretcher-bearers put down their burdens and knelt beside them. Suddenly, looking around, Gavin saw that he and Freddy were the only two still on their feet. "Our Father," declaimed the priest, "who art in heaven, hallowed be Thy name."

"Our Father," repeated the crowd, in dutiful fervor, "who art in heaven, hallowed be Thy name."

Gavin looked at Freddy, who seemed about to follow everyone else and kneel down. But then, catching his eye, Freddy winked. Godless guardsmen of the rational view, they stood erect in a two-man mutiny, aware that the kneeling people around them were filled with resentment at their posture. One of the kneelers, the priest who led the prayer, glared directly at Gavin, seeming to declaim his appeal to the Almighty as though it were a stream of insults against this mutinous, mortally sinning boy. Kneel, pleaded the White Angel. You may be blown up in the next half hour. A principle, said the Black Angel, is a principle. Good man, yourself. You're not afraid now of bombs, or priests of Our Father or your father or anybody. You've changed, Gavin.

Changed, changed utterly. He smiled at Freddy, who smiled back. Remembering: his father calling after him across the allotment. Remembering: his lack of fear, earlier, on the roof of the Nurses' Home. "And forgive us our trespasses as we forgive those who trespass against us." He could forgive them all, his father, these people, this city, for, after tonight, nothing they could say or do would hurt him again. There and then, in the drone of the priest's "but deliver us from evil," he vowed to deliver himself from the sham of church attendance, of pretending belief for his parents' sake, of the pretenses and compromises which had helped keep him becalmed in indecision between adolescence and adult life. Tonight, he felt, at last that he had grown up, escaped . . .

But at that moment, the prayer ended, and the people stood up. He and Freddy bent to lift their stretcher and, as they moved forward with it, he saw, on a stairway above him, a group of nurses getting up off their knees. And then *her* face, staring at him. He saw her run downstairs, two at a time, running toward him.

"You!" she said. "I saw you. Who do you think you

are, what a big baby you are, standing there, showing off at a time like this? Oh, I'm sick of you."

"Hello," Freddy said. "Is this your mysterious girl friend?"

"Girl friend," said she. *"His* girl friend? Not any more."

And ran off down the corridor, lost among nuns, patients, porters, ran away—perhaps forever. How now? asked the angels, in unison. Was your gesture really worth it? Or have you also escaped from her?

eighteen

Far off down the Lough, antiaircraft guns were firing with a noise like slamming doors. Yet the guns seemed uncertain, aiming into emptiness. For seven hours, attacking in waves, more than one hundred German bombers had flown in over Cave Hill and the Lough, dropping incendiaries and heavy explosives. The city was ablaze, the skies above it visible for miles around in a red, burning glow. But there was no longer the terrible thump of exploding bombs. And when, in the first light of dawn, the sirens sounded the thin, exhausted note of the all clear, they merely confirmed what the guns had said an hour before. The Germans had gone, at last.

For Gavin, Freddy, and the other A.R.P. stretcher-bearers, the raid's end brought no change in the routine of work. Ambulance drivers continued to bring in casualties, reporting, as they did, that whole districts of the city had been wiped out. An injured Heavy Rescue worker told them he had seen the engines of the Dublin Fire Brigade, pumping away in the York Street area, their peace-time headlamps blazing. His story was confirmed by others, and, soon, the hospital nuns, very pleased by this news, were telling patients how the Dublin Fire Brigade, God bless them, their headlamps blazing, had driven one hundred and thirteen miles, crossing the border from neutral Eire, to help with the conflagration. A loyal pro-British patient countered with the intelligence that the English had loaded fire engines on ships in Liverpool and that those ships were already on their way across the Irish sea. Another patient told how she had seen a Canadian aircraft carrier, in dock for refitting, blaze away at the enemy until all its ammunition was spent. There were other stories too: stories of looting and cowardice. An English naval rating, who died shortly after Gavin and Freddy carried him to the operating room, told them that he had heard two men cheering in a pub as Lord Haw-Haw, the Nazis' English-speaking commentator, reported on the German radio that Belfast would be completely wiped out.

Reports and rumors continued to circulate well into the morning, but, by then, Gavin and Freddy were too exhausted for listening. Their hands had developed blisters, their feet were wet with perspiration, their limbs ached, and each time they sat for a minute, it seemed they would not have the energy to get back on their feet again. Craig, who carried few stretchers but was everywhere in evidence, shouting orders and harrying his staff, behaved in a demented manner if he saw any of the men taking a rest. "Youse have a job, get cracking!" His pale face glistened with the excitement of it all and, despite the grim sights all around him, his uneven teeth were revealed in a constant, pleased grin. Walking beside a stretcher, he would announce loudly, to no one in particular: "There'll be no more laughing now. I said, they'll be laughing on the other side of their faces now." Occasionally, he would frown and declare: "Letting them doctors give my men orders, that's not right, that needs fixing, yes, fixing. Next time, it will be different You'll see."

Around ten in the morning, one of the post ladies made tea and brought mugs around to all the men. Gavin, drinking the sweet, strong brew, thought he had never tasted anything so wonderful in his life. He lit his first cigarette in several hours and, without warning, fell asleep, tumbling onto the floor, the mug of tea spilling, scalding him.

"God, I'm tired."

"On your feet, there." It was Craig, coming up the corridor, shouting in a high voice. "Go in thon room there, the head doctor wants to talk to youse."

In the room, Big Frank Price, his face gray, sat slumped against a wall. Old Crutt, the stoolie, was beside him, similarly exhausted. Jimmy Lynan came in a few minutes later with his partner, Wee Bates. None of the other men could be found. Craig, closing the door, pompously blew his whistle for attention.

"Day shift has fully taken over now, so youse men can get some sleep. They'll be back the night, they said it on the wireless. I said, the Germans will be back tonight. But, before you go off, the head doctor. I said, the head doctor, wants to speak with youse. Stand to attention."

Gavin and Freddy joined the others in the semblance of men standing to attention. Craig went out and was heard saying: "All right, Doctor. My men is here."

Old Dr. MacLanahan came in. His white coat was smeared with blood, his pajama collar was similarly soiled. "Good morning," he said, in his usual brisk tone. "I know you boys are going off duty now. I know you need sleep. But I wonder if I could have two volunteers for a nasty job?"

He looked around as he spoke, his gaze coming to rest on Freddy Hargreaves. "What job, sir?" Freddy said, on cue.

"The dead. We're jammed up in the back there, no room at all. I've been in touch with the city authorities, and the plan is to put all the dead together in coffins, in a big hall downtown, bring them in from all over. Then identification can be done at one central place. Do you follow?"

Heads nodded, uncertainly.

"So, we've got to get our lot coffined and out of here by tonight. I've lined up three medical students to help our morgue man. But I need at least two more men. Will any of you help us?"

There was silence.

"What about you, Mister Craig?"

Craig's Adam's apple jiggled in his throat. "Well, Doctor, I'd be happy to oblige, only, you see, I'm in charge here, I have to be on duty again, the night."

Dr. MacLanahan's heavy eyebrows lifted expressively, causing Craig to shift his feet and utter an uneasy cough.

"I'll go," Freddy offered.

"Me too," Gavin heard himself say.

"Good lads," Dr. MacLanahan said. "Follow me." Pointedly ignoring Craig, he led them out of the room, across the extern hall, and into the hospital yard. At the far end of the yard, a canvas sheet had been tied from wall to wall, obscuring the entrance to the morgue. A policeman in a heavy black cape saluted as Dr. MacLanahan approached. "I want nobody in here, do you hear?" the doctor said. "Except the men who're working."

"Right, sir."

The policeman lifted a corner of the canvas and they all three ducked under it. At the entrance of the morgue, two young men in tweed jackets and flannels were smoking cigarettes. Medical students, they stiffened into poses of respect at the approach of the hospital superintendent. "Morning, sir."

"Morning, MacReady. And you, what's your name, I'm sorry?"

"Geary, sir."

"Ah, yes, Geary. Where's the other lad?"

MacReady, a tall young man with a wide clown's mouth and a lock of curly black hair falling over his forehead, said, in a Dublin brogue, "He was taken sick, sir. He asked to be excused."

"Hmm. Well that leaves only the four of you, you and these A.R.P. lads. You'll have your work cut out for you, I'd say. Where's Willie?"

One of the students opened the morgue door and bawled: "Willie?" The morgue attendant appeared. He was the same man Gavin had seen the night before, small, chain-smoking, his long rubber apron greasy with blood. "Morning, sir. Ah, it's a shocking mess, a shocking mess."

"Did Sister send over some whisky?"

"Yes, Doctor."

"Good. And the coffins?"

"They just come. They're out the back."

"You'll have to work outside," Dr. MacLanahan said. "I don't want anybody to see you, but the back yard's pretty well screened off. To bad about the rain, but it'll be easier for all of you to be out in the fresh air. Willie, do you have those antigas suits?"

"Yes, Doctor."

"Good. Give these lads a good jar of whisky to get them started. Remember, we want to identify people if we can. Thank you, gentlemen. I'll be back later to see how you're getting on."

"Okey-dokey," Willie said, when the doctor had disappeared back behind the canvas curtain. "You lads wait here and I'll get your duds. No sense in dirtying yourself."

He went back into the morgue and came out with an armload of Wellington boots and the yellow oilskins Gavin and Freddy had worn so often in Craig's decontamination drills. When they and the medical students had put these things on, Willie beckoned them inside. "Hold your snouts," he said.

Gavin had seen his first corpse when he was eleven years

old. Corpses were elderly relatives, dressed sometimes in brown shrouds, more often in their Sunday best. They lay in the downstairs bedroom on white linen sheets, their hands crossed over their breasts, fingers entwined in rosary beads or crucifixes, black-edged Mass cards strewn around them in tribute. People knelt and said prayers or looked silently at the waxy, dead face, before withdrawing to the sitting room for tea, whisky, and praise of the dear departed. The dead he had seen last night had not stiffened into *rigor mortis* and seemed like actors, shamming death. But now, in the stink of human excrement, in the acrid smell of disinfectant, these dead were heaped, body on body, flung arm, twisted feet, open mouth, staring eyes, old men on top of young women, a child lying on a policeman's back, a soldier's hand resting on a woman's thigh, a carter, still wearing his coal sacks, on top of a pile of arms and legs, his own arm outstretched, finger pointing, as though he warned of some unseen horror. Forbidding and clumsy, the dead cluttered the morgue room from floor to ceiling, seeming to stage some mass lie-down against the living men who now faced them in the doorway.

"Jaysus," said the tall medical student. "How many are there?"

"There was eighty-seven the last time I looked in my book," Willie said. "But the ambulance men was shoving them in sometimes when I was out the back. There's more in the yard. Here, have a wet."

He produced a bottle of whisky and passed it around. "Take a good swig," he advised. "It's all buckshee, and there's more where that comes from."

Waiting his turn at the whisky, Gavin gazed on the dead, his attention caught by the bare, callused feet of an old woman, sticking out from the bottom of a pile of bodies.

> If her horny feet protrude, they come
> To show how cold she is, and dumb.
> Let the lamp affix its beam.
> The only emperor is the emperor of ice-cream.

"Here," Freddy said, passing the whisky, "have a swig."

The whisky, strong and biting, did not refresh, as had the tea. Gavin swallowed, then, his stomach heaving, threw up, the tea coming up, too. The medical student, Geary, was similarly sick. "You'll get used to it," Willie advised. "Now, here's what you have to do."

What they had to do was work in pairs. Two men would drag a corpse out of the morgue and into the back yard. One, using an old-fashioned cutthroat razor, would cut or loosen the corpse's clothes, while the other searched pockets for identification, money, and valuables. These, if found, were placed in a small canvas bag which was tied around the corpse's neck. If the corpse was fouled by excrement, the clothes were cut off. The corpse was then lifted and placed in a coffin and, if stripped, covered with a shroud. The head, unless mutilated, was left exposed. A lid was placed over the coffin but not nailed down. The coffin was then carried to the outer yard to be shipped to the central hall downtown, where casualties would be exhibited for identification.

The first body Gavin and Freddy took hold of was that of a mill girl in her twenties, a body picked because it was nearest to the entrance. Her cold, stiff hand in his, Gavin dragged her behind him out of the door, into the thick, foggy drizzle of rain, dragging her corpse across the cold, wet concrete of the yard. In death, her bowels had loosened, and so, cutthroat razor in hand, he cut away her skirt, sweater, and underclothes, revealing the first naked body of an adult woman he had ever really looked at in his life. Of course, he had seen female nakedness before, but fleetingly, as in a glimpse of his sister, or women on beaches inexpertly changing out of their clothes. But now, unurgent, cold in death, this woman's nipples sat on her skin like blind, brown eyes, and, sick, he gazed in fascination at the dark clump of pubic hair beneath her belly. He looked at Freddy, but Freddy merely picked up her skirt and threw it into a beginning heap in the corner. Freddy's glasses were misted with rain and sweat. He lit a cigarette. Naked, the woman lay on the cold, wet concrete and, naked, she sagged between Gavin's arms as he dragged her toward a coffin. Freddy helped lift her in and lay her down and Freddy covered the body. "Bloody Comrade MacLarnon," he said, suddenly. "And the other arseholes. So, they think this war is a good idea, do they? Capitalist killing capitalist. Look at this poor bitch, born and brought up on the means test and the dole. Bread and dripping all her bloody days. Some capitalist."

Gavin put the lid on the coffin.

The two medical students staggered past, carrying their first body. MacReady, the tall one, called out: "Gangway!" and added: "Jaysus, men, there's always a silver lining. Isn't this the first time in your life you can get stocious drunk and nobody will blame you one bit?"

The other student still looked sick.

"He's right," Freddy said. "Let's get a load in us."

But the stench in the morgue made whisky-drinking medicinal, rather than pleasurable. Putting down the bottle, they took hold of their second corpse and dragged it out into the rain. The corpse was that of an old man, and, again, stripping it, Gavin was struck by the ugliness of the naked body, the loose skin of old age, the veiny calves, the limp, somehow pathetic genitals. But the whisky was working now and, by the time he had coffined his fifth body and had two more drinks, he, like the others, had reached the strange light-headed state in which they worked all morning. Humor, a defensive morgue humor, became their shield against the horror of their occupation, and, soon, all four were exchanging grisly jokes.

"Come quietly, you!" the tall student cried, as he and his teammate lifted a stout policeman off a pile of bodies. "Lord Jaysus, lads, I'm interfering with an officer of the law."

"Tell us, is a cop's revolver, a 'valuable'?"

"Put it in his hand. And put his cap with it. No, not on his head, Geary, I said, on his chest. Let me like a policeman fall. There now, isn't that a grand sight?"

"Come on youse fellows, stop codding around," Willie called from inside the morgue. "People might hear youse."

"Let them bloody hear," the tall student shouted.

"Wait," Gavin said. "Keep it down. There's a cop out there behind the canvas blind."

"So there is." They worked for some minutes in silence. Then Freddy said: "Hey, just a minute. We're working our heads off, but what's old Willie doing in there? Drinking up all the whisky?"

The tall student made a face. "Never mind old Willie,"

he said. "If you're curious, go in the back room and see. But I wouldn't advise it."

"Why not?"

"He's working on the pieces."

The pieces. Don't think about that, the Black Angel warned. Don't think about anything. You're the youngest here, those students are five years older than you, and, besides, you worked all last night, nobody would blame you for dropping out. But he knew, Black Angel, or no Black Angel, that he, Freddy, and the students, they were all in this together. There could be no dropping out now. It was strange, but he felt that, in volunteering for this job, he had done the first really grownup thing in his life. Wait'll Sally heard what he was doing. She'd be sorry she sounded off like that last night. Big baby, indeed.

Two A.R.P. stretcher-bearers ducked under the canvas blind, carrying a corpse. They stopped at the sight of Gavin, razor in hand, cutting garments from a body; at the coffins stacked behind him; at the bodies in the rain. Freddy came down the yard toward them, portaging an empty coffin on his back as though it were a canoe. "Are you First Aid?" one of the stretcher-bearers asked.

"Right."

"The kid too?"

"Right."

"God, I hope they don't put *us* in a job like this," the second stretcher-bearer said.

"Don't worry, mate. We're volunteers."

"Oh? Well, the best of luck, lads."

The stretcher-bearers, depositing their burden, fled the yard. But, ten minutes later, more corpses were brought in. Freddy and the tall student, feeling their whisky, began to act out a grisly charade. As soon as they sighted the newcomers, picking their way timidly among the dead, the tall student called out to Freddy: "Hey, what about this leg?"

"Keep it a while. We'll find a match for it."

"Now, hold on youse fellows, cut that out," Willie, the morgue man, said, coming from his back room. "If it's legs youse want, I'll give you legs. But stop that codding around, it gives the hospital a bad name."

At noon, the policeman ducked under the canvas and

told them: "You lads are to go over to the hospital now for your dinner. The nun says it's ready."

The nun, an elderly woman, waited, huddled under a large black umbrella in the outside yard. After they had washed at a tap, she led them through a side entrance into the students' quarters. "In you go, boys," she said. "Doctor MacLanahan told me to give you a good dinner. We've done the best we can."

In a student dining room, a nun waited with plates of roast beef, roasted potatoes, Yorkshire pudding, and cabbage. There were bowls of thick broth and bottles of ale. "And after that, there's a chocolate pudding," the nun informed them, as she withdrew, leaving them with heaping plates.

Eat, the Black Angel said. The others are eating: it's no different from school. If you show how you feel, they'll make fun of you. What are you shaking for? The dead, dirty and pale, dried blood on their lips, their bowels loose in the final spasms, moved in afterimage behind his eyes. The food sat untasted. A year ago, I sat sick in the examination hall, sick because I couldn't do math, sick at the thought of failing my matric. To fail seemed the very worst thing that could happen to me. What had that sickness to do with this sickness? Yet, I was just as sick then: just as afraid. After lunch, we will go back to the yard, back to the coffins. The pieces must be coffined too. Tonight, the bombers will be back. More people will be killed. He thought of his parents, of Kathy and Owen. O God, he prayed, I hope they're safe in Dublin. Coward, said the Black Angel. You did pray, after all.

A tall doctor in a white coat came into the dining room and nodded familiarly to the two medical students. "Hello there, how's it going?"

"It makes dissection look like a piece of cake," said MacReady.

"Well, we've rounded up two final medicals to help you," the doctor said. "And, while I don't want to hurry you fellows, we've got to get the place cleared out by tonight."

"All bloody fine," said MacReady. "But I want the nun's chocolate pud."

The other student, Geary, got up from the table and ran out of the room. "He's been puking all morning," Mac-

Ready said, jerking his thumb after his departing friend. "Now, I ask you? Will that fellow ever make a surgeon? Why, this kid here has twice his guts."

Everyone looked at Gavin. Under those circumstances, a hard chaw, iron-gutted, tougher than any medical student, what was there to do, but eat the meal. Nonchalant, an actor on stage, he cut into the roast beef.

It rained all afternoon. In time weariness dulls everything, aches, fears, disgusts. The dead were heavy: they seemed, in their awkwardness, to resist the final indignity of coffining: their limbs stuck out, becoming entangled with other limbs; their arms stiffened, making it hard to search pockets. And, in time, seeing no end to these labors, the men who searched them became unnecessarily brutal in their handling of the bodies. Gavin found himself joining in the cruel, childish jokes of the others: he did not flinch even at the most sickening moment of the day, when he and Freddy, lifting the corpse of an R.A.F. officer, discovered that, through some freak of air blast, the body had separated down the middle, split from neck to genitals. Freddy, who, until then, had seemed indifferent to the sights around him, dropped his burden abruptly and turned away, his face sweating. Gavin did not turn away: it was he who finished the job of coffining the corpse.

It grew dark. The policeman brought kerosene lamps, which ringed the yard. Tea was brought out in workmen's billycans. They carried it into the morgue, now half empty, its floors covered with quicklime. They sat on a morgue table, smoking and drinking tea, too tired to speak. Willie, the morgue man, answered the phone.

"It's for you," he said to Gavin.

"Gavin, it's Sally. Are you all right?"

"How did you know I was here?"

"One of the girls was talking to Doctor Thompson. He told her and she told me. Oh, Gavin, I think you're a blinking hero. Is it awful?"

"It's all right," he said, and no sooner had he said it than the Black Angel sneered. Be heroic, the angel said, yes, over dead bodies you become a hero. But he was too tired to listen to the angel.

"You must be dead," she said, over the phone.

He laughed. "I'm not," he said. "I have reminders all about me that I'm very much alive."

"I mean, you must be dropping. We had a nap this afternoon. The Home's burned down, did you know? God knows where we're going to sleep."

Home. He saw his parents' house, empty, the windows broken, himself lord and master there, at last. "You could stay at my place," he said. "There's nobody there."

It was her turn to laugh. "I wonder what the nuns would say about that. Listen, Gav, I have to run now, but try and drop in for a moment before you go off duty."

"All right."

"And Gav? I'm sorry about last night."

"O.K."

He went back into the yard. Freddy and the others worked wearily in the rainy night, their shadows large in the light of the kerosene lamps. He thought of old films he had seen: perhaps, at this very moment, smiling German pilots were eating a hearty meal of sausage and beer in their mess hall, while, outside on the tarmac, German mechanics fueled the big bombers for their long run up the Continent and across the Irish Sea. He saw the German pilots exchanging gallant toasts across the mess hall table in a scene from *The Dawn Patrol*. But this was no film. There were no ugly corpses in films.

The policeman ducked under the canvas blind and came over. "There's a man here says he's a mate of yours. He wants in. Name of Gallagher."

"O.K.," Freddy said.

Your Man Mick Gallagher, his A.R.P. battle dress filthy with mud, his face and hair soaked by the rain, came out of the dark carrying a large flashlamp. "Get rid of the peeler," he whispered to Freddy. The policeman, hearing him, discreetly withdrew.

"Where's the bodies?"

"Why? Are you relieving us?"

"What do you mean?" Gallagher seemed about to burst into tears. "They bombed the Falls," he said, hoarsely. "Did you know they blew up the Falls."

"They bombed every part of town," Gavin said. "They didn't hold back just because the Falls Road is Catholic, if that's what you mean?" Freddy laughed.

"Shut your beak," Gallagher said, savagely. "I live in the Falls. Our house is gone. My wife and kids, I can't find them no place. I was in four hospitals today. I can't find them."

"I'm sorry," Freddy said.

"Maybe they're staying with neighbors," Gavin suggested.

"No. Nobody seen them after the bomb. There was some peelers and A.R.P. men come and took away some bodies."

"Did you try downtown?"

Gallagher nodded. "The bodies is not all in yet, down at yon big place. That's why I come here."

"Why don't you wait until tomorrow?" Freddy said. "You can hardly see here, it's so dark."

"I have this," Gallagher said. He snapped on his flashlamp and stared at it. The beam struck powerfully across the yard, pinpointing the wall opposite. "This," he repeated. "It was a curse of God, the day I bought it."

He wandered off, shining his flashlamp on the coffins. Gavin looked at Freddy. Last night Gallagher was alone in the attic. Hiding. He was always up in the attic. *My God.* "Freddy?"

"What?" Freddy said. His glasses were misted, obscuring his eyes. His tired, dirty face seemed a mask: it told nothing of his thoughts. Freddy was not a Catholic: Freddy might have justifiably harsh feeling toward I.R.A. sympathizers who flashed lights, hoping to guide the German bombers in. That was treason: traitors were hanged.

"What'd you say?" Freddy, turning from Gavin, watched Gallagher wandering in and out among the coffins.

"Nothing."

"Come on," Freddy said. "Let's finish this one off and have a smoke."

In silence, they lifted a boy's body and carried it toward its coffin.

They sat over by the wall, smoking, watching the flashlamp as it flickered in and out among the lines of coffins. Nothing had been said. Freddy flicked his cigarette butt, sparks crumbling on the concrete. "Jesus," he said.

So he did know. Gavin looked at him, quickly.

The Emperor of Ice-Cream • 193

"Sod it," Freddy said. "We have enough trouble here, without starting more."

Their cigarette butts glowed in the dark. "Jesus," Freddy said, again. "I'm asleep on my feet."

"Me too."

They had never been better friends.

At half-past five, Dr. MacLanahan came down to inspect the work. He brought four volunteers with him, medical students, to finish off the job. When he caught sight of Gavin and Freddy, he stopped and said: "You lads have been here all day?"

"Yes, sir."

"And you carried stretchers last night. Have you had no sleep?"

"No, sir."

"Well, you'd better go home. I'll tell that A.R.P. fellow I sent you home."

"Thank you, sir."

"Thank *you*," Dr. MacLanahan said. "I just hope your beauty sleep isn't interrupted. What are your names, again?"

They told him.

"Good. I'll see you lads get some sort of bonus or something. Now off to bed."

They handed their filthy yellow oilskins over to two of the newcomers and, after a freezing wash at the tap, ducked under the canvas blind and out to freedom. "I'll be glad to get home," Freddy said. "My parents are pretty ancient. I hope they're still all right. See you tomorrow, Gav."

" 'Bye, Freddy."

He should pop in and see Sally, for a moment. After all, if another raid came tonight, they might never see each other again. He went into the hospital and a nun told him that Nurse Shannon was up in Ward Six. He began to climb the stairs, his body so tired it no longer seemed to belong to him. He moved as though drunk, bumping against the banisters.

In Ward Six, four student nurses were in the ward kitchen having tea. They had taken off their starched white aprons and collars and sat, untidy and schoolgirlish, in their blue nursing smocks. When Sally saw Gavin in the doorway, she got up and went to him. "Gavin, come on in. Josie, give this fellow a cup of tea."

Josie, a plump girl with fair skin and red hair which straggled in untidy spirals about her neck, removed a cigarette butt from the corner of her mouth and reached for the teapot. She heaped two spoonfuls of sugar into a large mug and said: "God, you're desperate young to be doing the morgue stretch. You're the fellow, aren't you?"

"He's the fellow, all right," Sally said, smiling at Gavin. She turned to the others. "Did you know, most of our students refused the job? Doctor MacLanahan was fit to be tied."

The nurses nodded sleepily. They sprawled on the kitchen chairs, legs outstretched, nursing their mugs of tea.

"Including your pal, Clooney," said a third nurse, a sensible older girl. "I never knew what you could see in that fellow."

Sally blushed. She turned to Gavin. "Tell me, Gav, are your family all right? Have you heard from them?"

The hot tea burned his mouth, but he swallowed it down. "They've run off to Dublin," he said.

"Weren't they dead right," Josie said. "I hear half the North of Ireland is running toward the Eire border. Tell us, Gavin. Will we have another raid tonight?"

"Lord Haw-Haw says so. He said it on the wireless."

"You're joking?" They stared at him, four girls, afraid. "You're not joking us now? Did he say that?"

"He did."

"Dammit," said the sensible nurse. "Why can't the Brits send up a few fighter planes to protect us."

"They don't have them," Gavin said. He was aware that his uniform gave him some authority in the eyes of these girls. It was pleasant being a hero, if only he could keep awake. It was nice to think that Sally was proud of him at last, was showing him off to her friends. Nice, too, that Clooney had turned out to be a coward about the corpses. No surprise, of course, but nice . . .

"Look at that." Josie's voice came to him through a mist. "The poor kid, he's out on his feet."

He had dozed off, slipping off his chair. Sally was holding him, her arm around him. He let his head fall on her warm, soft breast. "He needs a bed, that's what he needs," Sally told the others. "He's been on the go since the raid started. Maybe we could fix him up in the student quarters?"

"No." He sat up, groggy, trying to remember his plan. "No, I'm going home."

"To your house?" Sally said. "But you'll be all alone there. What about the raid tonight? I'd be scared stiff, all alone in an empty house."

"I'll be all right."

"But how will you get home? Have you got a lift?"

"I'll take the bus."

His eyelids drooped: he heard their laughter. "Would you listen to the man?" Josie said. "Sure, the buses aren't running. The city's in a shambles."

"You should see it, outside. Royal Avenue's all bricks and rubble and burst water mains."

"And gas mains. There's rats running in the streets."

"Rats, ugh!" Josie squealed.

"Come on, you girls." A nun's voice, official and firm. "There's beds to be made. Back to work."

He saw the nun in the doorway, saw that she stared disapprovingly at Sally, who took her arm away from his shoulder. "Sister," Sally said. "This boy's a friend of mine, he's been working all day in the morgue. Do you think I could go downstairs and help him get a lift home?"

"Ah, the poor lad," the nun said. "Go on, then, but don't be all night about it. And put your apron and collar on, before you go out. I don't want this hospital becoming a madhouse. Bad enough, as it is."

Sally, wearing her cap and apron, walked him down the corridor. He wished she could come home with him. *Home.* The house where he had been born, in whose rooms he had played as a child, home was the only place he wanted. Away from this hospital, away from the dead faces, the blood, the intestines, the reek of ether and quicklime. Home. And sleep.

At the turn of the stairs, they met a doctor, a small man with a pipe sticking out of the breast pocket of his white medical coat. Sally, at once, let go of Gavin's arm. She said something to the doctor, whispering. The doctor looked at Gavin and smiled. "Of course," he said.

"That's wonderful," he heard Sally say. "Yes, the Antrim Road. Sure, it's on your way. Thanks very much, Doctor Dancey."

"Not at all," the doctor said.

"Good-bye, then, Gavin," Sally said. "Doctor Dancey will give you a lift home."

"Sally?"

"What?"

"Give me a kiss," he whispered, taking her hand in his. She squeezed his hand. "Don't be silly. See you tomorrow." She turned and ran back upstairs. The little doctor grinned. She couldn't kiss him in front of the doctor, that was it. The whole bloody world was being blown up, but Sally Shannon couldn't kiss him in front of a doctor. Sally Shannon would never change. Tired as he was, he knew that now. No sense dreaming of having her come home with him some night to his parents' empty house. No sense . . . He was too tired to think, but, watching her run off up the flight of stairs, watching those black-stockinged legs which had so often provoked his lust, he felt a small, empty feeling inside him. A voice, not the voice of his angels, but a new grown-up voice, said: You're over that, you know. You're over her. It's true. People get over things.

Dr. Dancey, not waiting to let him think about the voice's warning, took his arm and walked him downstairs. "My car's outside the front entrance, second car on the left. You go ahead, I'll be with you in a minute."

Outside, it was very dark. He found the car and sat in it. Were the German pilots already airborne, coming up through Holland and Belgium, their compasses set on Ulster? He mustn't fall asleep. He heard the car door open and turned to see Dr. Dancey sitting beside him, the pipe now in his mouth.

The car had started. Its taped headlamps threw their tiny beam on the road ahead. They drove down a street he had known all his life, a street which once looked familiar, but now, like a broken set of teeth, revealed strange cavities. They passed the Nurses' Home, a blackened, windowless ruin. As the car turned left in the Antrim Road, going toward the Cliftonville Road, The Swan, the pub he had passed last night, The Swan wasn't there. He wondered, idly, if there were whisky bottles in the rubble and broken barrels of porter oozing in the mud and dust. Or had Captain Lambert rescued the spirits? Beside him, Dr. Dancey was saying something. He tried to concentrate.

"And York Street's worse. Leveled, completely leveled."

"Oh."

"Is your house all right?" Dr. Dancey asked.

"I don't know."

He looked back again, as the car went up the Cliftonville Road. There was a moon tonight, a bombers' moon. Every morning of his school life he had passed The Swan. He remembered hiding at the entrance to the Family Bar, playing hide-and-seek with other boys. Now, The Swan was gone.

"I'll let you off on the corner," Dr. Dancey said. The car came to a stop. "Good luck. I hope everything's all right at your place."

"Thank you."

He stood alone in the avenue, remembering last night, walking along the pavement toward the house in which he had been born. In the moonlight, the roofs of the houses on either side of the avenue presented an even, unbroken façade. And then, coming closer, he saw that there was a gap. He stopped, caught in a moment's panic, but, no, it was not his house, it was the Miss Dempsters' house, four doors down. Like The Swan, it was no longer there. He began to run.

The iron railings in front of his parents' house had been removed last year to be melted down for guns. He remembered his father's angry complaints at the time. He jumped over the low stone plinth in which the railings had been embedded and ran up the narrow strip of grass which was the front garden. He saw that the front door was ajar, pushed it inward, and reached familiarly for the light switch. The light did not work. Striking a match, he went down the hall, finding the switch at the dining room entrance. Again, it did not work. He remembered that his mother kept candles in a cupboard over the kitchen door. He struck his second-to-last match, but the wind blew it out.

The house was very cold. Moonlight came in through the broken windows of the dining room, striking down on the dining room table, showing slivers of glass and dust on its surface. He turned back into the blackness of the hall, forgot the step down into the kitchen and stumbled when he met it. The kitchen was moonlit, and, looking out of the shattered window at the silent, empty back yard, he wondered if there were people in any of the other houses in the avenue. Had everyone gone away? Mr. Hamilton, the dentist next door, was a staunch Churchill man, not likely to run. But still, there was a haunted, empty silence all around. He turned, found the cupboard and the candles, and carefully lit his last match.

He dripped hot wax from the candle end onto the kitchen table and anchored the candle in it. The candle flame cowered from the cold wind at the window. Lighting two fresh candles, he went out of the kitchen and began to climb the stairs. At the turn of the stairs, leading to the breakfast room, his father's favorite print, a framed engraving of the Parthenon, had fallen, face down, its glass shattered. Hot candle wax dripped on his fingers. He was reminded of books he had read: a boy alone, holding a candle in either hand, going upstairs in a haunted house. Yet this house was not haunted. Its dangers were real. The sirens had not sounded yet, but Lord Haw-Haw had spoken. Somewhere, above the clouds, the bombers roared over the Continent, coming in for the kill.

The window in the breakfast room was not broken. Dicky-Bird's cage was gone. His family had not forgotten the canary in their flight across a neutral border. He thought of his father—was it only seven months ago—sitting there, below Dicky-Bird's cage, his father's weary blue eyes, forgiving yet not forgiving, his father announcing that he, Gavin, a stupid boy, was only fit for some minor role in this, the grown-ups' world. Dicky-Bird sang, applauding his father's decision. Gavin turned away.

He went up a second flight of stairs. There was dirt on the stair carpet, and, looking up at the ceiling, he saw a long, jagged crack in the plaster. He paused on the landing and went in at the sitting room door. On a tallboy, just inside, he picked up a silver christening mug, given to Owen by Aunt Agnes. He stuck one of the candles in this mug and placed the mug on a Sheraton table near the window. Almost at once, a whistle blew in the street below. A voice called out. "Hey, you. Put that light out."

He looked through the broken window pane and saw a warden standing in the middle of the avenue, a stout elderly man, the same warden who had helped him with last night's casualties. "What are you doing there?" the warden called. "That house is condemned."

Condemned. "I live here," he shouted down.

"Not any more, you don't. It's not safe. Put that light out and get out of there."

He pulled down the blackout blinds and listened to the retreating sound of the warden's footsteps. The room was all shadows, half lit by the pale flickering light of the candles. This house is condemned.

He went toward the fireplace, holding a candle aloft and, in the round looking glass, saw himself, dirty and strange, his steel helmet askew. In that world, encircled by the looking glass, he had acted and reacted, had left his mark and had, in turn, been marked. His bare knees had helped wear down the old Turkey carpet, battleground of a thousand childhood games of Snap. From that gramophone, he had heard his first record. Over his mother's writing desk, the fierce stag still peered from a dark forest glade. But the picture which had hung beside it, a framed Raphael print, had fallen behind his father's bookcase. The looking glass room, unchanged since his childhood, had changed at last. This house is condemned.

Condemned, the house was his. He could sleep in any bed he chose: he could break open the dining room sideboard and drink his father's port. Yet, standing in the cowering light of the candles, he feared the house. It had died, its life had fled. The dead, their faces dirty and pale, dried blood on their lips, their bowels loose in the final spasm, sat on his mother's sofas and chairs, moved in the shadows, lay out there on the landing in a stiff jumble of arms and legs. He trembled: he could not stop the trembling.

And then, sudden, the sound of footsteps in the hall. He must not scream: it was the warden, come back to make sure he had gone. But it was not the warden. The step was heavy and strange: the step of the dead. It came up. It came on.

His hand, holding the candle, shook so that he had to put the candle down. He turned to face the sitting room door and, suddenly, defending himself against this unknown, ran to the fireplace and took a brass poker from the set of fire tongs. In panic, his mouth dry, he turned again to face the door.

His father, wearing a heavy tweed overcoat, a woolen

scarf knotted around his neck, his head bare, stood for a moment in the doorway, then came forward. "Gavin." His father's arms were around him. His hands, holding his father's shoulders, felt those shoulders tremble. They stood for a moment, embracing and then, with no words said, both needed to sit down. They sat, side by side, on the dusty slipcovers of the sofa.

"You're all right, then?" his father said.

"Yes, Daddy."

"I went to the hospital first," his father said. "Nobody knew anything about you. I went to the A.R.P. place. Same thing. Then I met a fellow as I was going out to the car. He said you'd spent the day burying people. Is that right, son?"

"Coffining them."

"O, dear God," his father said.

"Did you get to Dublin, all right?"

"Yes. They're all with your Aunt Agnes. Did you see the Miss Dempsters' house down the street?"

"Yes. Daddy, why did you come back?"

"Why?" his father said. "I was worried about you, that's why."

In the candlelight, he saw that his father was crying. He had never seen his father cry before. Did his father know that the house was condemned, did his father know that everything had changed, that things would never be the same again? A new voice, a cold grown-up voice within him said: "No." His father was the child now; his father's world was dead. He looked over at the wireless set, remembering his father, ear cocked for England's troubles, pleased at news of other, faraway disasters. Forget that, the grown-up voice said. He heeded that voice, heeded it as he had never heeded the childish voices of his angels. Black Angel, White Angel: they had gone forever. His father was crying. The voice would tell him what to do. From now on, he would know these things.

His father seemed aware of this change. He leaned his untidy, gray head on Gavin's shoulder, nodding, weeping, confirming. "Oh, Gavin," his father said. "I've been a fool. Such a fool."

The new voice counseled silence. He took his father's hand.